WRIGHT RIVAL

WRIGHT RIVAL

K.A. LINDE

ALSO BY K. A. LINDE

WRIGHT

The Wright Brother

The Wright Boss

The Wright Mistake

The Wright Secret

The Wright Love

The Wright One

A Wright Christmas

One Wright Stand

Wright with Benefits

Serves Me Wright

Wright Rival

Wright that Got Away

All the Wright Moves

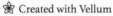 Created with Vellum

PART I

MY OWN WORST ENEMY

1

PIPER

"It's not that I hate Wright Vineyard," I said, gesturing to the interior of the barn I was currently drinking in with my friends. I shot a pointed look at Jordan and Julian Wright, the owners of said establishment.

Jordan quirked a smile. "I appreciate that, considering you're here for our one-year anniversary event."

I held up my wineglass. "See, Julian, I don't hate it here."

Julian held his hands up and said, "Hey, I didn't say that you hate us." He slid his arm around his girlfriend, Jennifer. "That's what Hollin has been spouting."

I seethed at the very mention of his name. Hollin Abbey was...trouble. He was a thorn in my side on a good day and a huge pain in the ass every other day. It was unfortunate that he was the hottest guy in town. He swaggered around like he was some Greek god to be worshipped. And worse, he knew how to push every one of my buttons.

"Hollin is an asshole," I spat.

Julian laughed. "Obviously."

Jordan nodded.

His girlfriend, Annie, flipped her long red hair off of her shoulder and leaned forward. "Yeah? You're not new here."

"It *is* kind of his specialty," my best friend and roommate, Blaire, said.

She'd ditched her signature baseball cap for the night and looked stunning in jeans with her dark curtain bangs falling into her blue eyes.

Bradley shot me a dopey grin. "You should just ignore him, sweetheart. Don't let him get under your skin."

I gritted my teeth at the words coming out of my boyfriend's mouth. It had been six months since Bradley and I had decided to try this for real. After years of on-again, off-again, it was now or never. He was perfectly nice and normal and everything. The kind of guy I should *want* happily ever after with. Then why did every word out of his mouth make me want to cringe? Why did the thought of continuing this for another six months seem more like a business arrangement than anything with passion? Why was I even *doing* this?

"Sure. Ignore him," I said. "That's a good idea."

Blaire hid a smile behind her wineglass. Jennifer coughed to try to cover her own laugh. The three of us were roommates, and they'd heard the long diatribe of *should I or shouldn't I dump my boyfriend*.

"Hollin isn't great at being ignored," Julian said with a smile of his own.

Jordan took a sip of his wine. "We have the entire winery because he was that persistent."

Jordan and Julian had all of that Wright charm with the dark hair and eyes, enough charisma to spare, and the dominance of someone who always got what he wanted. But the knowing look on both of their faces said that they'd heard about the worst of my relationship, too. Wonderful.

"Just ask every girl he's three-date-ruled," I said with an arched eyebrow.

"Three-date rule?" Bradley asked.

I shook my head. "It doesn't matter. What he said isn't true. I like it here. It's just not Sinclair Cellars."

"Touché," Julian said.

My father had worked at Sinclair Cellars since the '70s. He'd met my mom around the same time that she and Abuelita had immigrated from Mexico. After the owner's kids had shown no interest in the property, my dad had worked his way up and been rewarded with ownership of one of the best vineyards in West Texas. I'd been working there since I was a kid—putting up Christmas lights for our annual display, serving hot chocolate, and giving tours— and I now managed the entire property. It was in my blood.

"You have to admit, the barn is great here though," Bradley said obliviously.

"Sure," I ground out. Whose side was he on? "But the wine is better at Sinclair."

Jordan winced. "Hey, our new vintage is impeccable."

"And yet we're not drinking that."

"Take that up with Hollin," Julian said with a smirk.

Blaire snorted, Jennifer kicked her foot, and Annie looked like she was going to interrupt. I didn't want to hear it from them. It wasn't fair that they knew all my problems when they were all so happy. Well, not Blaire. She was single. But the other two!

"Whatever," I got out before Annie could speak up. "I'm going to go to the restroom."

"Hey," Bradley said. He leaned into me and planted a sloppy kiss on my cheek. "Come back soon."

Then, he tipped a little farther forward. Everything happened in slow motion as he lost control of his wineglass.

I jerked back but wasn't fast enough. The glass slipped out of his hand, and the red wine splashed out...all over my white shirt.

"Fuck," I cried.

I jumped backward and threw my hands into the air. The glass fell onto the hardwood floor and shattered into a thousand pieces.

"Oh shit," Bradley said.

I stared down in horror at the huge red stain spreading across my favorite shirt. There was no way it was salvageable. Not with this much blood-red wine all over it. I'd have to toss it. Fuck.

I was still staring down at my shirt as everyone went into motion. Julian and Jordan ran for something to clean up the mess. Annie pulled the chairs away from the spreading wine. Blaire and Jennifer pressed napkins to my ruined shirt. And Bradley...he just sat there, his mouth hanging open, utterly helpless. This was far from the first time that wine had spilled on me. It was sort of an occupational hazard, considering I worked at a winery. But this had been avoidable. My anger threatened to boil up and unleash on him.

Blaire stepped between us, as if she could see what was about to happen. "I think I have a jacket in my car."

"I...I have a shirt. A gray shirt in the side of my gym bag," Bradley said with a cough. It was as if he had suddenly realized he should do something. "I can go get it."

"No. I'll get it. I don't want to stay here any longer."

"I can go with you," Bradley offered, a little manically.

But Julian came back with a broom in hand. Jordan threw a towel at Bradley. I'd never been so thankful for the Wrights.

I didn't so much as flee as stomp angrily through the

crowded barn and outside into the chilly night air. My hands were clenched into fists. I wanted to kick something. Mostly my boyfriend.

Bradley's truck was parked at the back of the lot, wedged between two other giant trucks. I jerked open the back door and grabbed for the gym bag. His shirt wasn't going to fit me, but it would be better than wearing something soaked in wine. Maybe Blaire could work her magic and make it look okay. After all, she was the famous influencer.

I'd just ripped my blouse off when I heard a low whistle, and a gravelly voice said, "Well, well, well, what do we have here?"

My head jolted upward as Hollin Abbey came into view. Just the sight of him made my knees wobble. I wasn't short by any stretch of the imagination, and still he towered over me. He had on jeans and a white T-shirt, revealing the inky-black lines of his full sleeve. His beard had recently been trimmed. His hair was a soft blond, and his eyes were so blue, as if reaching the endless depths of the ocean. When they caught sight of me, shirtless, my breasts half-spilling out of the nude bra, they rounded wide.

I was too angry to be self-conscious. I balled up my shirt, threw it into the cab of the truck, and put my hands on my hips. "Like the view, Abbey?"

He smirked with the cocky, annoying look he always gave me. "Yeah, I do."

I huffed. "I don't want to deal with you tonight."

He leaned against the truck next to Bradley's, which I belatedly realized was his. He crossed his muscled arms across his chest. I averted my gaze, so I wouldn't stare at the bulging biceps and incredible chest.

"Why are you naked out here? If you want more people to come to Sinclair, this probably isn't the way to do it."

"Fuck off, Hollin." I yanked out a gym towel and patted down my skin. "Bradley spilled a glass of wine all over me. I'm getting a shirt."

He snorted. "Smooth."

"I didn't think you were coming out tonight. Missing the one-year anniversary of your own winery for a date." That was what Julian had said. It seemed low, even for Hollin.

He took a few steps toward me. Always in my fucking personal space. "Jealous?"

"Not in a million years." I went back to rummaging through the bag to find that damn shirt. "I was hoping that I wouldn't have to be graced with your presence."

"Don't worry, Medina," he said, his voice silky smooth. "I'll always be around for you."

I rolled my eyes. "Save it for your next conquest."

When I didn't find what I was looking for, I opened the side of the bag. I sank my hand into it, and it closed around a box at the bottom. I froze.

Hollin must have read my change in body language. "What?"

With a gulp, I withdrew the box from the bag, praying to all things holy that it wasn't what I thought it was. In the parking lot light, the black box was very clearly for a ring.

"Oh fuck," Hollin said with wide eyes. "Is that..."

I gaped and popped it open. A glittering diamond ring peered back up at me. It was...not at all something that I would have picked out for myself. I'd always liked simple things. I wasn't one for grand displays or crazy jewelry. This thing was almost gaudy.

"Fuck, fuck, fuck," I breathed.

"Bradley's proposing?" Hollin asked, his voice had an edge to it that I'd never heard before.

"He sure as fuck better not."

I closed the ring box and threw it back into the bag like it was a grenade with the pin pulled. I shook my hands out. Fear blossomed in my stomach.

"Sure looks like he's going to."

"And why do you care?" I snapped at him.

Hollin chuckled. "Still got three dates with you, babe."

"You're going to get three dates with me over my dead body."

"We'll see." All confident, as if it were inevitable. He nodded his head at the bag. "What are you going to do about that?"

"None of your business."

I found the gray shirt I'd been looking for and drew it over my head. It smelled like Bradley, and for a second, I felt nauseated. He'd bought an *engagement* ring. He must have thought that I'd say yes. I couldn't even fathom it. Was this his now or never?

Hollin frowned down at my shirt. "Not that."

He popped open the passenger door of his truck and tossed me a shirt from inside. It was a white button-up, three sizes too big for me. It smelled like musky cologne that made my toes curl in my boots. Hollin. It smelled like *Hollin*.

For the first time in our long acquaintance, I didn't argue. I slipped Bradley's shirt back off and pulled Hollin's onto my curvy frame. I worked on the buttons, and when I was done, he stepped forward. I stilled, wondering what the hell he was doing. He took my arm in his hands and slowly rolled the sleeve up to my elbow. His eye caught mine for a split second, and I stopped breathing. Then, he switched to the other arm, drawing the fabric up inch after precious inch. My body tingled at every brush of his skin against mine. And I swore that he knew it, too.

He grinned. "Tuck it in, in the front."

I did as he'd instructed with an eye roll. "This?"

He appraised me with a hungry glint in his eyes. "You look good in my clothes, Medina."

I took a step toward him. His eyes rounded slightly in surprise before settling back to his arrogant know-it-all look. "When we get back inside, you're going to keep your mouth shut about everything that happened out here."

"And if I don't?"

"I'll take a baseball bat to your Harley."

He hissed. "Cold-blooded, babe."

I arched an eyebrow. Then, I sauntered back inside, as if I hadn't just seen an engagement ring or been completely frazzled by Hollin Abbey, of all people.

2

HOLLIN

The last thing I'd expected to see today was Piper Medina, half-naked.

I wasn't complaining. Not by a long stretch.

When I'd rounded that corner and seen her in nothing but a nude bra, her tits spilling out of the top of it, my brain had short-circuited. Piper had always been fucking gorgeous, but it was her anger that fired me up. The way she held her temper back for everyone but me. As if my very presence lit a fire under her. It was hot. It was why I kept doing it.

My brain came back online the moment I saw that ring though. Piper and I were oil and water. We poked and pressed and fought. We didn't mix. But one look at that ring, and...I had no fucking clue what came over me. All I knew was that there was *no way* she was marrying that brain-dead loser. Luckily, she had the same idea.

She wrapped that lush, curvy body in his stupid shirt. I could have let it go. I should have...probably. But when it came to Piper, I always pushed the envelope. Giving her my shirt could have backfire, but what was most surprising was that she let me.

She did up every little button in front of me and looked at me with those enormous brown eyes. I couldn't help but push it a little further. That look on her face when I rolled up her sleeves...she might have threatened me right afterward, but I'd seen it nonetheless.

Piper Medina might hate me, but she wanted me, too.

And I could live with that.

I adjusted my cock inside my jeans. I needed to stop thinking about her tits in that bra and the way she'd looked, doing up the buttons on my shirt, and those huge eyes as I touched her skin. I had to follow her inside. I needed to talk to Jordan and Julian about my trip. I couldn't do that with a semi in my fucking pants.

"Get it together, Abbey," I grumbled under my breath.

After another moment, I rolled my shoulders back and strode toward my winery. *My* winery. Sometimes, it was too much to consider.

I'd worked at West Texas Winery all through college and after graduation. It was a dump that just happened to have good wine. No one cared about it, and the owners chased the college crowd to cover their debts. When it went under, I swore that I'd get it back up and running again. I loved it too much to let go.

Somehow, I'd convinced my cousins, Jordan and Julian, to drop the money on renovating it. I ran day-to-day operations and had all the experience while they had the business acumen and finances to get it off the ground. Now, we were a year out from the first day we'd opened, and it had never been better.

I strode inside and was immediately greeted.

"Aye, Abbey," the burly, tatted man at the entrance said.

"Good to see you, man," I said, clapping hands with my buddy Zach, who sometimes worked security for the vineyard.

He nodded at me, and I continued through the barn, shaking hands and offering hellos to everyone. The Wrights might have their name on the place, but I was the heart of the operation.

Lubbock, Texas was a dusty, windy small town, five hours away from the rest of civilization, but it was home. I'd grown up here with my two siblings, Campbell and Nora. I'd gone to college at Texas Tech. I'd stuck around when most of my friends had ditched, including my brother.

Finally, I shoved through the last of the crowd to where my cousins were seated. Piper glanced up at me and then hastily away, returning her attention to her boyfriend. An irritated scowl crossed her face. I barely suppressed laughing at it.

"You made it!" Julian said. He hopped out of his seat. We slapped hands, and then he pulled me into a hug. "How'd it go?"

Jordan held his hand out, and we shook. "Give him some room, Julian."

Julian laughed. "Just excited."

I liked that about my cousin. Julian was enthusiastic. Jordan wasn't quite solemn, but he was serious. He'd had to grow up fast to protect Julian from their father. That was a sentiment that I understood. Even if I hadn't gone down the same route. I always found it hard to subdue my larger-than-life personality. When my cousins had first moved to Lubbock about five years ago, I'd thought that it would put them off, but they hadn't missed a beat. It was as if they had always been in my life. I couldn't imagine Lubbock without them now.

I sank into a spare seat next to Blaire.

"Hey, Hollin."

I nodded my head at her.

She looked good tonight. Normally, she hid behind baseball caps and oversize T-shirts, but now, she was in some tight dress. She was some high-profile influencer on social media, but I so rarely saw her like this that I sometimes forgot. She was just *Blaire*, the striker on our soccer team, the girl who ate more pizza than me and who could drink more beer than should have been humanly possible for someone her size. She was practically one of the guys.

"Piper was just saying you were nice enough to let her borrow your shirt," Blaire said with mirth on her lips.

My eyes flicked to Piper's. "Is that what she said?"

"No," Piper said flatly.

Blaire arched an eyebrow. "She might not have said it that way."

"What can I say?" I said with a shit-eating grin. "I'm a giver."

Blaire practically choked on her drink. Piper bristled but said nothing. Bradley, the poor guy, looked flummoxed. His gaze shifted between us, as if he were trying to decipher the meaning of life.

"So," Julian prompted, "how'd it go in Austin?"

Piper was still looking at me. She thought I'd gone to Austin for a date. Julian had told her that. It was our cover story, of sorts. We didn't need one, but we weren't sure that our plan would work. We didn't want to tell anyone other than Jordan before we were ready. And they'd both agreed not to tell their girlfriends, which was the biggest bet that it would get out. But Piper *had* sounded jealous at the prospect of me going out of town for a date. I should disabuse her of the notion, but what fun would that be?

My grin doubled in size. "It went excellent. I'm definitely in."

"Yeah?" Julian asked. "No complications?"

"None at all. It was even easier than I'd thought it would be."

Piper rolled her eyes but said nothing. That wouldn't do. I wanted a reaction from her.

"That's good," Jordan said. "You were worried for nothing."

"I wouldn't say I was worried. I always get what I want."

Piper snorted this time. "Classy."

Blaire scrunched up her face. Jennifer looked to Annie, and Annie shrugged. Well, at least the guys had held up to their word.

"You got something to say, Medina?" I asked with an arched eyebrow.

"No," she said.

Jordan picked up on what was happening first. He shot me a look. "We should tell them."

"Ah, Jor, let me have my fun," I said with a laugh.

Julian glanced around and then made a comical O with his lips. "Ohhh." He cleared his throat. "I guess I should do the honors."

All the girls looked even more confused. I winked at Piper, and she glared back at me. She could look at me that way all she wanted. But I remembered the one second when her guard had come down and she gazed under those thick lashes without any bullshit between us.

"I'll do it," I said, coming to my feet.

"No one cares about your date, Hollin," Piper said. "Keep it in your pants."

Blaire muffled a laugh. "She's not wrong."

"I'll have you all know that I didn't go to Austin to get some ass."

Jennifer choked. "Good for you?"

Annie cackled and nudged her friend. "I love you."

Jennifer reddened. Julian was wearing off on the shy girl. Julian drew her in closer and pressed a kiss to her temple.

"I can get ass just fine here," I told them.

Jordan groaned. "Get on with it, Hollin."

"Right," I said, tipping my head at him. "I entered Wright Vineyard into the IWAA Texas Wine Award Competition in Austin."

"What?" Annie gasped. She swatted at Jordan. "You didn't tell me."

Jennifer's eyes lit up. "That's amazing."

Blaire pulled me into a hug. "Really? That's incredible!"

But Piper...Piper did nothing. Bradley was up, shaking hands with Jordan and Julian. Piper remained seated in my fucking shirt, looking hot as fucking hell. I had no idea what was running through her head. Was she processing that I hadn't been talking about a date at all? Was she mad about the competition? Why was she blank-faced?

"Hey," I said, drawing her eyes up to me. "This means I wasn't on a date."

She scowled. "Like I give a fuck."

"What's with the face? Can't even be happy for us?"

The others had grown quiet at my words. No one else had realized that Piper wasn't jumping up and down with excitement. There was no guarantee that we'd win this award. It was a huge competition. But it was a possibility. The wine I'd entered was our newest vintage, and it was above and beyond what West Texas Winery had ever made. Everything had come together in the last year. The grapes had yielded better than any before that. It was as if we'd sacrificed the old winery to some ancient deity and Wright Vineyard had been reincarnated out of the ashes. Blessed in some way.

But that didn't explain Piper's reaction. Yeah, she managed a separate winery, but we were a small enough operation not to dip into Sinclair Cellars' profits or anything. They'd been around for decades. They were a huge operation. A national name. It didn't change the rivalry. How could it when we were both so antagonistic?

"I'm happy for you," she said without a hint of emotion.

"What is it?" I asked, taking a step toward her. "Say what's on your mind."

She met my step by coming to her feet and lifting her chin. A slow smile curled on her lips. There she was. There was the fire heart.

"It's nice that you entered, but you've no chance of winning."

My eyebrows shot up at her gall. The rest of the room disappeared as I got into it with her. I didn't know what the others were doing or saying. When we got like this, tunnel vision narrowed in, and I forgot everything but the fight.

"And why is that?"

"Because I entered last week."

3

PIPER

*H*ollin's stupid smirk dropped for an entire second as my words registered. His brows furrowed, and he tilted his head slightly, the soft strands of his blond hair falling across his forehead before he pushed it out of the way. It was like a victory. Until it disappeared and he smiled again, bigger and brighter than before.

"We're competitors, Medina."

"I guess we are."

"I'll be your Wright rival," he crooned.

He held his hand out. I warily looked at it before putting mine in his. I stared him down. Heat bloomed between us. Something potent and commanding. A binding spell cast over this handshake. Magic of old sealing our words.

The contact made my hand tingle. As if magic had really been flung over us. Ribbon tied around our wrists to connect us. And I didn't know how I felt about that. How I felt about having *any* connection to Hollin Abbey.

I jerked my hand back first. "I'm going to win."

"We'll see," he said with a smirk.

Julian clapped a hand on Hollin's back, and everything

crashed down all at once. As if a bubble had been burst and the last stray traces of glitter fluttered to the ground, forgotten. Noise returned to our reality. Our friends huddled around us to congratulate us both for even entering. And somehow, I was still trapped in that in-between place. Not quite ready to give up whatever had come over us.

I made the mistake of looking up into his endless blue eyes. He was still Hollin, of course. Still a hundred and ten percent arrogance, wrapped up in a towering, tatted bow. But for a second, I thought he felt it, too. That nowhere in which nothing else existed but our rivalry.

He raised one eyebrow. A question and an invitation. Not that I could ever answer that particular question or RSVP to whatever he was inviting me to. Not with Hollin. Not ever. I knew what he did to girls who showed an ounce of interest. Just one ounce. I wouldn't be one of those girls. No matter what had happened between us.

"Good luck," I said without a touch of goodwill in my voice.

He laughed. The sunshine to my grumpy brooding. "I don't need it. But you might."

Then, Julian and Jordan pulled him away to get champagne for a toast. My friends bombarded me a second later. Thankfully, Bradley was shoved out of the way as the girls each drew me into an excited hug.

"When did you decide to do this?" Annie asked. "And why weren't we informed?"

Annie was the bossiest one of the bunch. She was in residency as an ER doctor and radiated confident energy. She somehow exuded enough of that for all the rest of us.

"Yeah," Blaire said. "I'm your bestie."

I shrugged. "We enter competitions every year. Usually

smaller regional competitions. Our wines do all right, but I wanted to go bigger this year."

Jennifer tucked a strand of her light-brown hair behind her hair and smiled. "We want to celebrate every achievement. You know that."

I should have known that. But sometimes, I didn't think that applied to me. Jennifer was a wedding photographer for Wright Vineyard, but she had also recently started working with Hollin's rockstar brother, Campbell. After her photo of him had gone viral last year, their record label had hired her to do the photography for the cover of their latest album. They were now on an international tour for said album, and her photography was *everywhere*.

That felt like something to celebrate. Entering an award competition felt like nothing.

"A toast," Jordan interrupted the conversation.

The guys passed out champagne, and we all held our glasses aloft. Bradley returned to my side, sliding a hand across my hips. I was self-conscious about it, knowing what I now knew awaited me in his gym bag. He wasn't happy about me wearing Hollin's shirt after I came back—*what guy would?*—but he'd shrugged it off quickly. As if me wearing another guy's shirt didn't even matter. Was he that secure in us?

"To one year at Wright Vineyard," Jordan said.

"One phenomenal year," Julian added.

"And friendly competition to follow," Hollin said.

He tipped his head at me, and I just stared back blankly. What part of this made him think it would be friendly?

Still, I held my glass aloft and clinked it with my friends' glasses. I took a sip of my champagne. The Wrights had splurged on a vintage Veuve Clicquot, and I could appreciate every single delicious note of the champagne. Wright

Vineyard didn't make a sparkling yet, but few could compare to the historical French wineries anyway.

We settled back into our seats. Bradley scooted his chair even closer to mine, draping his arm across the back of it. I was ready to leave. I needed to get this over with. But Jordan was still standing and speaking, and I should focus. I couldn't leave yet. Even if I wanted to.

"While I have your attention," Jordan said with a wide grin, "I'd thank everyone for joining us on this adventure. It's had its highs and lows. I never believed I'd move out of Vancouver, but now, I'm here, and I couldn't imagine being anywhere else."

A few, "Hear, hear!" were chorused as others listened in on his speech.

Other Wrights were in attendance. Jordan and Julian's cousins—Jensen, Austin, Landon, Morgan, and Sutton Wright—ran Wright Construction in town and were the reason that the Wright name was associated with Texas royalty. Jensen's wife, Emery, was hugely pregnant while their one-year-old tottered around their feet. Landon had his three-year-old, Holden, with him, who was happily playing with Sutton's seven-year-old, Jason, and two-year-old, Madison. Landon's wife, Heidi, wasn't in attendance since she had recently had twin boys—Hudson and Harrison. The number of Wrights in this town was growing exponentially.

Morgan and Patrick had set a date for their wedding for this fall. Everyone kept looking to Austin and Julia, wondering when they were going to tie the knot. But they had always done their own thing, and I appreciated that.

My twin brother, Peter, was in attendance with his boyfriend, Chester. He looked up, as if sensing my eyes on him across the room. Twin thing. He flipped me off, and my hardened veneer dropped. I laughed and covered it by taking another sip of my wine. Bradley glanced at me in confusion.

Jordan had been talking all this time. Giving the fancy Wright speech the family was known for. It was a good one. I was sure it was. I hadn't been paying attention, but still...

The crowd gasped all at once.

My eyes snapped back to Jordan Wright, who had gotten down onto one knee. My jaw dropped as he removed a red ring box from his pocket.

Time slowed as he faced Annie Donoghue with a stunning Cartier ring. Her hands flew to her mouth. Tears came to her eyes. Shock rippled through the crowd. They'd only been together for a year. But when you knew, you knew.

Didn't you?

Bradley's eyes were on me. I looked over at him, and he was giving me giant puppy-dog eyes. Ones full of hope and awe. As if he saw *us* in what was happening right now.

My eyes didn't mirror his. I felt...horror. Riotous, dawning, gaping horror in the pit of my stomach. This couldn't be happening. Bradley couldn't propose to me. I imagined myself in Annie's shoes for a minute and thought I might be physically ill. I'd say no.

No.

It was so final. The end of everything we had. And yet I knew it without a shadow of a doubt.

I'd touched that ring box in his gym bag and tossed it aside like it didn't matter. But now, it was an immediate visceral reaction. I *had* to do something about this. I couldn't sit here and pretend things were okay.

"Yes!" Annie cried.

Everyone was up and applauding as Jordan slid the diamond onto her finger. They embraced as if this were the best day of their entire lives. A year ago, everything had started in this very room for them. It was magical.

If only there wasn't a distress signal in my head. A loud beeping, telling me to escape.

I stepped out of Bradley's arm when I got to my feet, and as I stumbled forward to congratulate Annie, my foot caught on something imaginary. I tripped, barely catching myself before face-planting on the hardwood floor of the recently renovated barn.

Then, there was a strong pair of arms on my hips, steadying me. I was hardly the clumsy damsel in distress.

So, my first instinct was to push the person away. "I'm fine."

I looked up to find Hollin arching a pointed eyebrow at me. "Medina," he said, rolling my surname across his tongue.

"Don't touch me," I said.

Every inch he touched was on fire.

"You're welcome," he said cheekily. "You almost fell on your face."

"I had it."

He finally released me. "Seem flustered."

"Hollin," I growled. "Shut your face."

"Just saying," he purred under his breath. "You went into straight panic mode at the sight of that ring."

Had it been that obvious? "I did not."

"Okay, fine. Only I saw it."

"You can't read me that well."

"You almost fell on your face," he repeated.

"I'm happy for Jordan and Annie."

"Of course. How could you not be? They were made for each other."

"Exactly."

"Are you agreeing with me?"

"No," I said automatically.

He chuckled. His hand slid to the sleeve of my shirt. I looked up at him as he fixed where the sleeve had come undone.

"Abbey," Bradley said, suddenly appearing at my side.

Hollin dropped the shirt and smiled at my boyfriend. "Had to fix my shirt. Looks good on her, doesn't it?"

Bradley looked between me and Hollin, as if he couldn't figure out whether or not he should punch him. Of course, that would be a real problem. Since Hollin probably had a hundred pounds of muscle on Bradley. Frankly, it was obscene.

"Shut up, Hollin," I growled and turned back to my boyfriend. "Come on. Let's congratulate the happy couple."

Bradley followed me away. "Is...something happening with y'all?"

I blinked at him. "With *Hollin*?"

He laughed softly at my incredulity. "I know you say you hate him, but..."

"But I'm wearing his shirt?"

"Yeah. And he riles you so easily."

"You know why that is."

Bradley nodded. "Yeah. I mean, I know what you told me. It just felt different."

It had, hadn't it? Fuck.

"Don't worry about it. He's the same Hollin."

I glanced back at Hollin Abbey. A flash of possessiveness came into Hollin's eyes, and my cheeks heated from the one look. It didn't matter how attractive he was or that he looked at me like every book boyfriend I'd ever read about. He was still Hollin Abbey, and I wouldn't ever go there.

4

HOLLIN

*M*y new life mission was to see how often I could make Piper blush. I'd never seen her do it until that look back. Now, it was something I absolutely had to see more often. Mostly, she scowled at me and told me to fuck off. This was a whole new look.

And sure, I'd been a dick to say that shit to Bradley. I'd never been able to hide my feelings about the guy. But taunting him was a new low. I'd thought he might swing on me. Would have been a waste of energy anyway. Piper looked like she was long over him.

Finally, I tore my gaze from her to return to the moment. My friends were engaged.

"We have to celebrate," I cheered. "Let's open a bottle of the new vintage."

Julian nodded eagerly. "Yes, bro. Let's do it."

Jordan shot us both a stern look. "Before we find out about the award?"

"It's not like we're opening it up to the entire party. Just us."

Annie nudged her new fiancé. "Come on. I haven't even tried it! And we used to taste-test all the wine."

She winked at him, and I had a feeling she was talking about something else entirely.

Jordan's face softened at her words. She had that effect on him. "All right. We are celebrating."

Julian and I clapped hands and then barreled through the party and out the side door. We didn't keep the newest wine in the barn yet. We'd bring it out as a special-edition vintage after we found out about the award. But we had a few cases in the cellar, and we trekked across the lawn to grab the bottles.

Julian shot me a look. "What's going on with you and Piper?"

"Nothing more than normal."

"So, you're antagonizing her for no reason?"

"Not for *no* reason," I said with a laugh.

Julian punched in the code to open the cellar, and we entered the long line of wooden wine barrels. The machinery was on one end of the cellar with offices on the other end, and a storage unit was in the middle for processed wine to sell. For the last year, it had been predominantly empty since for our first harvest, we had been using the slightly neglected grapes from when the place was West Texas Winery. Now that we had our own operation, from harvest to bottling, it was running much smoother. And the wine was exponentially better as a result.

"I have a case in my office," I told Julian. We passed the barrels and headed into my office. I grabbed two bottles, handing them to my cousin. "Should be enough?"

"Probably."

I grabbed another bottle for safe measure. "Just in case."

He laughed. "You mean, more for you?"

"This red is the shit. If I do say so myself."

"It's your baby."

I winked. "Obviously."

I took great pride in looking down at the first bottle that had been all my doing. The label was cream in color with *Wright Vineyard* written in a fancy blood-red script and a red wax seal with the *WV* inside it. Under that, it said the vintage—*Abbey*. *My* wine. We'd decided a year ago to give the wines names and then describe them under the label. So, the red was Abbey, and the first white, we'd named Annie. Guess that should have been my first clue about the pending engagement.

"So, what is this reason you're being a dick to Piper?" Julian asked.

"Oh, because it's fun."

Julian laughed. "Wow."

"Yeah. I'm really mature for my age."

"Sure. *Mature*. That's the word I'd use to describe you."

"Thanks. I try."

We both laughed as we walked back to the barn. I filched a corkscrew from the bar on our way and had a bottle uncorked when we arrived. One of our bartenders for the night followed us over with a set of new glasses.

I poured tasting portions in each glass and passed them out to our friends. Piper held her hand out for a glass, and Julian offered one out to her. I had no idea what came over me, but I put myself between her and the wine. Julian fumbled the glass with a curse.

"Piper doesn't get any," I said with a devilish grin.

"What?" she asked in obvious shock.

"Hollin," Julian grumbled.

"She's the enemy."

"The *enemy*?" Piper all but growled. Her eyes narrowed in annoyance. "What the hell?"

"We're competitors now. I can't let you sample the goods."

"As if that's going to change *anything* about the competition. We've already submitted the wine for sampling."

I shrugged, unperturbed by the facts of the situation. "So?"

She blinked at me. "You're really not going to let me have any?"

I crossed my arms over my chest, my biceps bulging against the confines of my white T-shirt. "Nope."

"You're *unbelievable*."

"Not the first time I've heard that before, babe."

Her displeasure turned straight primal. She looked half-ready to claw my eyes out at the insinuation in my voice. And there *was* insinuation in my voice. I couldn't help it around her. I'd told Julian it was fun. It was. But there was something about poking at Piper. She reacted the best. The soft heave of her chest at the indignation. The dilation of her eyes when she realized I was fucking serious. The clench of her hand for the moment when she was deciding whether or not it was worth dealing with me. There was always a point where she'd tell me to fuck off and walk away, but it was like threading a needle to wait to get there with her.

Today, she chose sass.

"Like I want your shit wine anyway. I'll stick to French champagne. Since they know what they're actually doing."

She rolled her eyes at me and walked back to her awaiting boyfriend and the Veuve we'd been using to celebrate. She thought that she'd won that round. But the look on her face had been success enough.

"Leave her alone," Julian hissed.

I turned back to my cousin with pure innocence on my face. "I don't know what you mean."

"Must you antagonize her?" Jordan drawled, hefting a bottle of Abbey to examine it.

"I must," I said with a grin.

"Oh. My. God," a voice squealed. "Hollin?"

I glanced up at the unfamiliar voice. A petite blonde stared up at me with bright blue eyes and a sizable rack spilling out of some frilly pink dress. She looked vaguely familiar. Emily? Emma? Emmie? Fuck.

"Hey," I said with a charming smile. "Can I help you?"

She strode forward two steps in white booties that Julian had claimed were in right now. Whatever that meant. He was the fashion guy.

"It's Emily."

Ha! I'd been right the first time.

She waited for a response to that, but I didn't give one. "Remember, we went on a few dates in January? You said you'd call..."

"Right," I said, rubbing my hand on the back of my head. I didn't always remember the girls I had gone on dates with two months prior. "Sorry about that."

"It's totally okay. It's good to see you. I came with a few girlfriends who love the winery."

"Glad they like it."

"So..." She bit her lip and looked down, trying to be suggestive.

I remembered that about her now. That she'd been really into biting her lip. As if it was the only seduction tactic she'd picked up. Her big tits and blonde hair and heart-shaped face usually got her whatever she wanted.

We'd gone on three dates, hooked up, and then I'd given

up. As I so often did. Most girls like Emily couldn't keep my attention for that long. I'd given her the benefit of the doubt for a third date based on her rack alone.

"So?" I prompted.

"Well, do you want to meet up again?"

Julian barely suppressed a laugh next to me. I shot him a look. He already knew my motto with things. It wasn't that I had a three date rule *exactly*. I just got bored so easily, and I wasn't interested in anything serious. I hadn't been interested in that in a long fucking time. Most girls weren't relationship material anyway. They weren't for me at least. I was down with fucking around for longer than that. But I wasn't a *feelings* guy.

My dipshit friends called it my three-date rule. But that made it seem like I was looking for a relationship. Like I was giving up on girls because I hadn't found *the one*. When the opposite was true. I had no interest in finding *the one*, and I was pretty sure that person didn't even exist.

Yeah, Jordan and Julian had each found their person, but they'd gone through a whole hell of a lot of shit to get there. I wasn't willing to invest that much into anyone but myself. Sure, it made me look like a dick, but I wasn't leading anyone on. People knew who I was upfront. Was it my fault if they wanted to change me?

"Thanks for the offer, Emily, but I'm going to pass."

Her cheeks reddened. "Oh. You're going to pass?"

"Yeah."

She gulped and her head swiveled to her friends. They waved her back over, and she bit her fucking lip again. "Are you sure?"

"Pretty sure."

"I, um...okay."

"Could you have an ounce of sympathy?" Annie said with an eye roll as the poor girl scurried back to her friends.

"What? She knew when we tried that in January that I wasn't Mr. Relationship," I said to Annie.

"Yeah, but do you know how hard it is for a girl to ask a guy out?"

"And so I'm obligated to say yes when she asks?"

"No," Annie said, smacking my arm. "But you could let her down easy."

Jordan held his hand out to his fiancée, and she stepped into his embrace. "Listen to the doctor. She knows what she's talking about."

"I said thanks for the offer," I said with a shrug.

"It's a waste of time," Piper chimed in.

My gaze found her. "And why is that?"

"Because you're tactless. You can't teach an old dog new tricks."

I grinned, taking a step forward, ready to lay back into her, but Julian smacked me in the chest. "Do *not* say whatever just came to your mind."

I shot my friend a look and laughed. "What was I going to say?"

"Something obscene," he guessed.

True. I was about to tell her that I could teach *her* new tricks. If she'd just let me instead of always mouthing off. Who the fuck was I kidding? I'd teach her new tricks while she mouthed off, and I'd enjoy all of it.

She must have seen all of that cross my face in a split second because she suddenly stood. Her chair knocked backward, scraping against the hardwood. "It's time for me to head out. As much fun as it is to watch Hollin three-date-rule some poor girl *and* not get to drink at a winery, I have to work in the morning."

Bradley rose to his feet as well. He hadn't touched his wine out of solidarity, apparently. He set it down on the table we were all sitting around and dusted his hands off on his cargo pants. "Y'all have a good night."

The girls all pulled Piper in for a hug before she headed out. Blaire whispered something in her ear, and they plotted for a minute before Piper waved at everyone and then left with her boyfriend. I watched her walk away, enjoying the sway of her ass, clothed in her tight jeans.

Julian shook his head. "Never going to happen, bro."

I laughed and tilted my head for a better view. "It might."

"No way. She's way out of your league."

That, at least, was true. "Maybe."

Didn't stop me from wondering if a few orgasms would loosen her up.

5

PIPER

"You can't drive," I said, snatching the keys out of Bradley's hand.

"Come on. I'm fine."

I ignored him. He'd spilled a glass of wine on me. He wasn't fine. And sure, he'd sobered up some since then, but I wasn't going to risk it. I'd drive him home. I opened the driver's side, grasped the oh-shit bar, and towed myself into his truck. It was a lifted F-250 that he used on construction sites, where he worked for Wright Construction. He'd been promoted to a site manager, but it was still day-to-day construction work. It wore on him, which was why he always drank so much. I almost always drove us home.

He climbed into the passenger seat with a grumble. "I could have driven."

"Whatever. We're out in the middle of nowhere."

"You're staying at my place tonight?" he asked, dropping his hand onto my thigh.

"Yeah. We're going to your place."

I never said I was staying there because I wouldn't. But I wasn't having that conversation while we drove to his house in Tech Terrace. I lived on the other side of the popular neighborhood right off of the Texas Tech campus. Though my house was slightly nicer and a lot bigger. Close enough that I could walk, far enough away that I usually didn't.

Bradley put on the country station, and I let the heart-break tunes serenade us on the drive home. I remained silent as I parked the truck in his driveway. The garage was too packed with all of his construction tools that he couldn't get anything else in there.

He hopped out, and I followed him out of the truck. He strode right up to the front door but only stopped when he realized I wasn't beside him.

"Piper?" he asked.

I took a deep breath. I'd prepared myself for this. I knew what was coming. It didn't make it any easier to do. "This is over, Bradley."

His eyes widened, and he stumbled back down the steps. "What are you talking about?"

"This isn't working."

"Why not?"

I didn't even know where to begin. "It just isn't."

"Is this because of Hollin? Is that why you're wearing his shirt?"

My face was a mask of disbelief. "What? No, of course not. I'm not interested in Hollin Abbey. I'd never do that to you. It's about you and me."

"It's awfully suspicious that you're wearing his shirt and you were flirting with him all night, and now, you're breaking up with me."

"For one, *you* poured wine all over my shirt. Two, we weren't flirting."

He laughed hoarsely. "You were flirting."

"This isn't about Hollin," I insisted. "This isn't working

for me anymore. We said when we started dating again that this was the now or never. This was our chance. We'd been dating like this—on-again, off-again—for five years, Bradley. If it's not working yet, when is it going to start working?"

"I thought it was working," he said miserably.

"Not for me."

"What can I do to change your mind?"

I closed my eyes and breathed out heavily in exasperation. "There's nothing you can do. This is my decision."

"Let's decide together, Piper. Come on. You're going to throw away all of this time?"

"I'm not throwing it away. I've thought about it, and I'm making a decision. This is what's right for me."

"Please," he said, reaching for my hand and pulling me toward him. "Please. I'm nothing without you, Piper. Nothing."

"Bradley," I said on a sigh. "No, I can't keep doing this."

"Sweetheart, we can work this out."

I wrenched my hand back from him. My heart should have been rending in two, but I felt...done. I was already done with this. "I can't. We can't."

"Why not? Please..."

"I found more than your shirt in your gym bag," I blurted out.

Bradley went deathly still. He knew exactly what I'd found when I rummaged around in there. The ring that he'd purchased. I'd just admonished Hollin for not having any tact, and then I'd thrown that in Bradley's face. I had to be blunt. I had to make it perfectly clear where I stood. And if that meant telling him about the ring, then I'd do it. Was that how Hollin justified things too?

"You did?" Bradley said softly, warily.

"I did. And...I don't want that."

He winced at my words. "I see."

"I'm sorry. I...I'm just done."

He nodded, speechless. As if I'd put the nail in the coffin. There was no coming back from saying that I didn't ever want to marry him. Jesus.

I handed him the keys to his truck. I considered hugging him one last time, but I couldn't make myself do it. I didn't want him to think it was encouragement. So, I swallowed hard and walked away.

Blaire pulled up beside me on the road. She rolled the window down. "That was faster than I thought it would be."

I got into the passenger seat. "Longer than I wanted it to take."

"He didn't take it well?"

I shook my head and stared out the window. "I found an engagement ring."

"What?" Blaire gasped.

Blaire had been my best friend since college. Even though she was three years younger than me, we'd hit it off and never looked back. I'd been there to help her get her business, Blaire Blush, off the ground. And watch her cross a million followers on Instagram. I'd seen her recently hit three and a half million on TikTok. She was infectious and incredible and empowering for all women everywhere. I loved that about her. And that she'd never told me to ditch Bradley long ago when I was still trying to figure out what the hell we were doing.

"Yeah. That's why I was outside so long and why I took Hollin's shirt. Because Bradley was going to propose."

"Talk about a curveball," Blaire said as she parked her silver Lexus in the garage beside my blue Jeep Wrangler.

"Yeah. Hollin asked if Bradley was going to propose, and I freaked out."

"Wait," Blaire said as we entered my house, "Hollin *saw* the engagement ring?"

"He did."

"Ah." She blew out a breath. "No wonder."

"What?"

"He was in rare form tonight."

"He was the same asshole as always."

Blaire flipped her long black hair off her shoulder. "If you say so."

"I don't want to talk about Hollin."

"Fine. Tell me about Bradley."

"I don't want to talk about him either."

Blaire laughed. "I bet I have some ice cream in the freezer."

She went to look, and I went into my bedroom to change out of these clothes. I chucked the tight jeans onto my bed and slowly unbuttoned Hollin's shirt. I brought the fabric up to my nose and inhaled. It smelled like him. I didn't know what cologne he used, but it made my mouth water. It was so heady. As if I could fall back into a forever dream at the mere scent of it.

I hastily stripped out of the shirt and threw it on top of my jeans. I needed to get this under control. It didn't matter that Hollin's cologne turned me on. Or that I'd worn the shirt all night. Or that Blaire had been right...that he'd been in rare form. He'd pressed every single button and not backed off all night. He'd wanted a reaction from me, and I'd given them all to him.

"Okay," Blaire called from the kitchen. "Looks like Jennifer killed the cookie dough."

I tugged on sweats and a Texas Tech sweatshirt. "Strawberry?"

"Yes. There's a pint of strawberry and chocolate, cherry, pecan."

"A scoop of both?"

"You got it."

She doled out ice cream into fancy martini glasses and brought them over to the couch. She positioned them just this way, snapping a few shots.

She guiltily looked up at me. "Sorry, work..."

"I'm used to you taking pictures of everything before we can enjoy it."

She laughed. "Yeah. Well, after a breakup is different. I should be in the moment."

"You're here. You have ice cream. Good enough for me."

No matter how laid-back Blaire was, she always worried that her carefully curated life interfered too much in real life. But I didn't care. It never changed anything about our time together.

My mind snagged on one thing that Blaire had said. "What do you mean, no wonder about Hollin? That he was in rare form?"

"Well, he's into you," Blaire said with an unapologetic shrug. "Like...he was acting like that because the ring freaked him out."

I dug my spoon into the ice cream. "Hollin is just pissed that I'm one of the few girls who won't give him the time of day."

"He doesn't act like that around me," she pointed out.

"Yeah, but it's different."

"Not to play the minor celebrity card"—she gestured to

herself—"but after a few million followers, I have discovered that guys *and* girls find me attractive. I could be dating right now. But Hollin Abbey doesn't even look at me. He's into *you*."

"So? I'm not into him," I insisted.

Blaire pointed her spoon at me. "You think he's hot."

"He is."

"You like the way he smells."

I bit the inside of my cheek. I hated that I'd told Blaire that once. "And? It doesn't change what he did."

Before Blaire and I lived together, I'd lived with these two girls, Quinn and Khloe. When Quinn asked me about Hollin, I told her what I knew about him. He was a year older than me in school. We'd never associated before the Wright cousins moved here, but I'd heard that he was a good guy. He hadn't had his sleeve tattoo. He was still *so* tall but less muscular. I told her to go for it.

Unbeknownst to Quinn, he was already dating Khloe as well. When it all came out, the friendship ended over a guy who three-date-ruled them both and then threw them away. We had to break the lease because they wouldn't even talk to one another. It was when I decided to get my own place. I'd never do the drama or deal with Hollin Abbey.

"That was a few years ago."

"You think he's different? You saw how he was with that Emily girl tonight. If anything, that proves that he's exactly the same. He'd probably even tell you that he is."

Blaire sighed. "All right. You win."

"Good. I like winning."

"You better win the wine competition."

I chanced a glance at her. "Was the wine that good?"

"Really fucking good."

"Ugh!" I was still irritated that Hollin hadn't let me try it.

He'd even called me the enemy. Jerk. "I'd better fucking win."

"Yeah," Blaire said with laughter sparkling in her eyes, "or you're never going to hear the end of it."

She wasn't wrong. Hollin would never let me live that down. Not ever.

6

PIPER

*T*he good thing about Lubbock was that a person could get to anything they wanted within twenty minutes. Sinclair Cellars was just on the border of that time limit. Built on land the Sinclairs had acquired in the '60s in the south part of Lubbock, it had acres and acres of vineyards. What had once been a small family operation had bloomed under their careful tutelage and my father's burgeoning enthusiasm for the property.

Driving onto the land each morning was like coming home. I'd grown up running through the grapevines, had my first kiss on a tractor ride through the fields in the fall, and learned the feeling of a hard day's work. When I was having a bad day, the first thing I wanted to do was go out and walk through the grapes. I found peace here. I understood how family farmers felt, connected to their entire world in this dirt. It had sustained me for a long time.

So, when I parked my blue Jeep Wrangler at the front of the property Saturday morning, the land was calling to me. I took my coffee out of the center console and trekked out into my fields. The vines were empty of the bountiful fruit that would start growing this summer.

But it settled something inside me.

I'd broken up with Bradley last night. For the last time. I wasn't sad about it exactly. It felt like a lot of wasted time. It wasn't, of course. It had shaped me in many ways. I'd dated a bunch of idiots before him, and he'd been good to me for the last couple of years. We just hadn't had *forever* stamped on us. As hard as it was to let go, it was the right choice.

I took a sip of my drink and let the early morning rays crash over my golden skin. The mornings were still too cold to go without a jacket. I snuggled into the North Face and let the coffee heat me up.

After a few minutes, a throat cleared behind me. "Thought I'd find you out here."

I smiled at my dad. "*Buenos días*, Papa."

Matthew Medina wrapped an arm around my shoulders. "Did it call to you too?"

"*Sí.*" I dropped my head on his shoulder. "Always."

We stood there until the sun crested the horizon, bathing our fields in orange and pink. This was what we had in common. This was who we were. Our name might not be on the wine label, but it was our blood, sweat, and tears that created the incredible blends.

"Come, *mija.* It's time for work."

I nodded and followed my father back out of the crops. He veered off to his office, and I went down to the cellar. There was always something to do at this point. We were experimenting with a small batch of natural yeast fermentation wine. It was risky and tricky, as it likely wouldn't be reproducible. But we were a large enough operation that we could try out ideas, even if they didn't come to fruition, as long as we hit the quotas. Our product was in stores all across Texas as well as specialty stores across the rest of the southwest.

It was nearly noon before I looked up from my work to find my sister, Peyton, standing with her hands on her hips. "Pipes, did you forget?"

I blinked at her as comprehension dawned on me. "We're meeting the wedding planner."

"Yep. Were you going to come? Dad said that you'd be down here."

"I'm coming," I told her instantly. I put aside my work and followed her out of the processing center.

Peyton was five years older than me and Peter and a classically trained ballerina. She'd left us at seventeen for the School of American Ballet full-time in New York City. She was a principal for the New York City Ballet until suffering a knee injury. She'd retired last summer and moved back to Lubbock to be with her high school sweetheart, Isaac Donoghue.

I was so happy for them for working it out after all these years. It sometimes felt too cute to be true. I hadn't even *had* a high school sweetheart. I'd been more interested in my studies and working at the winery to get into anything serious. And my experience in college with a series of terrible boyfriends had taught me that what Isaac and Peyton had was special and utterly unrealistic. The expectations I had from my parents and sister made all my relationships look like chump change.

"Okay, seester," I teased. "Let's go show you around the vineyard you grew up in."

She rolled her eyes, tugging her cardigan tighter around her body. She was the artistic director for the Lubbock Ballet Company and still looked every inch the dancer from her perfect posture to her strict ballet bun. "It's not about a tour. Nora wants to focus on the layout."

"Whatever you want."

Peyton and Isaac would be married at the end of May right here at Sinclair Cellars. We didn't do a ton of weddings on-site anymore. Not since we'd expanded into higher production. Dad kept talking about opening a venue downtown that served food and our wine during the week and did events as a side project. But it had never happened.

It was one of the differences between us and Wright Vineyard. They'd immediately hired Nora to be their on-site wedding planner and dove straight into event planning while they got the wine side of the business off the ground. It helped that Nora was Hollin's sister.

Peyton and I headed back up toward the main building. It was a large with a church facade and terra-cotta roof. We used it for our annual tractor rides in the fall, Christmas light rides, and wine tasting year-round.

Nora waited for us at the front entrance with her face buried in an iPad. She had on a green-and-white floral number on her barely five-foot frame. The platform heels made her look much taller than she actually was. She wore them basically everywhere, except the soccer field. I found it baffling. Her blonde bob was parted straight down the middle and had been recently cut to just under her chin. She looked up at our approach, and her blue eyes were nearly the same color as Hollin's. I had to push aside that thought instantly.

"Hey, Nora," I said, holding out a hand.

Nora swatted it away and gave me a hug. "We're all family here."

"Thanks for coming, Nora," Peyton said.

She smiled wide. "I'm so excited for y'all. This is going to be so much fun. Y'all ready?"

"Sure," I said.

Nora had only graduated last year, but she'd worked for a wedding planner all through college. She was *good* at her job. She walked us through all of the technical business—layouts, arrangements, flow. I was the maid of honor and promised to be there for Peyton through all of it, but I was starting to wonder if Nora was a magician. She juggled every little thing as if it were so easy.

"That about covers it," she said an hour later as we sat around a table inside. "What do you think?"

"You're a godsend," Peyton said honestly.

Nora laughed. "It's what I've always wanted to do." She pointed at me and frowned. "Oh, one thing I forgot to ask about. Is Bradley still on for building the altar? The one that I thought we had on hold was scooped up. You said that he'd be interested if I couldn't get the arch we wanted."

I opened my mouth and then closed it. Well, fuck.

"What happened?" Peyton asked intuitively.

"We kind of broke up last night."

"Again?"

I winced. "Yeah, but for real this time."

"I've heard that before," Peyton said.

"Well," I said with a cringe, "I found an engagement ring in his bag."

Nora put her hand to her mouth, and Peyton's entire face softened.

"I realized that I could never marry him. So, yeah, it's over."

"I'm sorry," Peyton said, putting her hand on mine. "You were together a long time."

"That's hard, Piper," Nora said. She scribbled on her

iPad. "I'll handle talking to Bradley. Don't even worry about it."

"Okay, great."

"But I guess that explains why you were wearing my brother's shirt last night."

"You were *what*?" Peyton asked. She fully faced me. "Is something going on with you and Hollin?"

"No. I wish people would stop asking me that," I grumbled. "Bradley spilled a glass of wine on me, and Hollin had a spare shirt."

"They were flirting," Nora said with a grin.

"We weren't flirting."

"Would you be aware if you were flirting?" Peyton asked with a laugh. "You're kind of oblivious, Pipes."

"This conversation isn't about me. We're here about the wedding," I reminded them. "Hollin is a manwhore. No offense, Nora."

Nora raised her hands. "None taken. I know who he is, and I'd love to see someone put him on the straight and narrow."

"No one can make another person change. That's not how it works." I shrugged as I came to my feet. "I don't care what Hollin does as long as he's not hurting people. But that doesn't mean I'm interested."

I wasn't interested. He'd called me the enemy, and I felt the same way. We were on opposite sides of a war. He was hot and made me fucking blush with his looks, but that was sexual. That wasn't anything important about a relationship, except my body's reaction to him. I was smarter than that.

"Forget I mentioned it," Nora said easily. "I'll take care of the specifics for the wedding, Peyton. If you have any questions, feel free to message me at any time. I'm always available."

"Thanks, Nora," Peyton said.

"Seriously, thank you."

"It's no problem."

"You all got the gala invite, right?" Peyton asked as we cleared the table and stood to leave.

"Got it," I told her.

She was excited. Lubbock had acquired our first professional sports team, a Division II soccer team—FC Lubbock, the Prairie Dogs. Jordan had been in charge of the contract through Wright Construction, and Isaac had been the project manager alongside him. They were hosting a huge welcome event at the Buddy Holly Center. The ballet was performing a mini set for the audience and everything.

"August and I will be there," Nora confirmed. "We're excited."

"Me too," Peyton said.

We followed Nora outside to see a truck parked next to her CR-V. Her boyfriend, August, leaned against it in Wranglers, a gray T-shirt, and cowboy boots. His floppy surfer hair blew in the wind, but his heart-melting grin was all for his girlfriend. Nora squealed and trotted over to him as fast as she could in her heels. He picked her up and twirled her around, planting a firm kiss on her lips.

"Couldn't wait for you to be done. Brought you Starbucks," August said.

Nora looked up at him with hero worship in her eyes. "Gah, I love you."

"Love you, too, baby girl."

He passed her the coffee he'd driven out to the middle of nowhere to bring her and then waved at us. "Hey, y'all."

"Hey, August," I said.

Peyton waved next to me.

"They're cute," Peyton said.

"Young."

Peyton laughed. "You're so cynical."

"Practical," I argued.

"Whatever you say." She faced me. "Are you sure you're okay about Bradley?"

"Totally. It was a long time coming."

"Well, if you need to talk, I'm around." She checked her phone. "But I need to get to the studio. They knew I was coming in late, but still...things get out of control in a matter of hours."

I hugged my sister and watched her leave, too. Maybe I was cynical. After all, wasn't Peyton proof that young love could last? It'd just taken fifteen years for them to get back to it. Was it because I didn't have anyone like that in my life that I felt so jaded about it?

Things hadn't worked out with Bradley after trying time and time again. Was it me? Or was I over the bullshit? Over settling?

My thoughts were clouded as I walked back inside and grabbed another water. I didn't have time to think about all of this. I had work to do. I was heading to my office when I nearly ran into a face I hadn't seen in a good long while.

"Chase?" I asked.

Chase Sinclair blinked when he saw me. "Oh, hey, Piper."

"What are you doing here?" I asked in confusion.

Chase was the grandson of Ray Sinclair, who had bequeathed Sinclair Cellars to my father. He was also a lawyer and Annie's ex. I wondered if he'd heard about Annie and Jordan yet.

"Just meeting with your father."

"About what?"

"Going over some paperwork," he said with a shrug. "He

wanted a second opinion on the legal documents. It's a smart idea to keep everything up to date."

"That makes sense. I didn't see you at the Wright party last night."

He shot me a pointed look. "I don't go to many Wright events."

"Did you...hear what happened?"

Chase sighed. "If you're asking me if I know that Jordan and Annie got engaged, then yes."

I held my hands up with a sly smile on my face. "I was just curious. I didn't want to be the bearer of bad news."

"It's fine. Annie and I are friends. She called to let me know. I'm happy for her."

"Well, good," I said.

He hadn't exactly sounded *enthused*. But I hardly blamed him. Chase wasn't a bad guy. Not like his evil sister, Ashleigh. He'd just missed his opportunity with Annie. Someone else would come and steal his heart.

"Thanks for helping out my dad."

"Anytime." He patted my shoulder. "See you around, Piper."

I found my dad's office and knocked twice on the door. "Hey, just saw Chase."

His head popped up. "Yeah? He's a nice guy."

"He is."

"You could do well with a guy like that," he said with a teasing smile. "*Mira,* a lawyer, too."

I rolled my eyes. "You overheard that Bradley and I broke up?"

"Just looking out for you."

"*Ay Dios mio!*"

He chuckled at my disinterest. "You're coming to church

49

tomorrow morning, right? Abuelita Nina misses you. You're going to break her poor heart."

I huffed out a breath. I adored my *abuelita*. She was in her eighties with more life than most people half her age. But church and I didn't always get along, and it was her favorite place outside of the kitchen, where she admitted to worshipping Jesus with her cooking.

"I don't know, Papa."

"Don't *Papa* me," he said, pointing a pen at me. "Make your grandmother happy. Pray that we have many more years with her, but you need to spend the time with her now."

"Fine," I told him, feeling much younger than my twenty-nine years as he admonished me.

This was the best and worst part about working with my father. I loved him dearly, but the guilt trips sometimes put me over the edge.

I waved him off and returned to my own work. I had too much to do, and now, I had to attend church tomorrow instead of coming here like the workaholic I was.

"*L*ook at you," Nora said when she entered the living room of our childhood home. "You almost look like an adult."

"Almost?"

"You'd be a full adult in a tie," she teased.

I ruffled her blonde bob, and she hopped away from me in her unbelievably high heels.

"Hey!"

"I put on a whole suit, and you're upset over a tie?"

"Just saying," she said with a grin. "Tell him, August."

August, dressed in a black suit with a tie that complemented Nora's teal dress, held his hands up. "Keep me out of this. I just do what she says."

"See, he's the smart one," Nora said.

"Luckily, I'm not tied down to someone who requires a tie."

It was a rare enough occasion for me to even be wearing a suit. A tie was next level. I'd do it for important nights, but I preferred to wear jeans and T-shirts. I liked cowboy boots and hats and belt buckles. It was Julian who had gone with me to get a few suits that were up to the Wright standards. I represented the winery now after all.

"You look nice," my dad, Gregg, said as he ambled into the living room. He still wasn't very fast on his feet and stepped into the room, clutching a cane.

Bad knees ran in our family, but my dad's had started to fall apart at a young age. He was well past due for total knee replacements. He hated asking for help or admitting he was in pain. Instead, he suffered through most of it with a smile.

"Thanks, Dad," I said. "You ready to go to church?"

"Waiting on one more," he said, his smile widening.

"One more?"

At that moment, the doorbell rang, and a second later, the door banged inward. In walked my brother, Campbell.

"What the hell?"

Nora's face lit up. "Campbell!"

She threw herself into his arms, and he laughed, wrapping her in a hug.

"Hey, y'all."

"What are you doing here?" We fist-bumped and then hugged.

Campbell was easily the luckiest bastard in the world. The minute he'd graduated high school, he'd ditched Lubbock like a bad breakup and gone straight to LA with nothing but a few hundred bucks and his guitar. Five years later, he'd was part of one of the biggest bands in the *world*. They'd been this huge for three years, and it was unbelievable. Cosmere was his baby. He wrote all the lyrics, was the lead singer, and played guitar. As far as I knew, he was currently on a world tour for their latest album.

"I did two shows at Red Rocks in Denver and had two whole days off before I needed to be in Salt Lake City. So, I took a jet home," Campbell said.

"Casual," Nora said, but she was smiling like a kid in a candy store.

We hadn't seen Campbell since January, when he kicked off the tour in Lubbock, of all places. He'd barely even checked in. And while it had only been a few short months, we'd gotten used to having him around again. It was one thing when he was in LA and Lubbock was the last place in the world he wanted to be. It was another to finally have him back and for him to leave again. That felt much worse.

"He called me when he got on the plane," our dad said.

"It's the best," Nora said.

"A hundred percent," I agreed. "Are you going to church with us?"

"Don't I look like I am?" he asked with a smirk. The shithead was in ripped black jeans, a ripped black T-shirt, and a leather jacket. He looked like he was going to step his Converse-clad feet onstage.

"No," Dad said. "But it's okay. We're just glad you're going."

"Glad to be here. And I have a surprise." He reached into the small duffel he was carrying and withdrew a handful of lanyards. He passed them to me.

"Backstage passes?"

"Yeah. For the Dallas show. It's this weekend after we play Salt Lake City. I asked for a box for my friends and family, and they gave me one. So, you'll be in the Owner's Club. The tickets are on my phone. I'll send them over. You can all come backstage, too, but the view is better from the box. Plus, free food and booze."

Nora's eyes were wide. She snatched a backstage pass from my hand. "Are you serious?"

"Of course. They give me whatever I want. So, if y'all

want to come to another show, let me know. I can make it happen. I thought Dallas would be easiest."

I stared down at the pass. It had Campbell's face featured prominently on the front. A picture that I recognized as Jennifer's work. "This is great, man."

"You'll invite everyone for me?"

"Of course. I'll send a group text and see who is free on such short notice."

"Oh, right." Campbell ran his hand back through his artfully messy hair. "I forgot about that part. This was when they gave me the tickets."

"It's perfect," Dad said. "It's very generous."

Campbell smiled warily at our dad. He'd always gotten along better with Mom before she'd died in a hit and run his senior year of high school. Mom and Dad had been fighting, like normal, and she'd stormed out of the house. We'd never seen her again. Campbell's relationship with our dad had been strained since then and half the reason he'd left for LA. They were only now getting back on track.

"It was nothing," Campbell said.

"Let's get to church," I said, getting between them before it got awkward.

We piled into my truck, and I drove us the few short miles to the church my dad had been going to on and off for years. He'd stopped for a while when they were shitty to my aunt Lori for marrying her girlfriend, Vail. With a change in pastor, the place had become more accepting. It had lost some of the older parts of the congregation, but Lori and Vail had returned. I still found it amazing that they'd wanted to come back after all that. But it was enough of a change that they felt welcome again and let old wounds heal.

I parked in the back of the lot next to Lori's bright

orange classic Volkswagen Beetle that Vail had helped her refurbish. Vail was smoking a cigarette, leaning back against the hood. She had full sleeves down both arms with short, cropped hair and a nose ring. She was one of the coolest people I'd ever met. I was lucky to have her as an aunt.

"I thought you were quitting," I admonished as I dropped out of the truck.

Vail winked at me. "I'm always quitting."

"I told her to stop it, or she couldn't come home with me," Lori said. She crossed her arms and shook her head at her wife.

Lori was tall and thin. She'd recently dyed her hair dark red and had grown it out past her shoulders. Vail had on jeans that were ripped from working as a mechanic and a collared polo. While Lori had on a blue sundress. They were night and day, total opposites, and it worked so well for them.

"You like the bad girls, Lori Bug," Vail said. She stamped out her cigarette and kissed her wife. They twined their hands together. "Come on. Let's go praise the Lord."

Lori laughed. "Gregg, is Helene coming too?"

Jordan and Julian's mother, Helene, had moved back to town from Vancouver for cancer treatments. She'd wanted to be closer to her siblings, Gregg and Lori. She'd had a scare last year, and we'd all been worried we'd lose her. Luckily, she was still with us. After her second round of treatments, she'd been better but fragile.

"No," Dad said. "She wasn't feeling up to it."

Lori frowned. "All right. We'll go see her after."

A throat cleared behind me, and Lori and Vail glanced at the same time. Smiles burst onto their faces.

"Campbell!" Lori cried, rushing to pull him into a hug. "What are you doing here?"

"Quick trip to see y'all before I head back out. I was in Denver."

Vail fist-bumped him. "Hey, kid. Nice jacket."

He laughed. "Hey, Vail."

"You bring us anything from Denver?" she asked with a wink.

Campbell grinned and opened his mouth to say something that our dad clearly did not want to hear.

He butted in. "Church," he reminded the lot of us.

"Yes. Let's head in," Lori agreed.

Campbell sidled up with Vail and spoke in whispers. Nora and I exchanged a glance. We'd gotten closer over the last year. We could read each other's moods. And when it came to Campbell, we'd had that intuition a lot longer.

"I'll watch Dad," she said, teetering on her heels.

I nodded and watched her pull August forward.

Dad might seem like everything was okay with him and Campbell, but we all knew that it was a volcano waiting to explode. Talking drugs with Vail certainly wasn't going to help anything. Even if Campbell was the one who had gotten Helene marijuana to help with her cancer treatments. He'd thanked him then. He wouldn't for this. We all walked on a razor's edge.

It was quite a conversation to have right before we all strode into church.

We always sat on the far-left side of the nave, and I followed my family over to their seats. The Wrights were already in attendance, splayed out across the front pews. They'd gone from five lonely siblings without parents to five siblings, five significant others, and seven kids with one more on the way. Even Jensen's oldest, Colton, was in attendance, sulking broodily, the farthest he could get from his dad.

Morgan came over to speak with Nora about her upcoming nuptials. I sat down next to Campbell. He drummed his fingers on the back of the pew in front of us. He was in a constant state of motion. He had always been like that. A fidgety kid who had always gotten in trouble for never being able to sit still. Now, he'd taken that energy and made a career out of it.

I watched the rest of the congregation fill the space. That was when I saw her. I blinked in shock. I didn't come to church every Sunday, but I came enough with Dad to know most of the people in attendance.

And I'd never seen Piper Medina here.

Before I could think better of it, I was on my feet and striding across the room. I should have thought it through before I blundered in her presence. She was with her family. She probably didn't want me to bother her. Did I care?

"Hey, Piper," I said with a smirk, stopping her before she could reach the pews.

She was fucking stunning. It was a statement of fact. Her full, dark hair was loose, down around her shoulders. Her dark eyes were rimmed in kohl, and her lips were painted a soft pink color that made me want to lick it off of her. She wore high-waisted black trousers with a white blouse tucked in, pulled tight across her chest. She'd shucked off a jacket, and she held it in one arm.

But it was the way she froze at the sight of me. Her eyes traveled down my body, as if she were interested in what I looked like under this suit. I wanted that look. I wanted to bottle it up and devour it.

"Hollin," she finally said in a breathy voice.

And I was done for.

8

PIPER

*H*ollin Abbey was in a...suit.

I'd never seen him in anything but T-shirt with jeans or soccer shorts. The way his muscled thighs were revealed in the red shorts as he ran powerfully across the field. The arch of his ass in the fitted jeans that had been made for working and admiration. But a suit...I could hardly process this Hollin.

Charcoal molded to his shoulders like an artist had taken their instruments to draw the sharp definition of him. His trousers cut him in tight at the waist and hung on those hips and over the powerful thighs. Then opened the collar of his shirt to reveal a few inches of tanned skin.

I normally hated the smirk on his stupid, pretty face. The one that said he was going to try to drive a scalpel under my skin and pull up until I screamed at him. The teasing that drove me crazy and also made me wonder if all this anger could be fuel for something potentially delicious.

My eyes glazed over at the sight of him. My toes curled in their little pumps. Dammit, why was he so hot?

"Who's this, *amorcita*?" Abuelita asked, stepping gingerly

up to my side. She reached out and took my arm to steady herself. She'd been doing that more and more lately, as if her own feet weren't enough.

I jerked out of my reverie and crashed back down to reality. His smile only grew as he watched my anger light a fuse between us. I didn't want to want him. What was *wrong* with me?

I clenched my hand and released it. "Abuelita Nina, this is Hollin Abbey."

"Well, why didn't they make men this handsome in my day?"

I scoffed. "You were married for fifty years."

"Shush," Nina teased. "He might not know."

Hollin barely held back his laughter. There was a new light in his eyes at the sight of my grandmother. As if he couldn't believe my eighty-something-year-old grandma was flirting with him. Well, neither could I.

"Can I help you to your seat?" he asked, holding his arm out.

My eyes rounded in shock. He was going to go along with this?

Abuelita preened under his attention and put her hand on his. "Isn't that sweet of you?" Abuelita looked back up at me with a wink. "Find yourself one of these."

I shook my head as Hollin escorted my grandmother down the aisle. And they were actually flirting. Jesus Christ, strike me down for taking your name in vain inside your house, but who was this man? Hollin Abbey was acting distinctly like a gentleman, and I didn't know what to think of it. It was quite unfathomable.

Abuelita sat down with a wide grin on her face. I hadn't seen her look like that since Peyton had moved home. What kind of magic had he worked on my poor grandmother?

My hackles immediately came up. "What are you doing?"

He raised his eyebrows. As if he were innocent. "What do you mean?"

"Nothing," I grumbled. Abuelita grinned toothily at the both of us. "Just leave us alone."

"*Piper*," Abuelita gasped. "Where are your manners?"

I straightened further, resigned to the fact that I could say nothing against Hollin while my grandmother sat there. Nothing at all. Abuelita was right anyway. Hollin wasn't doing anything wrong. I was anticipating him doing something or having a motive that I couldn't yet see.

Finally, I shot him a rare smile. "Thank you."

He looked taken aback for a split second before grinning down at me. "Anytime, Medina. Anytime."

He tipped his head at my grandmother again and then returned to his family. Campbell was sitting next to him. Wasn't he on tour?

I didn't have a chance to find out as piano music filled the atrium, signaling for everyone to return to their seat for the service to begin. I sat between Abuelita and my mother. Mom shot me a questioning look as soon as I sat down, but thankfully, I wouldn't have to answer that until later. Hopefully much later. Or never.

When the service ended, I helped Abuelita back out into the narthex, where she immediately began to gossip with all of her friends. We wouldn't move her from there for another half hour. I stepped out of the cross fire inside and outside, where it had begun to drizzle. There was possible snow on the radar for tonight. A late snowstorm always swept through Lubbock in March, blanketing everything just enough to be annoying. I was hoping it wouldn't happen this year. But the rain was making me reconsider. Maybe I'd stop at the store on the way home for provisions just to be safe.

"So," Hollin said at my back.

I raised my eyes to the heavens and sighed. "What?"

"Nina is nice."

"*Mi abuelita* is the best of us," I said automatically.

She was the strongest and bravest and the best cook. She was my entire childhood, wrapped up in one teeny package. She was only four foot nine, and we used to have a holiday when any of us got taller than her. We'd celebrate while she reminded us that she was still the smartest of us all. She'd looked utterly ridiculous on Hollin's arm, considering he was easily six and a half feet tall.

"Surprised you were missing your other half," he teased.

"Peter?" I asked in confusion.

My twin had somehow weaseled his way out of church this morning. Jerk.

Hollin laughed. "I was thinking Bradley, but yeah, it's weird that Peter isn't here either."

"Oh." I glanced down at the spattering of rain on the concrete. "We broke up."

"Good," Hollin said, hunger in his voice.

My chin jerked back up at his tone. "*Good*?"

"Yeah. You were way too good for him."

I narrowed my eyes. "You do know that you're supposed to show sympathy, right?"

"For what? A guy you were over before it ended?"

My glare faltered at his words. He wasn't wrong. I had been over him. He wasn't the only person who had noticed. But still, I hadn't expected him to. "Don't act like you know me."

"Of course not, Pipes."

"That's my family's nickname for me. You can't call me that."

"Why not?"

"You're not family."

He raised his hands in defense, but I could only see the predator scrawled on his face. He liked when I got defensive. He liked working my anger out of me. I needed to calm down, but he made it so goddamn hard.

"What do you *want*, Hollin?" I demanded now that no one else was around to admonish me for my tone. "You're here, bothering me. I didn't ask for this. I've had a very long weekend. So, get to your point."

"My point can't just be this?" he asked.

"No," I snapped.

He laughed casually. "All right. Well, I'm glad that you and Bradley broke up. That makes this easier."

I furrowed my brow as he pulled a lanyard from his pocket. "What's that?"

"Campbell got me a bunch of backstage passes and the Owner's Club for his Dallas show next weekend. Want to go?"

"With you?" I stammered out.

"I would be going, yes. He's my brother."

I stared at the pass with blatant desire. I wanted that pass. I *loved* Cosmere's music. I wasn't as into it as Jennifer and Annie. They'd always been obsessed. But I knew all their songs and loved to listen to their latest album. Even if critics were saying it wasn't as good as the last. Plus, *backstage.* I had never been backstage at a show before. Or in a box for that matter. Both were big dreams of mine. Still...it was Hollin.

"I'm not going on a date with you," I said stiffly, still eyeing the pass.

"You sure?"

"If that's the requirement to go, then have a nice time." I took a step away from him, but he grasped my elbow. He was laughing.

"Christ, Piper, I'm kidding." He stuffed the pass in my hand. "I know you love Cosmere. You're coming with us."

I gingerly took it in my fingers and stared down at it. "What's the catch, Hollin?"

"You think so little of me?"

I arched an eyebrow. When had he shown me otherwise?

He shrugged. "Look, I'm inviting everyone. You're the first person I saw. Actually," he said, reaching into his pocket, "give these to Blaire and Jennifer when you get home. I was planning to invite them, too."

Now, I had three backstage passes to the most antici-pated concert of the year.

My eyes lifted to Hollin's, and he grinned. That same fuck-me smile. But there was no catch. I was confused. And why did he have to look at me like he wanted to eat me alive? And I needed to cut down those thoughts. Right the fuck now.

"Well, thank you. I'll...I'll tell the girls."

"Piper!" Campbell called as he barreled out of the church toward us, stopping right before the rain. "You're coming to the show, right?"

"I just invited her," Hollin said.

I held up the passes. "Thank you so much. This is incredible."

Campbell sexily ruffled his hair. "Hey, it's no problem. I want all y'all there."

"Well, I'll ask Blaire and Jennifer, too. I'm sure they're free."

Campbell's Adam's apple bobbed in his throat. "Blaire? You think she'll go? I didn't think she liked our music."

My gaze shifted to Hollin, but he was looking pointedly at his brother. Something had happened with Blaire, but I had no idea what. Maybe some unrequited shit from high school. They'd been in the same grade in the same school, and *everyone* had loved Campbell, even then, from what I'd heard. But Blaire never talked about it. Not even to me, and I was her best friend.

"She'll be there," I told him. "How could she say no?"

Campbell grinned. It was an onstage smile. One he used for cameras and fans. "Good. I'm glad you'll be there." He patted Hollin on his back. "Come on, bro. I have some merchandise to pick up for Vail."

Hollin grumbled under his breath, smacking his brother upside the head. "You're an idiot."

Campbell laughed and ducked under his arm. Hollin smiled at me. A real one this time. Then, he tipped his head at me and disappeared.

I stared down at the backstage passes in my hands. Next weekend was sure as hell going to be interesting.

PART II

BAD HABITS

9

PIPER

*M*y eyes were wide as I stood on the tarmac outside the hanger where the Wrights kept their private jet. Some part of me had *known* that the Wrights had their own jet. I'd heard it mentioned that Jensen Wright flew up to New York City on the regular to see his son. That Jordan and Annie had flown to Seattle in it. Still, somehow, I hadn't *known*. And I'd certainly never thought I'd be on it.

But Jordan shrugged like it was nothing and said, "I got us the jet. It made more sense."

I blinked at Blaire. "It just made sense."

She cracked up and pushed me. "I'm not going to argue with him, are you?"

"Nope!"

I slung my weekend bag over my shoulder and followed Blaire up the stairs onto the Wright jet. Dallas was five hours away. We would have needed two cars to get all of us there. This was a hundred percent preferable even if it felt *ridiculous*.

Jordan, Julian, Annie, and Jennifer were already on

board when Blaire and I entered the plane. It was bigger than I'd imagined with a long couch and seats larger than ones I'd seen in first class of most commercial planes. A flight attendant stored our bags and offered us drinks.

"Oh, I'll have a Bombay and lime," Blaire said.

"Excellent," the man said. "And for you?"

"Uh, just water."

Blaire nudged me. "Free booze, Piper. Live a little."

I laughed. "All right, fine. I'll have what she's having."

"Coming right up."

I'd just gotten my drink when Nora stepped onto the plane in crazy high heels. She handed off her bag and took the seat next to me.

"Where's August?" I asked. "Isn't he always at your side?"

Nora wrinkled her nose. "He had to work. So annoying. I asked Tamara to go, too, but she already had plans. Why are my friends so lame?"

"Excellent question," Blaire said, raising her glass.

Nora removed her trusty iPad and a stylus. Then, she opened a document, where she started shading in the barn at Wright Vineyard.

"Whoa, did you draw that?"

Nora waved her hand noncommittally. "Yeah."

"It's really good."

"Nah, it's just doodling. I like to draw all of my ideas for my clients. This is for Morgan and Patrick." She turned the screen fully to me. "See how I want the chairs to be set up?" She flipped to the next page. "And this is the altar view."

"Wow. Do you do this for all your weddings?"

"Not all of them, but the big ones, I include it in the package. You really like it?"

"Yeah. Did you do this for Peyton, too?"

"I didn't. She didn't ask for it. But I could! If you wanted to see it."

"Not if it's a lot of work."

"Girl, I love it. It's the best part of the job," she said with a laugh.

Blaire leaned over. "Wow, Nora, you're so good."

Nora flushed. "Thanks. You think so?"

"Definitely. Would you be interested in designing some logos like this for Blaire Blush?"

Nora's eyes widened. "Seriously?"

"Yeah. I have Honey doing so much of the behind-the-scenes stuff, but she doesn't have a design eye like this."

"Oh, Honey," I said with a laugh.

Blaire had gotten a new assistant at the beginning of the year. She'd been handling her *Blaire Blush* blog and all her social media platforms herself for so long that she claimed she didn't need anyone. But when she took over Jennifer's photography accounts, it had been too much. Enter Honey. Yes, that was what she asked to be called. Honey, despite the name, was a godsend for Blaire's work. She'd had a few virtual assistants, but it was so much better to have someone in town.

"She's nice," Blaire said.

"She's enthusiastic," I offered.

"Maybe more accurate."

"Hey, where's your brother?" Julian called over the seat. "He was supposed to be here first."

Nora held her hands out. "I don't know. I'm not his keeper."

"He has the tickets. So, we can't leave without him," Julian said.

"You were planning to leave without me?" Hollin asked as he climbed on board.

My mouth went dry. He looked...so fucking good. How could a man in jeans and a black T-shirt look like him? He shot me a half-smile filled with a dangerous energy that tore straight through me. I looked back down at Nora's iPad and pretended not to notice.

"Course not," Julian said. They clapped hands.

"You're perpetually late right now," Jordan said, low and slightly annoyed.

"Ah, Jor," Hollin said, ruffling Jordan's hair. Jordan looked ready to knock his teeth out for the gesture. He wasn't exactly the kind of person used to being trifled with. "You know you love me."

Jordan reared back from his hand. "You're lucky I do."

Annie chuckled. "Poor baby. Need me to fix your hair?"

He shot his fiancée a look, and her smile widened as she reached out to fix his hair. He grabbed both of her wrists. She squeaked as he kissed her.

Ugh. The level of cuteness. Sometimes, I was so jealous of other people's happiness that it ate away inside of me. Blaire never seemed to care. Her followers liked that she was single. She got enough marriage proposals on the weekly that she felt perfectly loved. But I wanted that...that *right there*.

The guys joked around for a while as we prepared to take off. We looked over some more of Nora's designs and then took our seats. I rummaged in my bag for my Kindle as we taxied down the runway. I was in the middle of Sierra Simone's *A Lesson in Thorns*. The girls in my smut book club had recommended it, and I'd sunk into the story like inserting an IV into a vein.

We'd just lifted into the air when a voice spoke behind me. "Hey, what are you reading?"

I slapped the book down and looked into Hollin's face. "What?"

"What's the book?"

"Oh. *Pride and Prejudice*," I lied.

It had become a common pastime. Not that I was ashamed of the amazing books I read. But everyone was always so *weird* about the fact that I liked romance and erotica. They said that I didn't give off the right vibes. Whatever the hell that meant. Romance held the entire book industry afloat. It was single-handedly the best genre, and no one could convince me otherwise.

"Huh," he said. "Is it good?"

"Sure. Darcy. Lizzy. Pemberley."

I had read *Pride and Prejudice* in high school, but I was a bigger fan of the Keira Knightley version.

"Cool." His eyes swept my face before he leaned back in his seat and started talking to his sister.

I turned away from him. Blaire arched an eyebrow, and I shrugged. I couldn't explain Hollin Abbey.

With him occupied again, I pulled the book back up and began to read the sexiest truth-or-dare scene I'd ever read. A girl folded over a lap, skirt raised, getting spanked in front of all of her friends. I shifted in my seat and swallowed. Maybe this wasn't the best choice to read around company.

"You're free to move about the cabin," the pilot said, coming over the speakers.

Jordan, Julian, and Hollin unbuckled their seat belts and went to sit on the couch. Blaire and Nora settled into seats nearby. I could sort of hear their murmurs about possible design logos. Jennifer had her camera out and was snapping shots of us all up here in the private jet. Annie was posing like a model. Blaire laughed and adjusted her arms and feet for proper posing.

I lost the train of the conversation as Auden and Poe in the book took control of my entire world. I licked my lips and squeezed my legs together. I wanted to stop reading, so I wouldn't be this turned on, and I also had no interest in stopping at all. If I were home, I'd slip my hand into my jeans and get off right then and there. But...there was no chance of that here.

I was so consumed in my own world that I didn't even notice that Hollin had moved from his seat with the Wright brothers. Not until I felt his eyes reading over my shoulder.

"Well," he breathed, "that isn't the *Pride and Prejudice* I read."

My heart galloped ahead at the words. I was turning to castigate him for reading over my shoulder when plucked the Kindle out of my hand. I could barely react as he took the little Paperwhite in his massive hands.

"Hollin," I protested. "Give that back."

"What are you reading?"

I came to my feet, glaring. "Give. It. Back."

The others were looking at us now. Color was coming to my cheeks. They were going to ask. I'd have to explain. Jennifer knew what kind of books I read because she sometimes borrowed them from me. She wasn't in this particular smut book club though. Too dirty for her poor sensibilities.

"Hollin, stop being a jerk," Nora admonished.

Hollin's eyes skimmed the page I was on. The particularly filthy page where everyone watched the heroine get spanked. Like how bad of luck did I have?

"Hollin," I growled.

He smirked up at me and passed it back. "I was just curious."

"Asshole."

I flopped back into my seat with the Kindle in my lap. Hollin stepped around me and took Blaire's empty seat.

"What do you want?" I demanded.

He grinned. "Why did you lie about what you were reading?"

"Why do you care?"

"Well, I didn't pin you as a classics reader."

"What does that mean?"

"I don't know. I thought you'd read nonfiction or something."

"Like biographies?" I asked dryly.

"Or...I don't know...self-help or business or productivity stuff."

I narrowed my eyes at him. "Why?"

"You seem like you're a hundred and fifty percent on all the time."

"I am," I ground out.

He laughed darkly. A sound that went straight to my curling toes. "And yet you're reading...*that.*"

"I can like romance and be a smart businesswoman."

"Clearly."

But there was a sparkle in his eyes. A light that I hadn't seen before. It wasn't his teasing. It was something else, something sultrier. As if this had opened up his entire world. Like it had blown his mind that I read raunchy romance novels. And he...liked it.

He nodded his chin at the book. "That what you always read?"

"So what if it is?"

"Nothing wrong with it. It's just...hot."

My cheeks flamed at the word that had come out of his mouth. The way his eyes slid down to my lips. The tension in his body at the thought that I was reading about sex on the regular. Fuck.

Fuck, fuck, fuck.

I needed to somehow swim out of the deep end. Otherwise, I wasn't going to be able to breathe. Or think. Or exist.

This wasn't how things were supposed to go with Hollin. He was supposed to needle me, I'd tell him to fuck off, and we'd part. This was...personal. It was definitely so much more personal.

I pulled back from that thought. This was Hollin Abbey. He didn't care about anything but the chase. He didn't give a fuck about me. He was interested in the book because of sex and nothing else.

"Hot," I said flatly as I came to my feet. "Well, thanks. Needed to know you thought I was hot to survive today."

He huffed. "But didn't you?"

I rolled my eyes. "Whatever you want to believe."

Then, I made a hasty retreat to where my friends were sitting. I didn't turn my book back on the rest of the flight and tried to stay present as the girls chatted about logos, photography, and posing. But still, my brain was always a little aware of Hollin's presence at any given time.

10

HOLLIN

*M*y brain was on sex.

How the fuck was I supposed to focus when Piper was reading a girl getting her ass spanked? Because I sure as fuck could not focus on anything else. I kept getting flashes of me bending Piper over my lap and doing the same shit. But Piper's ass wasn't mine to spank until she came.

And she'd jumped away from me as quickly as she could when I told her it was hot. That *she* was hot.

Usually, I let the innuendo do its job.

Today, I hadn't been able to do shit.

We landed in DFW Airport and took a car to the hotel near AT&T Stadium. Campbell was already at the venue, doing sound checks for the show tonight. He'd gotten us all rooms at the hotel the band was staying at. Being in Campbell's world was something else,.

I'd come to a few of his shows in LA before he was famous. It wasn't a red carpet as they were fighting their way up. But after their first album took off, the first show I went to with Dad and Nora was a disaster of epic proportions.

Campbell and Dad had gotten into it, and a fire had been lit under all of us. Dad pretty much didn't come to shows anymore after that. He loved Campbell's fame enough to not want to cause any trouble for him.

Everyone was getting ready for the show. Campbell had promised to send a car for us to get to the venue. I had time to kill before we had to do that. And still, all I could think about was Piper.

My cock was already filling my pants. I pressed the heel of my palm against it to push it down. I was hard, just thinking about her. I'd seen her half-naked a week before, and now, *this*.

I'd enjoyed riling her up for a while. It was our dynamic. But something had changed when I saw that ring, when she let me put her in my shirt. Now, I wasn't just getting under her skin. I wanted to get under her. Or over her. Or put her over my knee. Whatever the fuck way she'd let me take her, I was up for.

And thinking about it right now was helping nothing. My cock certainly wasn't listening. Or maybe it was because my head was full of filthy thoughts of Piper Medina. It was stiff as a board now. So fucking hard that it was painful.

Jesus! I needed to get this under control before we went out again.

Which, of course, was the moment I considered how Piper could help me get it under control. I had a very vivid thought of watching her deep-throat my cock, and it was all I needed to pop the button on my jeans and slide down the zipper. Maybe I'd take care of this before we all left.

I'd just slipped my hand into my boxers when someone knocked on the door to my hotel room. I stared at the ceiling in dismay.

"Yeah?" I called out.

"Hey, Hollin." Piper's voice carried across the divide.

I groaned softly, my eyes rolling into the back of my head. Even her voice was turning me on right now. I was fucked. Seriously fucked.

I stuffed my cock back into my pants and adjusted them to hopefully hide the giant boner I had for her. Then, I opened the door, covering most of my lower half with the door.

"Yeah?"

Her eyes flitted across my face. Uncertainty in every glance.

And, fuck, she'd changed out of her jeans and T-shirt and into a fucking black minidress. She didn't wear a ton of dresses. But now, I got a full look at her toned golden legs. I jerked my head back up to meet her gaze.

She crossed her arms, which only pushed her tits up in the square cut of her dress. "Julian sent me down here to let you know that we're drinking in his suite. He's two doors down if you want to join us."

Julian must have gotten a sick pleasure out of asking Piper to get me. He'd seen the way I looked at her last weekend. The way I'd been around her on this trip. He was probably laughing his ass off right now.

"Sure," I said automatically. "Let me grab my...wallet. I'll meet you."

"Fine." She sashayed her tight ass away from me.

I bit back a groan at the sight. Fuck.

"Go down. Go down. Go down," I hissed at my dick as I stepped back into my room.

It had a mind of its own, but after a few minutes, it wasn't entirely noticeable, and I headed down the hall to Julian's suite. All I knew was that I was walking into a concert still so fucking turned on, with the woman I was interested in, wearing nothing but a skimpy dress, and I hadn't had time to take care of business. Fuck. Me.

Campbell hadn't sent a car. He'd sent a fucking stretch limo.

The girls giggled together as the driver came around to open the back door. "After you," he said.

It was a tight fit with eight of us in the back of the limo. Especially considering how tall I was. The girls scooted down further to give me more room, but no matter what happened, my entire left side was pressed firmly against Piper. She moved closer to Blaire again, but it was no use. There wasn't enough space. And none of it was helping how turned on I was. I adjusted my jeans and cleared my throat.

Julian caught my eye and smirked. I had given him so much shit when he and Jennifer first started out. He was deeply pleased that he could do the same for me. And Piper and I...we weren't anything like him and Jen. Piper had hardly even looked at me while we were drinking.

She wasn't looking at me now either. She was talking to Blaire and Nora, but she kept shifting and adjusting, which meant the bare skin of her thigh kept rubbing against my leg. I closed my eyes and tipped my head back, trying to stop thinking about her. What the hell was my problem?

I liked sex, but I wasn't normally this horny all the time. She'd lit a fire under me, and now, I couldn't make it stop. I couldn't keep from thinking about what she'd feel like. And it didn't help in these close quarters.

She'd just done it again, and I couldn't take it anymore. I urged her thigh down with the palm of my hand.

Her eyes jumped to mine. "What?" she gasped.

"Stop moving," I said, low and husky.

She gulped at the heat in my voice. Her pupils dilated as I held her firmly against the black leather seat. Her eyes traveled to where my large hand covered her leg and back up to me. Something sparked between us. Like the first heat of a firework before it burst into the sky.

Then, Piper came back to herself and shoved my hand away. "Don't touch me."

I grinned at her. "Sure thing, babe."

But she stopped moving around. In fact, she sat *very* still.

Blessedly, the drive to the venue wasn't too long. The last thing I wanted was to get hard again in the back of the limo. There would have been no escape and no way to hide it. I wasn't sure how obvious it was that I was horny.

When we rolled up in front of AT&T Stadium, we all piled back out of the limo. The driver gave Jordan his card to use for after the show when we were ready to come back. He pocketed the card and tipped the driver.

He nodded his head at the lot of us and said, "Shall we?"

I laughed. He was such a Wright. "Yeah. I have the tickets."

We walked through a metal detector, and I scanned all eight of our tickets from my phone. We were directed to the Owners Club one floor below. We took the stairs down and showed our tickets to the people manning the door. Each of us got a green wristband that allowed us entrance to this room, and we entered into a different world.

I tried to keep my jaw from dropping, but it was difficult. The Owners Club was an enormous central meeting space that branched off to each of the individual boxes. It was filled with lush couches, hundreds of televisions to watch the concert from any angle, a fully stocked bar with premium liquor, and a manned buffet for whatever your heart desired. It was pure luxury.

And that was before we even got to our seats.

"Whoa," Piper whispered next to me.

"I love it," Blaire said. She glanced at Jennifer. "Think we can take a few pictures for the blog?"

"I'd be insulted if you didn't want me to," she said.

"Pipes, you coming?" Blaire asked.

"I'm going to check out our seats," she said. "And then get some food. Is that prime rib?"

We watched a plate of succulent meat pass us. My stomach grumbled. I hadn't even realized I was that hungry.

"I like her plan," I said.

Piper looked at me and frowned. "On second thought, maybe I will come with you."

Then, she disappeared with the rest of the girls.

Julian clapped me on the back. "Better luck next time, bro."

"You're a dick."

Jordan furrowed a brow. "What am I missing?"

"Hollin has it bad for Piper."

Jordan snorted. "No way. All you two do is argue. You're constantly at each other's throats."

Julian arched an eyebrow. "Can you really talk? You and Annie argued every time you saw each other for three years."

"That was different," Jordan said smoothly. "We'd already hooked up. It was..." Julian crossed his arms and waited. Jordan huffed a breath. "Fine. It's similar. But Annie liked me at least. Doesn't Piper hate you?"

"Yeah. I guess she does."

We stepped into our own private suite off of the main Owners Club. My eyes widened at the perfect, uninterrupted view of the Cosmere setup on the Dallas Cowboys football field. It was spectacular. Hundreds of seats had been added to the floor around a giant stage with wings on either side and a long runway through the front. That way, Campbell could walk forward during some songs, as if he were a part of the audience. It was brilliant. I'd never seen anything like it, and it wasn't even lit up yet.

Jordan appreciatively ran his hand along the back of the first seat. "This is the way to live."

I laughed as Julian nodded. "Isn't this what you're used to?"

Jordan and Julian had been raised in Vancouver under the tutelage of their douche father, Owen. Jordan worked for Wright Construction as an executive vice president. They came from money…a lot of money.

They exchanged a look and shrugged.

"Sure," Julian said.

"I suppose," Jordan said. "I didn't have a whole lot of time to enjoy it though. That's the beauty of moving to Lubbock. I work a lot less, believe it or not."

That was hard to believe. Jordan was the biggest workaholic I knew. Even worse than Piper. Even worse than Annie, who was a doctor. But I was thankful that he had any time for the winery he'd helped us build from the ground up.

"Glad you have the time," I said. "I'm glad you're all here."

Jordan leaned back against the seat, facing away from the show as the opener was announced. He crossed his arms. "So, what are you going to do about Piper?"

I ran a hand back through my hair. "Fuck if I know."

"You can't play games with her," Julian said. "If you like her, you're going to have to be straight with her."

"Yeah. Sure. That sounds like me."

"She'll eat you alive if you pull the shit you pull on everyone else," Julian said.

"I concur," Jordan said, eyeing me suspiciously. "She seems like she'd be a match for you. Good luck."

Just then the girls prowled back inside, drinks in hand, laughing. Piper met my gaze, and she smiled. She was having a good time. And I *liked* that she was having a good time.

The guys were right about one thing at least.

If I wanted her, I'd have to tell her.

And I intended to do just that.

11

PIPER

*H*ollin wouldn't stop looking at me. I'd chanced a glance at him through the first two openers, and he'd quickly looked away. I had gone to grab another dessert, and his eyes had followed me. I'd sung along to the hit song for the second opener, and I could feel him staring at my lips.

I didn't know how to process this. How fast things had gone from us needling each other to *this*. Whatever this was, I had no idea. But I couldn't deny that I liked the attention. I liked him watching me. I liked him looking appreciatively. But I didn't know what it all meant. I didn't know if he was being a dickhead like normal and there was going to be some antagonistic punch line, because that seemed more like him.

Especially after he'd touched me. I could still vividly remember the way it'd felt to have his hand on my thigh. And not just...touched. He'd *held me down*. Held me in place with that one massive hand on my bare skin. It had set fire to my core like nothing else. I should have abhorred that touch. And now, I couldn't stop thinking about what else those powerful hands could do to me if I let them.

I hopped up from my seat. "I'm going to go look at the bar again. Anyone else want anything?"

"I'll take another gin and lime," Blaire said.

"You know the bartender can get that stuff for you," Jordan said.

Annie swatted at him. "The girl wants to move around and get another dessert. Just let her."

I laughed. She wasn't wrong. The desserts were delicious. I'd tried them all. I was a fan of the pecan pie.

"My bad," Jordan said.

"I'll go with you," Hollin said as he climbed out of his front row seat.

"Why?" I snapped before I could stop myself.

He raised an eyebrow. "I wanted to check out the whiskey selection. I heard they have an Owners Select Maker's Mark, which was crafted by Jerry Jones himself."

"Oh," I whispered. "Sure."

I wet my lips and backed out of the suite. Hollin fell into step with me. We rounded the corner out of the hallway for the suites and into the main area of the Owners Club.

"You like bourbon?" he asked.

"Yeah."

"Want to try the Maker's with me?"

I looked over at him, waiting for the antagonism. It didn't come. "Sure."

He ordered us both tasting samples while I requested the two gin and limes for me and Blaire. He swished the shot of bourbon around in its glass. I picked mine up and sniffed it. Smelled like Maker's to me. I didn't have a discerning palate for bourbon like I did for wine. But that was my job. This was just for fun.

He held his glass up to mine. "To free tickets."

"To Campbell," I offered.

He grinned. "That's right. To my asshole brother."

I chuckled and tipped the shot back. It burned on the way down. I liked it. It tasted sharp and clean, all at the same time.

"That's good." I set my glass down next to his. "I'd drink that."

He winked at me. "Excellent."

He raised his hand and ordered the Owners Select with Pepsi. Jennifer had complained that they didn't have Coke. She'd been hate-sipping 7-Up all night, and Julian had been poking fun.

"Is it weird that everyone is here to see your brother?" I asked before I could think better of it. "That there are thousands of girls here with his face plastered on their T-shirts? And that people have signs that say *Marry me, Campbell* on them?"

He thought about it and then shrugged. "Sometimes. I'm happy that he's doing what he loves. Most people don't get this opportunity. And when he's home, he's just my little brother, you know? It can't be that different than Peyton."

I hadn't even put two and two together, but it was remarkably similar to Peyton. She'd been a principal dancer. People from all over the world were obsessed with her work. She'd performed in front of thousands night after night. But at the end of the day, she was still just my sister. Somehow, Campbell felt bigger by magnitudes.

"I guess it is. Most people didn't wear my sister's face on their boobs though."

He chuckled. "No. But they bought her dirty shoes."

"Oh God," I said with a laugh. "They definitely did. It's so weird."

"Sometimes, it's weird. That's why it's important to treat him like everyone else. Otherwise, his head would get bigger than it already is."

"He seems pretty down-to-earth."

"You're welcome," Hollin said with a wink.

We headed back toward the suite. I passed my drink off to Blaire as the second opener finished.

She'd been deceptively upbeat about this whole thing. When I'd first invited her to the show, she'd thrown a pillow at my head. But eventually, I'd convinced her to come with us even if I hadn't gotten the story about her and Campbell.

Everyone hopped out of their seat to flood the Owners Club before Cosmere came onstage. I waved them off and found a seat. Instead of returning to where Hollin had sat earlier, he dropped into the seat next to mine.

We'd had an *actual* conversation. I hadn't known it was entirely possible for him to not get on my nerves every time he opened his mouth. But here we were. I didn't trust it. Even a temporary truce felt like a concession.

"What are you doing?" I asked.

"Sitting next to you."

"But why?"

"Because we're the only two people in here right now."

"So, you'll go back to your seat when people come back?"

He leaned his elbow on the armrest between us. "If you want me to."

"Good."

I glanced away from the Cupid's bow of his lips and the sensual way he looked at me.

"Can I ask you a question without you slapping me?"

I looked to the ceiling with a sigh. "Maybe."

"Are all the books you read like that?"

I whipped my head to him. "Are we back on this?"

"I mean, I watch a lot of 'books' like that."

"Are you equating romance to porn?" I snapped. This was why I didn't let my guard down, because he started saying stupid fucking shit like this.

"Are they that different?"

"It's not porn. Not that there's anything wrong with sex work. Women are vilified for anything they enjoy or anywhere they can make their own money. Romance and erotica are a female-dominated industry. Women make all the money in it. And God forbid that a woman chooses to read about women finding men who care for them and want them and are desperate to give them a happily ever after. Yes, there's sex. Yes, sometimes, the book is *just* about sex, but there's nothing wrong with anything that makes a woman feel powerful."

Hollin's mouth dropped open slightly. "Tell me how you really feel."

I laughed softly. "I've heard it before...the porn thing. It raises my hackles."

"Anytime you need to yell at someone about a woman feeling powerful, feel free to do it to me," he said with a smoldering look.

I swallowed. "Is that right? You don't seem like a man interested in a powerful woman. Considering how often you bag and ditch them."

"I don't meet many powerful women," he said. His voice was low and gravelly as his blue eyes bored into me. For a second, I was lost to him. Then, he smirked and opened his mouth. "So...have you done anything like you've read in these books before?"

I smacked him on the shoulder. "God, you're terrible. Is sex all you think about?"

"After reading over your shoulder..."

My eyes widened at the admission. Had he just admitted to thinking about sex because of reading my book? Was he thinking about *me*? Oh fuck. This was...this was bad.

Because suddenly, I had the vivid image of Hollin holding me down with those big hands of his. Doing all the dirty things that I read about on the regular that, despite not answering his question, no one had ever done to me. It had just been fantasy. An escape into a reality that was so far removed from my own. I never thought anyone would look at the books I read and wonder if *I* wanted to be held down and fucked.

I couldn't help it. I flushed all over and hastily looked away, but he caught the blush on my cheeks.

He grinned devilishly. "Mission accomplished."

"What?" I gasped out.

"I love to make you blush."

I shoved up out of my seat. "I am not one of your three-date-rule bimbos. I'm not falling for this stupidity, Hollin. Just...go bother someone else."

I left the room, nearly running into Julian and Jordan on the way out. They looked at me in confusion, but I brushed past them. I needed to get far, *far* away from Hollin and his lack of boundaries. Or the fact that I *liked* that he had none.

12

PIPER

*T*he Cosmere show was night and day to whatever Campbell had thrown together at the opening of the tour in Lubbock. That had practically been a personal party rather than a concert. *This* was a full stadium experience. Impressive light displays, perfect acoustics, backup dancers. The whole shebang.

I avoided Hollin through the rest of the show and drowned in Campbell's heartfelt lyrics with Annie and Jennifer. Blaire stayed on her feet through the show with the rest of us, but she spent as much time on her phone, doing Blaire Blush stuff, as she did, listening to the music. And at one point, she left right in the middle of their biggest hit, "I See the Real You."

And now, we were at the door to backstage. We flashed our passes to the bouncer and then were through. Even Hollin and Nora were excited about coming backstage even though they had to have been backstage for their brother a bunch.

An assistant found us at the door. She smiled wide. "Hi!

I'm Libba. Campbell sent me to get you. He said you could wait for him in the lounge."

"Great," Hollin said. "Show us the way."

We bypassed a line of eager fans, hoping to get one last glimpse of the band. We followed Libba away from the crowds and through the crush of workers, who had made sure the show went off without a hitch. Then, we were at the door of a lounge full of booze and women. The other members of the band were already there.

Viv played bass. She'd recently dyed her hair purple and shaved it on one side. She was smoking a joint and crowed when she saw Hollin. They hugged, and Hollin dropped into a seat on the couch next to her. A pang shot through me even though I knew Viv had a girlfriend, Kris. Yorke played guitar and was the hottest guy in the band after Campbell. He had this dark and mysterious thing to him. All hard edges and broody silent treatment. I rarely heard him speak, but when he did, everyone stopped to listen. Yorke was sitting next to Santi, who was the effervescent opposite of Yorke's taciturn demeanor. They were best friends and had met at a local LA talent competition when Santi showed up and played the drums so well that Travis Barker took him on as a prodigy. They'd paired up with Michael on keys shortly after that, who was currently video-chatting, likely with his wife and young daughter.

Viv had been introduced to them by the label. At the time, Santi had been singing lead, but it wasn't until they added Campbell as the lead singer and his incredible lyrical talent that they'd taken off like a rocket. And now, they were an international sensation.

We were just missing Campbell in the room.

The door creaked open behind us, and a boom of screaming girls hit us.

"Well, that'd be Campbell," Santi said with a laugh.

He elbowed Yorke, who looked back at him with a flat expression.

And then Campbell walked in the room, slamming the door behind him. He looked...tired. It had been a long day for him. He had to be exhausted.

"Good show, y'all," he said.

Viv gave him a thumbs-up. "I found your hot brother."

Campbell laughed. "Excellent."

Despite exhaustion etched into his features, Campbell hung out with all of us as if he weren't tired. He shook hands with Jordan and Julian, dragging them across the room to do shots. He hugged all of us, even signing the backstage passes for me, Jennifer, and Annie. Annie had asked, of course. She was the boldest of the lot of us. Jennifer had blushed from head to toe at the question.

"Seriously?" Campbell asked with a laugh. "It's your goddamn photo."

"It sure is," she said, biting her lip.

He shook his head, but he signed the pass. Blaire didn't offer hers up, and he carefully avoided looking at her.

I took a seat across the room from Hollin with another Bombay and lime. I'd done shots with Campbell, and the alcohol was finally hitting me. I had a high tolerance from all the wine, but even I couldn't compete with tequila shots. If I was honest, there was no one alive who could compete with tequila shots.

Santi leaned into Nora and was telling a story about the lot of them getting lost in Salt Lake City earlier that week. Everyone laughed as he regaled us with how they'd had to hike several miles through snow to find someone who finally recognized Campbell's face.

Campbell held his hand out. "Hey, it's not my fault that the car broke down."

"No, it's Yorke's," Viv said. "He should work better at a stick shift."

Yorke shrugged and kicked his feet up. "Sure."

"Why were you even driving around by yourself?" I asked.

All eyes shifted to Santi, who held his hands up. "Hey, hey, hey, I swore there was good Columbian food in that shopping center. Made by real Columbians."

"The food was delicious," Viv said with a sigh.

"Damn straight," Santi said. "Right back to my roots."

Santi winked at Nora, who flushed.

Campbell narrowed his eyes at Santi. "Hey, that's my little sister, dipshit. I know what that look means. Keep your hands to yourself."

Everyone cracked up, except Nora, who looked indignant.

"Nothing is happening, Campbell! I'm taken anyway."

"Yeah. Hands off our little sister," Hollin piped up.

Santi raised his hands and threw his arm over the other side of the couch, wrapping it around Blaire. "You taken, sexy?"

Blaire opened her mouth in shock. "I..."

Campbell jumped to his feet. Everyone stared at him, waiting to see what exactly he was going to say. I was the most eager to see how this was going to play out. There were enough slightly drunk, half-naked women in here, all vying for Campbell's attention. Blaire shouldn't have even been on his radar. Even in her mid-length designer dress and heels with her hair down straight as a board to her waist, her curtain bangs falling forward, nearly into her blue eyes. But she *was* on his radar. He looked ready to rip Santi's hands off of her. And he hadn't even been *that* upset about his own sister.

Blaire arched an eyebrow. "Got something to say?"

Campbell looked down at Blaire, who met his eyes defiantly. It was a *what are you going to do* look.

Finally, he sat back down, grinding his teeth together. "No. Nothing."

Conversation was stilted for a few moments after that. Jennifer yawned and gestured for them to leave. I should probably want to leave. Everyone else seemed done. Blaire certainly was ready to escape. She hadn't wanted to come in the first place. Nora even came to her feet to stand beside Jordan and Julian. Annie pouted a little about leaving so early...even though it was nearly midnight, but eventually, she relented when I caught Jordan squeeze her ass suggestively.

"Piper?" Blaire asked. "You coming?"

"No, come on," Campbell complained. "Someone should hang out a little longer."

"I think I'll stay," I said, which was a surprise, even to me.

"Me too," Hollin said. "I can make sure she gets back safe."

Blaire arched an eyebrow at me. "You sure?"

I was not. But this was *fun*. I was pleasantly drunk and not worrying about anything at all. I hadn't thought about work in hours. That never happened. What would a few extra hours hurt?

"Yeah. I'm good. Love you."

She squeezed me extra tight. "Have fun."

Campbell slung an arm around my shoulders as we both watched my best friend head out. "Glad you're staying."

"You going to tell me what happened with you and Blaire?"

Campbell blinked down at me, donning the casual rocker vibe immediately. "I don't know what you're talking about."

"Sure you don't."

He laughed. "Why worry about the past when the future is so bright?"

"You tell me."

Hollin interjected mid-conversation. "What are y'all whispering about?"

Campbell faced his brother with his arm still around my shoulders. "Your girl sure is blunt."

"I am *not* his girl," I said.

Hollin gestured to us. "The bluntest."

"Who said they wanted a blunt?" Viv cried. "I've got one or two here. Mostly joints though."

Campbell released me with a laugh. He took the joint she'd offered and took a puff. He passed it back to his bandmate and lounged on one of the couches. Girls crawled under his arms. Both looked ready to do whatever he asked right then and there. This was a side of Campbell I wasn't used to. Of course, there had been thousands of girls out there tonight who would have been just as happy to be in their position. It still wasn't how I saw him. This was showman Campbell. Not *back home in Lubbock* Campbell.

Hollin glanced my way. "Shots?"

"Might as well," I agreed.

Hollin ordered another round of tequila shots. Campbell hopped up almost instantly and was beside us as the shots were poured, as if he couldn't sit still for a second. The bartender added a third for him. We held them up, clinking glasses before tipping the drinks back.

I coughed around the tequila and reached for the lime on instinct. I bit hard into it. This was the most I'd had to drink in a long time. If I kept going at this pace, I was going to black out.

"How do you do this every night?" I asked Campbell.

"I don't know." He fluffed his hair. "It's the life."

Hollin laughed, jostling his brother. "Don't be an ass. There's no way you could drink this much every night and still perform the way you do."

"Hey, I can...sort of."

"He doesn't drink this much or smoke usually. This is Campbell's hosting skills."

Campbell snorted. "Hosting skills?"

"Yeah, you're like a housewife. Except for the concert."

"So, you're saying, he's showing off?" I asked.

"Obviously," the brothers said at the same time.

I couldn't help it; I laughed. "Well, that makes sense."

"Speaking of showing off," Campbell said, waggling his eyebrows, "want to see the tour bus?"

"Oh, yes!" I said, suddenly giddy with excitement. It was another thing I'd always wanted to see but never had.

Campbell and Hollin shared a look that I didn't comprehend. Brother thing.

"Yeah, let's go," Hollin said. "After you."

Campbell muttered something under his breath. Then, he gestured to the back of the room. "Let's go this way. Security is going to have to check for a clear walk-through."

We followed him through a maze of back hallways. Security stood in rapt attention at the door. They nodded at Campbell and checked for the all clear.

"Usually, the parking is pretty secure for the band," Campbell explained while we waited. "But sometimes, superfans find their way through all the security to get back here. It's happened a few times."

"Do they try to kill you?" I asked.

Campbell sputtered in surprise. "What? No. They want a picture and an autograph."

"You don't arrest them?"

Hollin's eyes were wide. "What do you think happens on tour?"

"There are lots of crazy people out there."

"We try not to resort to violence," Campbell said with a laugh. "Most people are cool, leaving when we tell them to. I've had a few stalkers and crazies, but security handles most of it." A security guard nodded at him. "All right. Let's go."

We stepped outside, and there was the Cosmere tour bus. It had their logo in blue and gold on the side, almost like graffiti. Campbell opened the front door, and we followed him inside.

"Well, this is it. Our little slice of home."

It was nice. Not anything fancy. I could see why they'd chosen to stay in a hotel while in Dallas. The beds were small though cozy. The space seemed cramped for five people to be stuck together all the time.

"This little nook is mine," Campbell pointed out. "Viv gets the back room. We offered to get her a solo bus, and she told us to fuck off. Michael asked if he could have the solo bus, so he wouldn't be with us all the fucking time."

"Or so his wife and kid could travel with y'all?"

Campbell gestured to me. "Or that. But the record label nixed it. Said they could do gendered buses but not family. I don't get the big deal, but here we are. One bus."

"It's not what I expected," I said as I settled into the plush couch and leaned my elbows on the table.

"Nah, it's nothing special. Gets us from point A to point

B," Campbell said. Then, his phone buzzed noisily in his pocket. He looked down at the screen and grinned. "I have to take this. I'll be back. Help yourself to the booze."

He disappeared down the stairs, leaving me and Hollin all alone.

13

PIPER

I was alone with Hollin Abbey. This was a bad idea.

I swallowed and glanced over at him. He'd taken the seat opposite me on the couch, manspreading his legs wide and resting his arms across the back of the cushions.

"I could get used to this," he said with a devilish grin in my direction.

"Most people could."

"No," he said calmly. "You."

"Me?"

"I could get used to you like this." His eyes crawled over me and answered the question on my lips. "A little wild."

A hoarse laugh escaped my lips. "I am not wild."

"You're here with me...alone."

"So?" I challenged him, coming to my feet defensively. "What? Are you going to put the moves on me?"

His smirk was so goddamn tempting. "I don't have to."

"And why not?"

"Because you want this as much as I do."

I gaped at him for a split second before laughing softly. "Wow. You're so confident."

He arched an eyebrow. "Prove me wrong."

"I don't have to prove anything to you." I had my hands on my hips, only a foot away from him.

He was so sure of himself. And, fuck, it was a turn-on. I liked it even if I wanted to throw it all back in his face in the same second.

Hollin leaned into me. "That right?"

I opened my mouth to say some other smart-ass response when his hands dragged my hips forward, and I tumbled into his lap. My skirt slid up dangerously high on my thighs. And I could tell immediately how much I'd affected him.

"What are you doing?" I demanded breathily.

I should be standing up right this minute. I should shove away from him and tell him to never touch me again. But I didn't. I sat there, straddling his powerful thighs, my hands on his shoulders and his face mere inches from my lips.

"I want you, Piper," he said, his voice like smoke.

"Hollin..." I gasped out.

"I want to kiss you right now. Clearly, that's a bad idea..."

Oh, fuck it.

Without an ounce of warning, I crashed my lips down onto his. It was like fireworks on the Fourth of July, wrapped up in opening presents on Christmas morning. It was everything I'd ever wanted in a kiss and more. His hands pushed up into my hair, sealing our lips together. His tongue roved against my lips until I opened for him, and then I was a goner. Utterly and completely gone. His tongue slid inside my mouth, taking control of the kiss I'd initiated. The first sweep of his tongue against my own sent shivers down my back. I squirmed against him, and he groaned, shifting his hips upward.

"I've been hard all day thinking about you," he growled against my lips.

"Oh God," I managed to get out as his lips ravaged across my jaw and down to my neck. The scratch of his beard made me hold on to him for dear life.

"Tell me you want me."

"Fuck."

"Yes, that's what I want to do to you," he said.

His hands slipped out of my hair and down my back. He grasped my hips and forced me hard against him. Holding me down into place over his cock. Fuck, fuck, fuck. I rolled my hips in micro circles against the thick length of him, wanting nothing but this friction to release all this pent-up energy.

Suddenly, his lips were back on mine. With the roll of his hips against my core and his mouth conquering me, I was close to releasing right then and there. It had been a long time since something other than my own hand and toy had gotten me off. I had a feeling Hollin would accept nothing less.

"Piper," he said as his hands trailed up and down my bare thighs, circling inward to my inner thighs and back up. He was getting closer and closer to where I wanted him.

"Hmm?" I gasped.

"I need your ass over that table."

I blinked at him, love-drunk on the endorphins coursing through me. "What?"

He didn't wait for another explanation. He lifted me with ease and flipped me around so that I was facing away from him in his lap. He'd picked me up as if I were weightless. Then, he pressed me forward until my face and chest were against the center table in the tour bus. My skirt hiked up nearly to my hips. From this angle, he had the perfect view of *everything*. My ass was on full display with the blue of my thong the only scrap of fabric covering my pussy.

His hands were on me, pushing my skirt up and out of the way. He appreciatively rubbed my ass a few times.

"You should always wear skirts," he informed me. "Though I sure do like your ass in your tight jeans."

I moaned as his hands slipped dangerously close to my thong. I clenched my hands on the table to keep myself from pushing back into his hands. To show exactly how desperate I was for his touch.

"How many do you want?"

"Want?"

His giant hand came down on my right ass cheek. I yelped softly at the sting, but pleasure flooded through me in the aftermath of the pain. Desire pooled in my core. I had already been wet from our kiss. I was going to soak through my panties now.

"That was one," he teased as he rubbed his hands all over my ass again. "How many?"

"More," was the only word I could get out.

I couldn't see the smirk that was likely on his face, but I heard his grunt of approval right before he brought his hand back down on the exact same spot on my ass. I whimpered at the second one, squirming to escape the pain, even as my entire body was set on fire.

He jerked me backward and braced an arm across my back. "Two."

Then, he swatted at me again on the other cheek. A quick series right, left, right. I gasped in pain as I tried to rub my legs together. I needed release. Holy shit. I needed it bad.

I was close, and he hadn't even touched me. But I wouldn't get there without rubbing my clit.

"That's six. Can you take it to ten?"

I moaned and bit down on my lip hard. I inched my ass back toward him. I didn't know how many I could take. I had no frame of reference. I just fucking wanted it. I wanted all of it.

"Seven," he said, bringing his hand down on the back of my thigh and then the other. "Eight."

I yelped. That was so much more potent than my ass. Tears welled in my eyes, even as everything built up so high that I might never come back down.

"Please," I whispered. "Oh God, please."

He finished off the last two in a brutal, merciless succession. My ass was on fire. It was going to be red and painful. I wouldn't be able to sit without thinking about him spanking me.

"There you go. That was very good," he said in the gentlest and most soothing voice I'd ever heard him use. He was rubbing and massaging the tender flesh. "Now, do you need to be taken care of?"

I couldn't even form the words. I nodded. If I'd had words, I would have begged him to let me release. I couldn't even believe I hadn't come from the spanking.

He tugged my thong to the side and dragged two fingers through the evidence of my arousal. "You're so wet," he groaned as if he could barely control himself.

He was hanging on by a thread. And so was I.

At the first touch of his finger against my clit, I bucked against his hand, and everything shivered through my body. "Yes," I gasped.

"Like this?" he asked, circling his finger around the swollen bud.

He stopped only briefly to remove my thong, so he could have better access. He brought his fingers back up to my clit, circling relentlessly, and I came hard and fast. I pulsed and pulsed, on and on. He never let up, until he drew out each shuddering breath from me as I climaxed higher than I'd ever reached.

Finally, he let me go, and I collapsed, releasing every ounce of pent-up energy. I was limp, and it was Hollin fucking Abbey who had teased it out of me.

"Fuck, Piper," he ground out. "I need...fuck, I need to fuck you."

"Yes," I said.

I heard the sound of a zipper, and I watched him pull his cock out of his boxers. My eyes widened. Considering how tall he was and the size of his hands, I'd maybe idly thought that he'd be big. But he was *huge*. Like I had no idea how he'd fit inside of me if I wasn't as wet as I'd ever been in my life.

He winked at me when he caught me staring and tore open a condom. I watched him sheathe the monster.

"I'll go slow," he promised as the head of his cock touched the lips of my pussy.

Our eyes were still locked together when I said, "Don't."

"Don't?" He stilled completely. The muscles of his arms tense. Ready to stop if I wanted him to. But that wasn't what I had in mind.

"Don't go slow," I begged.

"Fuck," he grunted and then slammed into me.

Even though I had been prepared for him, soaking wet and ready to be impaled on his cock, all the air whooshed out of my lungs at the first savage thrust. He didn't even make it all the way in, and I was still filled, but I squirmed to try to fit him in more. He grabbed each of my hands in one of his to keep me from moving. He drew back and pushed into me again. Inch by delicious inch, he fitted himself into my pussy.

"Fuck...fuck yes," he said breathlessly. "You're doing so good. Just like that, babe."

I had no words. His cock had stolen every single one of them.

He started to move. Thrusting in and out at a rapid pace until, against all odds, he built me right back up. This definitely shouldn't have been possible. I was not a second-orgasm girl. Nor was I an orgasm-during-sex kind of girl. What was happening?

"Oh God, Hollin, I'm going to come," I shouted into the empty tour bus.

"Come for me." He thrust harder and faster. Somehow lengthening even more inside me. "Come *with* me."

And that moment, we both unleashed at once. I saw stars as he emptied himself inside of me with a roar of pleasure. His grip on my arms was painful, and yet I didn't want to move. I had no interest in ever moving again.

Finally, he released me, and slowly—ever so slowly—he pulled out of me.

"Oh," I whispered helplessly as the fullness left me.

He pressed a kiss into my hip. "Such a good girl. My good girl."

Normally, the words would have been insulting. I would have seethed at him. Told him to fuck off with that misogynistic crap. But lying across a tour bus table after being properly fucked for the first time in my life, I *was* his good girl.

Somehow, I was Hollin Abbey's good girl.

14

HOLLIN

By the time Campbell returned, both of us were decent.

He shot me a look, and I just smirked.

"Sorry about that," he said. "Looks like we need to get back to the hotel. Thought we wouldn't be leaving Dallas until tomorrow afternoon, but they have us heading out bright and early for Austin."

"Sounds good," I said.

I offered my hand to Piper, which, shockingly, she took. She was in some kind of sex coma. A dopamine-induced high that made her all soft and pliant. I wanted to scoop her up in my arms and carry her right back to bed. This side of her triggered my protective instincts like nothing I'd known in years.

I helped her down the stairs, and we followed the band to an awaiting limo. Campbell told us that the tour bus would meet the band at the hotel at five tomorrow morning. We piled into the limo, and Piper sat, sandwiched between me and Campbell.

Santi had a girl under each arm and was going on about

some new sound he'd managed. Yorke kept shooting him *shut the fuck up* looks. But no one could make Santi be quiet before he was ready. Michael was half-asleep at the other end of the limo. Campbell and Viv were arguing like an old married couple. As per usual.

"How are you feeling?" I asked, slipping an arm around Piper's waist.

"Sore," she admitted. She leaned her head against my shoulder. Her eyes were half-lidded, as if she might pass out.

"Too sore?"

"Mmm," she murmured. Then shook her head.

"Good."

I tucked her in closer. I liked the way she fitted into my side. I was so enamored with every little move she made that I didn't even stop to question my behavior. I'd spanked her ass hard enough to bruise. She was shifting all over the place, so it must have hurt, and I didn't want to let her go without knowing that she would be all right.

I'd done some stuff like this before but never...*this*. It had always been more of a joke. The girl had seen some porn that she wanted to do and giggled through it. But Piper had been infected with it. It had catapulted through her veins and ripped through her skin. It made her this soft, weightless nymph instead of the proud, stubborn, glaring woman I was used to.

And in the middle of that shift, something had cracked inside me, too. I'd push her as far as she'd let me. But I wanted—no, needed—to be there to hold her and keep her safe once she was broken.

When the limo stopped in front of our hotel, I helped Piper out of the car. Even at an ungodly early hour of the morning, Campbell was looking around, as if anticipating a mob.

"I should probably enter from the back," he said.

"Shut up," Viv said, smacking him. "No one is even awake."

"And we have security," Michael added.

"Which makes us more suspicious," Campbell grumbled.

"Go around back," I told him. "Do what you think is best."

"All right," he said, nodding his head. "I guess this is good-bye. Can't imagine you'll be awake at five."

"Fuck no."

The rest of the band was already heading inside without Campbell. And as much as they acted nonchalant, he was the face of Cosmere. He was the one who got mobbed and stalked. When out for shows, it was safer for him to be cautious.

"You coming?" Piper asked, turning back to look at me as she followed Viv.

"Go on inside with everyone else," I told her. "I'll be there in a minute."

She shrugged and fell into step beside Viv. I watched her go with hungry eyes. What had I gotten myself into?

"So, you're welcome," Campbell said with a shit-eating grin when Piper was out of earshot.

"I have to admit, the tour bus was put to good use."

Campbell snorted. "I bet."

"Did you even have a call?"

"Yeah, bro. But I didn't have to be gone as long as I was."

"Little matchmaker."

Campbell laughed and rubbed the back of his head. "Yeah. I like to see everyone happy. And she seems to make you happy. Try not to fuck it up until I get back, will you?"

"No promises. I'm kind of a fuckup."

"No arguments there."

"When are you coming back?" I asked him.

"Tour ends in about two months. I'm supposed to go to LA, but maybe I'll swing by Lubbock first."

"Do that," I insisted.

"Tell Nora I said bye."

We hugged, and he returned to the limo to be escorted to a more discreet entrance. I'd miss him when he was gone. But I was glad that he'd made plans to come home. It was better having him in our lives.

I strode inside to find Piper waiting for me. The others had disappeared up the elevator, but she was still here.

"You ready to go to bed?"

Her eyes had slightly more life to them than she'd had in the limo. As if she were waking up from a long dream.

"Sure," she said and hit the button.

We took the elevator up to our floor.

"What did Campbell say?"

"Just that he'll be home in two months after the tour is over."

"That'll be good. You like having him in Lubbock."

"I do," I agreed.

She nodded and absently chewed on her lip. "I like having Peyton home, too. She'll be married in two months."

"Just in time for Campbell to crash the reception."

Her smile was light and airy. "She'd probably like that."

We left the elevator and strode down the hallway. My room was first. She hesitated at the door, as if anticipating me inviting her in. Which I wanted to do. Fuck, did I want that. But what was important was her getting some sleep and recovering. She wouldn't do that if she ended up in my bed. There was no way that I'd let her sleep. And I couldn't imagine she'd be begging for bed either.

So, I kept walking, and we landed at the room she shared with Blaire.

"Well, good night," she whispered.

My hand cupped her jaw. I turned her face up to mine. "Not yet."

She arched an eyebrow, a spark of that rampant stubbornness picking back up. But I smothered it when I slid my hand into her dark hair and captured her lips. She bowed into me like a boat on the water. I held her tight and firm, just the way she liked...needed to be handled. It wasn't the same kiss we'd had when she kissed me on the tour bus. This was slow, almost languid. It was a proper good-night kiss.

I pressed one more kiss to her swollen lips. Her eyes were still shut tight as I finally released her.

"Good night," I told her.

Her eyes fluttered open. "Okay," she murmured lazily.

"I'll see you in the morning."

She nodded. "Good night."

She scanned her card and slid into her room. I waited until the door closed behind her before heading back to my own room. It felt incredibly empty.

Why had I let her get away? Why had I decided that it made more sense for her to sleep alone?

Yes, it was the reasonable and responsible thing to do. But, fuck, it didn't mean I wanted it. I didn't want it at all.

I stripped out of my clothes and lay naked on top of the covers. I wanted her. Tonight. Tomorrow. The next night.

Fuck. I was in trouble.

I woke the next morning, feeling better than I had in years. With the amount of alcohol I'd imbibed with my little brother, I should have had the headache of all headaches. But instead, I felt incredible.

I showered the sex off of me and changed into jeans and a classic black T-shirt. We had to take the private jet back to Lubbock today. Campbell had already left. And I'd slept with Piper.

A grin hit my face.

Fuck. It had been amazing. And I'd done the right thing, tucking her away in her own bed. But I'd get to see her this morning. I hoped that her ass wasn't fighting her too much. Just enough to remember me every time she shifted in her seat.

I hauled my bag with me and went downstairs for breakfast. Piper was seated at a table with Blaire, Jennifer, and Annie. The guys and my sister were nowhere in sight.

Her head jerked up as if she knew the instant I walked into the room. I smiled at her. Not any of my stupid smirks that drove her bonkers, but the sincere one. The one that said I'd had a great fucking time last night and it was good to see her.

But as quickly as she looked at me, she dipped her head and stared down into her oatmeal.

I narrowed my eyes. What the fuck? She couldn't even meet my gaze?

A touch of pink was on her cheeks and she wasn't talking to the rest of the party. Was she embarrassed? Or ashamed? Had she remembered the amazing night of sex as something...bad? That didn't seem possible. Not after the way she'd acted when I took her back to the hotel. She'd been happy with me. Not the normal anger and fire, but actually happy.

Nora clapped me on the back, and I jumped. She chuckled. "How'd last night go?"

I glanced at Piper and back. "Uh, it was good. Campbell left at five. He told me to tell you bye."

"Yeah, I got a text. Glad you had fun."

She dropped her rolling bag off next to the girls and went to get breakfast. I added my duffel on top of her bag.

"Morning," I said to the table.

"Good morning!" Jennifer said, all chipper. "I am the only morning person at this table. You'll have to forgive everyone else who hates sunlight."

I laughed. "Sounds right. Y'all sleep all right?"

"The beds were amazing," Blaire said from under her baseball cap. "Piper has a massive hangover. We had to get her to take her sunglasses off indoors."

"Annie will bite you before talking to you without coffee," Jennifer added.

"Fascinating. I'm shockingly not hungover. After how much we drank last night, Piper, I'm surprised I'm not in the same mood as you."

Piper lifted her expression to mine, and none of the good girl I'd called her last night was visible in her expression. She was stubborn, angry Piper once more. A wall divided us.

"We're in very different moods," she said.

"Yeah?"

"Yes," she quipped.

And if she wanted to be like this, well, I could be the asshole she always thought I was.

"Sore?"

Her eyes rounded and then flattened. Her hand clenched into a fist.

"What?" Jennifer asked. "Did something happen?"

"Piper fell on her ass last night."

Piper shot me a death glare. If she could have had lasers shooting out of her eyes, she would have.

"Is that why you've been weird all morning?"

"I have a huge bruise," Piper said. She looked like she wanted to hit me. "Forgot about it until I showered."

Julian and Jordan appeared just as Nora brought her plate of food over.

"Eat up. It's almost time to go," Jordan said.

I tipped my head at Piper and walked away. I didn't know why I was so mad. Of course she hadn't told her friends that we'd slept together. Why would she? She had been adamantly against it up until the moment it'd happened last night. I shouldn't even fucking care. I did shit like that all the time. It wasn't even the first time it had happened to me. It just had felt...different.

Piper was different.

And I had no idea how to reconcile that.

"Could you be more obvious?" she demanded as she reached for a banana at the buffet.

"I didn't know we were hiding it."

"I fell on my ass? Jesus, Hollin."

I arched an eyebrow. "What did you want me to say?"

"Like normal, I'd prefer you said nothing," she snapped.

"So, this never happened."

"Sure, it happened. It was a one-night stand. I've come to my senses now that I'm not pumped full of alcohol."

"That wasn't the only thing you were pumped full of."

She made a disgusted look. "And this is why this never should have happened."

"And what about after? What about the ride home and the kiss at your door?"

"What do you want me to say?" She met my eyes with a dark gaze. "I was drunk."

"Fine," I said with the hedonistic smirk that she despised. "If you say so. How is your ass anyway? Still have my handprints on it, babe?"

"Fuck you, Hollin."

Then, she strode away.

And I cursed myself for being a perpetual dick as I watched her walk away.

15

PIPER

*H*ollin and I had gone from zero to a hundred. It had been a fucking master class in whiplash.

But what we'd done was a mistake. An incredible, soul-shattering mistake. I never, ever should have had sex with him, and he shouldn't have asked about it in front of all of our friends the next morning.

What had happened on the tour bus should have *stayed* on the tour bus.

So, I'd done the very mature thing—antagonized him and then avoided him entirely.

I had no idea what I was doing. I wanted more of what he'd offered. I wanted to feel the way I'd felt at the show, but I didn't even know how I'd gotten to that point. How I'd let my guard down enough to get there.

Hollin Abbey was the last person on the planet I wanted to be with. After what had happened with Quinn and Khloe, I'd written him off as the scum of the universe. We'd had mind-blowing sex, and I was just going to what? Forgive him? Forget about who he was? Not likely.

Not that he'd reached out. No texts. No calls. No stopping by. He wasn't exactly the pining type. After all, he was the guy who loved the chase and got over it once he got what he wanted. This wasn't any different.

"*Mija*, did you want to get lunch?" my dad asked, breaking me out of my thoughts.

I glanced at the time. "I'm supposed to meet Peyton. She wants to talk wedding arrangements."

Dad chuckled. "Does she know that you don't care?"

"She's Peyton. She knows." I pecked him on the cheek. "But also, I care that her wedding day is perfect."

"You're a good sister."

"I try. It's good to have Peyton back in town."

"We all feel like that. Go. Have fun."

"I will, Papa."

"Remember to pencil us in for Easter."

I squeezed his hand as I passed. "Always."

Easter was a big deal in my family. It always had been. Abuelita always talked about what it had been like in Mexico. Carnival before Lent and then all the amazing traditions leading up to Easter Sunday. I'd always wanted to go to her home in Mexico and experience it, but we'd never had the funds to make it happen. One day, I'd do it.

I jumped into my Jeep, glad that I'd taken the top off this morning when I drove into work. The weather was warming up, and I lived with my top off all summer. Rain or shine, it was the Jeep way.

I parked outside of Thai Pepper. They'd closed for a few months, and everyone had feared that they were going to close forever. It was the best Thai in town. It would have been a real travesty, but they had opened back up and were busier than ever.

Peyton had on a little skirt and cardigan over her leotard and tights when she met me at the door. A tall blonde trailed behind her in a burgundy dress and chunky heels.

"Pipes!" Peyton said with a Miss America wave. "Hope you don't mind that I invited Tori. She didn't have plans."

"The famous Tori," I said, holding my hand out. "I've heard so much about you."

Tori shook my hand with a wide smile. She was gorgeous in that dancer sort of way. Lean muscle mass on a narrow frame. Her legs were toned almost as much as Peyton's were. Though it was nearly impossible to be as fit as my sister. Her blonde hair was down in loose waves around her shoulders, and she had an easy smile that met her soft green eyes.

"Piper! God, it's so good to finally meet you."

Tori had been hired as the costume coordinator for Lubbock Ballet Company right before *The Nutcracker* season. She and Peyton had hit it off, and Peyton had insisted that we'd be fast friends.

We stepped inside the busy restaurant, put in our orders, and took a seat. Peyton pulled out a notepad filled with to-do lists.

"I have so many things left," she said with a sigh.

"You'll get through it," Tori said confidently.

Peyton smiled at her. "Thanks. I'm glad Nora is doing so much."

We talked through the cake choices and agreed on a half-dozen for her to taste-test with Isaac later that week. I'd agreed to watch Aly that afternoon so they could have some time together. His daughter was a dancer as well and quite a joy. I couldn't wait for her to be my niece for real. My mom and Isaac's parents had been doing double duty, watching her while they wedding-planned.

Our food came, and I ate the pad thai with gusto. Even if

I hadn't been starved, I'd have scarfed down the noodles like they were my life force. Sometimes, I wondered if they put something in them to make them taste this delicious. To make me always crave them.

"How was your concert, Pipes?" Peyton asked. "You never mentioned it."

I swallowed hard. "It was good. I went backstage with the band." I hesitated a moment. "Saw the tour bus."

"Really?" Tori asked. "That sounds so much fun. What band?"

"Cosmere."

Tori arched an eyebrow. "Wow. They're pretty huge."

"The lead singer is local," Peyton filled her in.

"I'd heard that."

"Why are you fidgeting?" Peyton asked. She pointed her chopsticks at me. "What happened? You're only like this when you're hiding something."

When I'd gotten home from the show, I'd confided in Blaire what had happened. She hadn't been that surprised, which I found mildly insulting, but she'd laughed it off. I'd begged her not to tell anyone else, but this was just Peyton. I could tell her. And I didn't know this Tori girl from anything. Made it easier.

"I might have done something rash."

"Oh?"

"Like hook up with someone on the tour bus."

Tori whooped. "Girl, get it!"

Peyton's jaw dropped. "You?"

"I know. Crazy, right?"

"Who was it?"

"Was it a band member?" Tori asked. She nudged Peyton. "You didn't tell me your sister was wild. I like her already."

Peyton eyed me with questions in her eyes. I wasn't wild. That wasn't me at all. And yet it had happened. This wasn't like me.

"It wasn't a band member. A band member's brother." Peyton's eyebrows shot up, and I gave her a look that said we'd talk about it later. "It doesn't matter."

"Well, was it at least good?" Tori asked, wiggling her eyebrows.

I couldn't hold in my own secret smile. "It was."

"What a way to get over Bradley," Peyton said.

Oh. Bradley. Right. I hadn't been thinking about him at all.

"I told you it was really over."

"You've proven your point," Peyton said gently. The big-sister voice.

"Ah, don't give her a hard time," Tori said. "Every girl needs to feel that thrill a little bit. Find that man who sets her blood on fire."

"Success," I said, returning to my food.

We returned to the safe topic of the wedding for the rest of the meal.

It wasn't until we left and Peyton hugged me good-bye that she whispered in my ear, "We'll talk later?"

I huffed. "I don't know, Peyton. Am I stupid for having done this?"

She glanced over at Tori to check that she was still on the phone. "Hollin?" she guessed.

"Am I that transparent?" I asked with a forced laugh.

"After that conversation with Nora, I've been wondering if more was going on than you let on. Is he why you broke up with Bradley?"

"What? No. Of course not. I was serious that I had no interest in him. He's not the kind of guy that I want."

"What kind of guy is that?"

I didn't know how to answer that. "Someone serious."

"Bradley was serious about you, and that didn't seem to matter."

"Yeah, but he wasn't...*serious*. And by the end, hearing him chew made me want to put a fork through his eye."

Peyton cracked up. "Yes, well, that sounds healthy. Look, I've been there. The last guy I dated was terrible. We had similar interests, and I had to see him for rehearsals, so I thought it worked. It wasn't until I saw Isaac again that I realized how wrong I'd been. Maybe...you should give Hollin a chance."

"Absolutely not."

"Then, why did you sleep with him, silly?"

I held my hands out. "I was drunk?"

"Well, if you just wanted some fun, then you got it. I'd say, it'd be smart to either take some time for yourself or actually *look* for that serious guy. Instead of inevitably falling back on Bradley."

I winced. Too real. "True. Thanks, seester."

She hugged me again. "I love you."

I returned to the office with my mind on anything but work. I grabbed the mail on the way in, leaving the bills for my dad to deal with. All my worries about Hollin fell away as I stared at the envelope in my hand. I ripped into it, pulling the letter from within.

It was the official confirmation that Sinclair Cellars would be in the IWAA Texas Wine Award Competition. We'd shipped wine down to Austin, and knowing that it had gotten there safe was a relief. The letter informed me that I'd receive further information if I was selected as a finalist. It all felt so real.

I tacked the letter up on my wall, feeling all the more focused for it.

I'd left work at a reasonable hour. Blaire was blaring music, doing some TikTok dance in the living room when I walked in on the whole thing. She shrieked like I was a horror movie villain coming to slaughter her. Then managed to trip and fall on her ass. She laughed hysterically at herself.

"Shit, shit, shit," Blaire said through her laughter. "You scared the hell out of me."

I was leaning over, laughing at her reaction. "I texted you that I was coming home."

Blaire got to her feet, killing the music and ending the video. She wiped tears from her eyes. "I've been learning that stupid dance for an hour. I didn't even check my messages."

"Well, you have to upload that one."

"I should. It might go viral if I include some slasher movie music when you walk into the door."

"Everything you do goes viral."

She shrugged. "Sometimes."

"Where's Jennifer?"

"Julian's." Blaire turned off the ring light, which had bathed our house in perfect artificial light. "She said she'd see us at the game later."

"The game?"

"Soccer. The Tacos."

My lips formed an O as I remembered that they had a soccer game tonight.

The Tacos was the team that Isaac had put together a few years ago. The roster had changed a few times, but

Blaire was their lead striker. She was really, *really* good. I loved coming to watch her. The only problem: Hollin played on the team. Running around in his short red shorts and ostentatious white cleats. Normally, I just ogled him from the sidelines. But I hadn't seen him since I'd gotten off of the jet Sunday afternoon. Avoiding him would be a lot harder in person.

"I might skip this one," I told her.

"No," she told me automatically.

"What do you mean, no?"

"I know what you're doing," Blaire said, crossing her arms over her matching coral athletic gear. "You can't just disappear. You were already acting suspicious the morning after the tour bus incident. If you stop coming around, someone else will figure it out."

"Ugh," I groaned, dropping my purse and falling on the couch. "Do I have to?"

"You said it didn't mean anything. Did it actually mean something?"

"No," I muttered.

"Then, it shouldn't matter that you see him."

"It's awkward."

Blaire sank into the seat next to me. "Well, you slept with your sworn enemy. I could see how that would be awkward."

I laughed. "Do I have to go?"

"Yep, you do."

"Fine," I said with a sigh. "But I'm not speaking to him."

Blaire grinned. "Yeah, right. He's going to be all up your ass, like normal."

"I won't rise to the bait."

She looked dubious. "Good luck."

Yeah, she was right. I was screwed.

16

HOLLIN

"Y ou're going to be late to your game," Alejandra called. She leaned against my office door. She was the winery manager, and I worked with her more directly than any of our other employees.

"Fuck," I grumbled.

"What's keeping you?"

I wrinkled my nose. "Tamara."

Alejandra laughed. "Is she coming on to you again?"

"When is she not?" I asked with a shudder. "She's the same age as my baby sister. I wish she would keep her hands to herself."

"You know that's sexual harassment. We could fire her."

"She's my sister's best friend. I'm not firing her."

"Plus, everyone loves her on the tours."

"She is our best guide."

"I'll talk to her," Ale said. "Again."

"Thanks." I headed into the bathroom to change into my soccer uniform. I threw my shirt, Wranglers, and boots into my bag and left.

And *there* was Tamara.

"Hey, big boy," she said with a wide grin.

She was a natural redhead with pouty lips and tons of makeup. She made it somehow look effortless. I couldn't deny that she was attractive, but again...same age as my sister. Not to mention, I had another woman constantly on my mind right now. Not that I'd heard a word from Piper.

"Tamara, you going to the game?"

"Yep. How could I miss you in shorts?"

I laughed with a head shake. "I'm your boss, Tamara."

"Oh, I know. All in good fun." Then, she winked at me to say that she'd bang me if I let her.

"Well, I'll see you at the game."

"Can't wait!" she chirped.

I hopped quickly into my truck. She always exaggerated her hips. It was like she knew I was an ass man. I didn't need any of that in my life right now. It was complicated enough as I tried to figure out what to do about Piper.

I parked my truck at the back of the lot and immediately looked around the field for Piper. I hadn't seen her very recognizable Jeep in the parking lot, but sometimes, Blaire drove. It didn't look like she was here yet.

"You're on time," Julian said with a grin.

"I'm always on time," I quipped.

"Not lately."

I found Annie sitting in the bleachers in her red uniform, next to Chase Sinclair. Jordan was on the other side, staring pointedly down at his phone.

"What's he doing here?"

Julian shrugged. "He and Annie are friends."

"And Jordan is chill with that?"

"Does he *look* happy about it?"

He did not. But he was trying at least. That was more than I would want to do. Chase and Annie had known each other since they were kids. It made sense that they'd stayed friends. It still would have been hard, knowing that he'd confessed his love for her.

"He's a better man than I am."

Julian arched an eyebrow. "Well, duh."

I punched him in the arm. "Shithead."

We warmed up for the game, but my eyes were still on the stands. I kept waiting for her to walk in and wondered what I'd do. It wasn't like I could go up to her and shake sense into her. I didn't even know what sense I would be shaking into her. But I wanted another taste. After Saturday, how could she pretend that she didn't?

She and Blaire strode out of the parking lot and toward our field. Blaire was a blur of red as I found Piper. My feet stilled, and I just stared. She was wearing tight jeans that fit her curvy figure and a skintight black tank top. A jean jacket was tucked under her arm. She hadn't seen me yet, or she was purposely avoiding my gaze.

Julian ran into me on the field. "Dude."

"What the fuck?"

Julian's gaze shifted to where I'd been looking. He found Piper and arched an eyebrow. "So, you and Piper?"

I ground my teeth together. I hadn't told him about what happened at the show. It had seemed like Piper didn't want me to. But I usually told him all about the girls I was into. Why was this any different?

"We might have hooked up at the concert."

"Might have?"

"On the tour bus."

Julian laughed. "Well, I didn't see that one coming."

"Thanks, dick."

"So, care to explain what's going on now?"

I gritted my teeth. I hated admitting the truth. "Nothing to explain."

"She's not looking at you. How did you already fuck this up?"

"I didn't fuck anything up."

Julian snorted. "I'm your best friend for a reason. I've seen you three-date-rule *a lot* of girls."

"I'm not three-date-ruling anyone."

"Yeah and you better not fucking do it to Piper."

I had no intention of doing anything to Piper that she didn't want me to do to her. But I didn't know how to explain what I was feeling. That I actually...wanted to date her. Or at least, I wanted more.

"Forget about it," I said. Julian dropped it and we went back to our warm-up.

Isaac called us in for a pregame pep talk. The ref blew his whistle for us to get on the pitch, and my blood started pumping. The Tacos was the best team I'd been on since college rec. Blaire and August played offense. Though August was mostly there to assist Blaire since girl goals counted for two. Isaac, Julian, and Nora played midfield. It was one of the few times my sister was out of her high heels. I sometimes forgot that she was so freaking tiny, but she was *fast*. I played defense with Annie and her doctor friend, Cézanne. And our goalie, Gerome, was Cézanne's boyfriend.

The rest of our friends watched from the stands as we all set up to play. When I looked up at the audience, Tamara waved and called my name. I cringed and let my gaze shift to Piper. She'd settled onto the bleachers next to Jennifer and their other close friend, Sutton Wright. Her husband, David, was on the sidelines with his adopted son, Jason, while Sutton sat with their daughter, Madison. Jennifer was cooing at her while Piper looked on uncertainly. She was here. She was sitting with her friends. She was acting like nothing had happened. What the fuck?

Then, the whistle blew, and I had no more time to think about it. I dove into the game headfirst. Taking out the days of pent-up frustration on the opposing team. It was a little too much energy, considering the other team was terrible. By the end of the first half, we were up thirteen to one. Blaire pulled back to let August shoot since the score was so embarrassing.

I took a water break and glanced back at Piper. But she was no longer sitting next to Jennifer. She'd slid across her seat and was next to Chase. Jordan had moved away from him, so the two of them were alone. All alone and looking awfully chummy.

What the fuck were they talking about? Chase said something with this big smile on his face. Piper was laughing. She was laughing at whatever he'd said. They weren't even touching, but already, I could see that she had none of the anger that I brought out in her. This was just Piper.

Piper flirting with Chase Sinclair.

My blood boiled.

"Hollin?" Julian called.

"I don't like that guy," I growled.

Julian looked up into the stands and grimaced. "Well, join the club. Us Wrights aren't too fond of the Sinclairs either."

Julian would know. He'd dated Ashleigh Sinclair before Jennifer. Before she'd gone off the deep end.

And even though I only needed a quarter of my brain to win this match, I played like we were in the finals. At one point, Isaac even came back to try to bench me if I didn't calm the fuck down. He rarely got mad, but apparently, humiliating our opponents was his line.

At the end of the game, Piper was still sitting with Chase. And I was still pissed.

I ripped off my shin guards, tossed them into my bag, and took a long swig of my water bottle.

"So, pizza?" Blaire asked with a little dance. "We should celebrate."

"It was a massacre," August said. "I've never scored so much in my life."

Nora leaned into him. "It was hot."

He grinned. "Thanks, baby girl."

"Can I invite Tamara, too?" Nora asked.

"Sure," Blaire said.

I grimaced. Great. Just what I needed. Then, my gaze shifted as Piper dropped out of the stands to head over to Blaire. "Nice game."

"Thanks! Pizza?" Blaire asked.

"Sure. I'm down." And she had this bubbly excitement to her.

"I'll pass," Isaac said. "Need to get home to Peyton and Aly."

Annie, Cézanne, and Gerome bowed out as well for work. Annie and Cézanne were on call, which always made the games up in the air if they'd be there at all. That left me, Julian, and Jennifer to go with Nora, August, Tamara, Blaire, and Piper.

"Sutton?" Blaire called. "Pizza?"

She groaned. "I'd kill for it. But the littles." She gestured to her children.

"I can take care of it," David said.

"You sure?" she asked.

"Go. Have fun."

Sutton skipped forward. "I'm in. Pizza sounds divine."

I wanted to talk to Piper, but she stayed purposefully

away from me. There was never an opportunity that wouldn't have been much too obvious for the company.

I ground my teeth together and left the parking lot. I followed behind Blaire's shiny silver Lexus until we reached Capital Pizza, which was The Tacos' typical after-game celebration. There were only two parking spots left by the time we got there. I pulled in next to Blaire with my door facing Piper in the passenger seat.

Blaire waved at me as I got out. She looked to Piper, who was stepping out of the car. "I'll see y'all inside," she chirped happily and then hightailed it away.

Piper crossed her arms. "What do you want?"

I slammed my door shut. "You've been avoiding me."

"Get over yourself. I haven't been anywhere *near* you all week."

"You're near me now," I growled, stepping into her personal space.

"And?" She tried to brush past me, but I put my arm out against my truck, blocking her way. "Real mature."

"What were you and Chase talking about at the game?"

She rolled her eyes. "Why? Jealous?"

Was I? Yes, that was that unfamiliar feeling. That want that went straight to my balls. I ached for her. I wanted to crawl back under her skin. She drove me out of my mind. And I wanted to drive her out of hers.

"I don't know why you're denying your attraction to me."

She laughed. "Do you hear yourself? Obviously, I find you attractive. But that doesn't change anything, Hollin. You and I would never, ever work out. You're so...*you*. Chase is nice, normal..." She paused before saying the final word, "Serious. He's serious. And that's what I want. He asked me out, and I said yes."

"That's stupid," I told her.

She scoffed. "Thanks."

"He's not *serious*. He's a goddamn Sinclair."

"I don't need this," she said.

I pinned her back against my truck. Her breath came out all huffy, and her eyes dipped to my lips before back up again. She wet her lips, as if waiting for me to kiss her.

"Go out with me," I said in a soft voice, an earnest one.

"What?" she whispered.

"Go on a date with me."

"No."

"Why not?"

"I don't want to date you, Hollin."

"Then, whatever happened Saturday, I want that."

She pushed against my chest. I released her easily. "I don't want to just fuck you either."

"I can't date you. I can't fuck you. What can I do with you?"

"Nothing," she spat. "It doesn't matter what happened, Hollin. We had sex. We both enjoyed it. But that was it."

"Why are you denying this?"

"Why are you pursuing it?"

"Because I'm fucking interested in you, Piper."

"For how long? Until the chase is over? Until you get bored? Until you fuck me over? No thanks. I'll pass."

She shoved my hand aside and stormed off. I was missing a huge part of the conversation. I'd dated a lot of women who wanted more than I was willing to give. People I'd slept with and moved on from. She'd made it seem personal. As if it had happened to her. As if I'd done that shit to her in the past. But I clearly hadn't. Now, I was left out here, more confused than ever.

17

PIPER

*M*y date was going fine.
Fine.

Chase Sinclair was personable, easy to talk to, and even charming. He was definitely serious. A lawyer who had moved back to Lubbock last year to be closer to home. He was also handsome. Very handsome. He had on a suit and tie, slicked his hair up, and had on those fancy shoes that only rich kids wore.

It was exactly what I'd told Peyton I wanted.

That was the main reason I'd agreed to go out with him. I'd said I wanted serious, and then bam! There was Chase, asking me out like a fucking adult.

It had nothing to do with making Hollin jealous. Nothing at all.

Though seeing his face when I'd told him was satisfying. I shouldn't have blown up on him the way that I had. I'd shown my cards even if he had no idea about Quinn and Khloe. Now, he knew there was a *reason* for how I always acted around him.

And look, there went my mind again...focusing on

Hollin and not my date, who had just paid the check at the nicest steak house in Lubbock.

"That was delicious," I managed, getting my head back in the game.

"It was." He finished off his wine and set his glass down. "I was glad you suggested the Willamette Valley pinot noir. It was a great match."

"Wine is what I know."

"I like that about you." He pushed his chair back and held his hand out for me. I put mine in his and let him help me to my feet. I'd worn heels, and Blaire had picked out my pink dress. I'd felt pretty when I left the house, and Chase had been flattering me all night.

We headed back to his car, and he held the door open for me. He'd rushed around earlier to get my door and everything. True gentleman.

We chatted about the winery as he drove to my house. At least that was something I could talk about forever. Our conversation had been kind of flat throughout much of dinner.

Once we parked, he jogged around again to open my door, and I let him walk me up to the porch.

"I had a great time," I told him.

"Me too." His smile was wide. "We should do this again."

"Definitely."

He waited at the front door, as if anticipating me asking him inside. The entire night stretched before me if I did that. I knew every step that would lead to my bedroom. And part of me just...couldn't...do it.

"I'll call you," I told him instead.

"Great," he said, his face falling slightly. "Yes. Maybe next weekend."

"Yeah," I said with a nod as he pulled me into him.

He was going to kiss me. And with a shock, I realized that I didn't *want* to kiss him. There was no part of me that thought this was a good idea. I didn't owe him a kiss for taking me out to dinner. We'd tried this date, and it hadn't been it for me.

So, at the last second, I turned my face, and he landed a soft kiss on my cheek.

I reached for the door handle. "Have a good night."

"You too," he said, as if startled.

Then, I was through the door, slamming it shut behind me with a huff. I kicked my heels off and flicked the clasp on my strapless bra in a matter of seconds.

"Thank fuck," I grumbled.

Luckily, no one else was home. Jennifer had date night with Julian. Blaire had gone out with Honey for something for the blog. They'd left in case I wanted the house to myself with Chase. But that clearly had not happened. No matter how much I'd put into that date, I couldn't make myself interested in him. He was exactly what I should want, but I just didn't. I was frustrated with myself as I grabbed a bottle of merlot and stomped back to my room.

I changed out of my dress and into an oversize T-shirt. Then, I sank down under the covers, flicked the television onto something mindless, and drank the wine straight from the bottle, like an adult.

What was I going to do? I'd had the date that I'd claimed I wanted. And it hadn't been anything that I wanted. It should have been perfect. Still, it hadn't been.

This had to be Hollin's fault. Everything had been fine in my life until he inserted himself into it. I avoided him and antagonized him enough to hope he would never turn his sights on me. And then he did. It had all gone downhill from there.

The worst part was that I couldn't. Stop. Thinking. About. Him.

Like, *why*?

Sure, he'd given me the best orgasms of my life. But I didn't even want him. Not after what had happened to my friends. Not with who he was as a person. He wasn't suddenly going to change. He'd never even been *in* a relationship. And I didn't want one with him even if he had. It was a recipe for disaster.

Still, as I lay in that bed all alone, I couldn't stop my mind from slipping back to that tour bus. The way he'd held me down against him. The ferocity of his kiss. The way he'd bent me over the table and spanked me like he'd been doing it his whole life. The way he'd come undone when I asked him not to go slow. How gentle he'd been after. He'd taken care of me the entire night until I got back into my room and promptly passed out.

All of it sent a shiver through me. I'd gotten off a few times, just thinking about him holding me down on that table.

I was considering sliding my fingers into my panties again when my phone began to buzz noisily. I sighed and set my merlot down on a side table. I hoped this wasn't Chase. It would suck if he was more into me than I was into him.

But when I turned my phone over, the name on the front said *Hollin*.

Jesus, had he read my mind? Had he known that I was thinking about him? Or was he just an asshole, calling when he knew I had a date?

Probably the latter. And I should ignore him.

I bit my lip in indecision, silenced the TV, and pressed the green phone icon.

"Hello?"

"Hey, Piper," he said into the line, his voice dark and sultry.

I swallowed. "Did you need something?"

"Just seeing how your date is going."

Did I tell him? Fuck.

"Why?" I asked, diverting the conversation.

"You made sure I knew, and I wanted to make sure that you were getting taken care of." He laughed softly in the phone. "So, is Chase standing right there, wondering who you're talking to?"

I glanced around my empty room. "No."

"Ah. Smart. Decided to take the call in the restroom?" he teased.

"Did you call to be an asshole?"

Hollin paused for a beat before laughing. "I can't be concerned for you?"

"Hollin," I grumbled.

"All right, all right. Get back to your date."

"Did you really call to see how my date went?"

"Well, I was hoping you'd tell me it was awful," he admitted. "And that you needed me to come make it all better."

I snorted. "I do not need you to come over."

He was silent for a few seconds. "You didn't say whether or not the date was going well."

Well, fuck. I hadn't, had I? I didn't want to lie. There was no point. It wasn't like he wouldn't find out anyway.

"It was okay," I finally said.

"Was," he said, catching on to the past tense. "Is it already over?"

"Yes, Hollin, it's over. Is that what you wanted to hear?"

"If I admit that I'm happy to hear that, will you hang up?" he asked with a soft laugh.

I rolled my eyes and burrowed down a little more under the covers. Of course he was happy about it. He'd been pissed that I was even going on a date with Chase.

"He was the perfect gentleman," I added like it was a consolation prize.

"So, not your type," he shot back.

I gnashed my teeth together. "It was just a first date."

Even though I had *no* interest in a second.

"Did he kiss you good night?"

I narrowed my eyes. "Why?" I snapped. "Jealous?"

Hollin laughed, and I had to close my eyes to ignore the pulsing in my core at the sound. It was the same one he'd used right before he spanked me. Seductive and possessive. And it did things to me.

"Aww, poor baby," he purred. "He didn't take care of you?"

"Maybe he did."

No, he really hadn't.

Why was I pushing Hollin? Why did I always push him?

But he wasn't finished. "Oh, I know he didn't."

"You're awfully sure of yourself."

"I have firsthand experience, knowing what you sound like after you've been fucked properly, Piper," he drawled, low and gravelly. I squeezed my legs together. "The sleepy sound you make when you're completely satisfied. You don't have this much anger when I'm done with you."

"Hollin," I said, reaching for admonishment, but instead, it came out like a whimper.

"So, I see only one option: he didn't satisfy you."

"Try *we never even got that far*," I admitted over the line.

Somehow, the phone kept enough distance between us that I could admit it. I shouldn't have, but hearing him mutter into my ear in that deep voice had made my body shudder with need.

"How far?" he demanded.

"Kiss on the cheek."

He coughed out a laugh. "How very chaste of you, Medina."

"Fuck you, Hollin."

"You could let me help."

It was an offer as much as an invitation. It was Pandora's box, just waiting to be opened. I should keep it closed.

"You can't come over here," I told him.

"Who said I needed to?"

"What?"

"Spread your legs, babe."

"What?" I repeated in a breathy rasp.

"Spread your legs," he said, slow and deliberate.

My brain short-circuited. Was I going to do this? I'd gone on a date with someone else. Granted, it was never going to go anywhere else. There would never be a second date. But I'd sworn off Hollin Abbey after the concert. Except, God, it was so hard. I wanted more of what he was offering. My brain kept shutting off and only listening to what was pulsing between my legs.

"Now," Hollin said.

It was a command. There was no question in his voice. No room for disagreement. I could try, but, fuck, I didn't want to.

So, I slowly spread my legs under the covers.

"Piper?" His voice returned to a gentle coaxing. "Did you do it?"

I closed my eyes and whispered, "Yes."

"Good. That's a good girl."

I huffed at the words. The ones that I'd loved so much

after we had sex last weekend. And now, here I was... wanting to hear them all over again.

"Imagine my hands are running down your body, over your tits, down your stomach."

I put Hollin on speaker and did as he'd said. I touched myself where he'd told me to touch, and with his voice in my ears and my eyes closed, I could almost feel his hands on me and not mine.

"Slip into your panties," he said, "and tell me how wet you are for me."

A groan escaped my lips as I ran a finger through my slicked wetness. "So wet."

He grunted, and for a second, I imagined him in his own bed at home, his giant cock out of his jeans, his fist wrapped around it. The fierce pumping as he worked himself up to meet the sound of my moans.

The thought turned me on even more. I'd replayed what we'd done a lot, but I hadn't considered him jacking off to the memory of me bent over for him.

"Tell me how you get off when you're alone," he told me.

"I..." A flush hit my cheeks. "I work my clit in slow circles."

"Yes," he said as I did exactly what I'd told him.

"I slip a finger in and out of my pussy to build up the pleasure."

"Do it. Imagine my fingers thrusting into you."

My head tipped back as I used my own fingers to draw me closer to climax. "I think about you holding me down."

A thud on the other side of the line. "Fuck, Piper."

He sounded breathless. As if we were in the same room, breathing the same heated air, drinking down the same euphoric energy. Everything in me wanted to release for him, wanted to feel his fingers inside of me, his mouth on my clit, his hand braced against me.

"What do you think about?" I asked boldly.

"You begging me not to take you slow."

I moaned at the words as everything drew in sharper.

"Me slamming my cock deep into your pretty pink pussy."

I picked up speed to match his filthy words. If I didn't have his voice in my ear, I would have pulled out my vibrator and fucking finished it already. I would have wanted the sweet release. But with his gravelly voice and the soft smacking sound of him working his cock, I couldn't help but want to drag it out. To feel like he was actually there, holding off my orgasm until he said I could have it.

"Your handprint on my ass?" I asked in a half-gasp.

"Fuck yes, babe. Fuck," he said. "I don't want you to be able to walk for days after I've finished with you."

I worked faster and faster. Something peaked inside of me, and everything was hazy. My orgasm came harder and faster than I'd expected it. I couldn't even stall it out. It was a tidal wave. Everything in me contracting and releasing all at once.

I moaned out my orgasm as I came undone.

"Oh fuck, fuck," he said. "Did you just come?"

"Yes," I gasped.

And then I heard him grunt on the other line as he came undone. We weren't in the same room. We were miles apart. And yet it was like having him emptying himself inside of me all over again.

"That was...wow," he finally said. "I came hard."

"Me too," I whispered, slow and sleepy. I crashed back on the bed, curling into a ball. Sleep crept up on me out of nowhere. I hadn't even been tired before.

"You sound tired," he said.

"Mmm."

"Did I fuck all the anger out of you again?"

I merely swatted at him as if he were there and not on the other end of the phone. "Shush you."

He laughed softly. "Good. You're my good girl. Now, get some sleep. Dream about me."

I didn't even have it in me to contradict him. I was definitely going to dream about what had just happened.

PART III

I HATE YOU, I LOVE YOU

18

PIPER

*H*ollin was a problem. I hadn't heard from him since our phone sexcapade, but I couldn't stop thinking about him. In fact, I couldn't stop *dreaming* about him. As if his last command had lingered long past that first night. Hung on by a thread strung between us that I didn't understand in the slightest.

I'd done everything that I could to not think about him. I'd gone for a run with Blaire, who'd looked at me like I was nuts since I hated running. I'd worked myself to the bone. I'd even volunteered to handle the weekly booth at the Lubbock Farmers Market.

Sinclair Cellars had a permanent booth at the market. Usually, we rotated who was in charge of it. We each took a weekend and blocked it out on the calendar. But when one of our workers, Eliza, had tried to get out of going so that she could see her boyfriend in Amarillo, I'd jumped at the chance to do anything but sit around and obsess all Saturday morning.

Eliza had promised to take one of my shifts to repay me. My dad had asked me if I was feeling well. I'd ducked my head and acted like everything was fine. I couldn't explain anyway.

So, that was how I was standing in the brisk April morning weather with a Sinclair Cellars jacket tight around my shoulders, waiting for the sun to break through the unusual morning clouds. Lubbock had sunshine ninety percent of the year, and I never looked forward to the weird gloomy weather in the spring.

The best part of working the booth though was seeing all my friends and regulars of the winery. We brought six of our most popular wines—three red and three white—and gave out samples all day. People stopped by for tasting and to purchase wine and Sinclair Cellar apparel. Today, of all days, Peter had agreed to show up to help me.

"You never work the booth," I accused.

My twin brother rolled his eyes. "I do, too."

"When?"

"When Dad makes me work it with him."

I snorted. "Naturally. So, why are you here today?"

"Dad made me work it with you."

"Of course he did."

"Hey, haven't you missed me?" He hip-checked me as he pulled out another bottle of our merlot, uncorking it like a pro.

"Sometimes. What have you been up to anyway? You and Chester too busy to hang with the likes of us?"

"Chess and I are too busy having sex," he deadpanned.

"Good for you."

"I'm kidding," he said with a laugh and then added, "Sort of."

"Typical."

Peter worked for Sinclair Cellars when he was in between his other gigs. He was a freelance writer. He did whatever work he could, but he always enjoyed working on comic books. He'd designed his own when he was ten and never broken the habit. His collection of comics was utterly impressive. But sometimes, the writing jobs were outstanding, and sometimes, everything dried up. He had to be in a bit of a desert if he was here with me today.

"No writing jobs?" I guessed.

He shrugged. "It's a volatile market. I'll get more work soon. But...I'm thinking of asking Chess to move in."

"Doesn't he already live there all the time?"

"Well, yeah, but officially."

"That's great. You never got there with Jeremy," I said of his last boyfriend.

"Definitely not. We would have killed each other. And Chess is brilliant and stable and out to his parents. So, it's going good."

"I like to hear that."

"And you?" he asked. "I heard about Bradley. And I got no phone call."

I laughed as I offered wine to a couple. After they were gone, I turned back to him. "Sorry. Old news. He was going to propose."

"Peyton said that."

"Yeah. Big clusterfuck there. I wasn't going to marry him."

"Dating anyone now?" he asked.

And when I looked up, Hollin Abbey was striding toward the Sinclair Cellars booth. My stomach dropped. He looked so fucking good. Like a tatted cowboy. And never in a million years would I have thought that would be my type, but here I was, salivating over Hollin in Wranglers, a fitted white T-shirt that showed off the length of his sleeve, brown cowboy boots, and a Stetson.

"Medina," he said as he stepped up to our booth.

"Hi."

Peter shot me a twin look and held his hand out to Hollin. "Hey, man."

"How's it going, Peter?"

Peter gestured to the wine before him. "So-so. You want to try the wine?"

Hollin's blue eyes met mine. "I'll take a red. Not quite a Wright vintage, is it?"

I rolled my eyes as I poured him the merlot. "You're right. It's better."

"Heard y'all entered the same competition," Peter said.

"We did," Hollin said. "We're rivals."

"How nice of you to say. Last time, you called me the enemy."

Peter chuckled. "Sounds right."

"He wouldn't even let me try the wine he submitted for the contest."

Hollin grinned. "All in good fun. If you want to come by sometime, I could let you sample it."

Our eyes met, and my stomach flipped. Why did I feel like we'd suddenly stopped talking about wine?

"Amazing," Peter said. "You two *can* be civilized with each other."

"We can. Can't we, Piper?" Hollin asked.

I forced a fake smile on my face. "Were you going to buy wine or commandeer the table?"

"I'll take a bottle of the merlot."

Peter nodded, glancing at me. "I'll get that together."

Peter disappeared into the trailer we had set up behind our booth, where we kept the majority of the wine. We only kept a bottle or two in front of us at any given time after a catastrophe last year when a car had literally crashed through the market and we'd lost the entire stock.

With Peter safely away for a minute, I could drop my fake smile. "Come to make small talk?"

"I wasn't expecting to see you here."

"I hadn't planned to come. One of our employees had to go to Amarillo. So, here I am."

He nodded. "And with that cheery disposition, I bet you're selling so much wine."

"Luckily, my resting bitch face doesn't sell the wine," I said flatly. "The wine sells itself."

Hollin chuckled and leaned against the table. "Are you coming to my birthday party tonight?"

His birthday party? Fuck, someone had mentioned that to me, but that was today?

"Today is your birthday?" I asked, my unease dissipating.

He held his arms out. "Yep. Big 3-0."

"Happy birthday," I said automatically.

"So, party?"

"I'd forgotten that was tonight."

"I want you there," he told me.

"Why?"

"Because I want you to be there."

I frowned and glanced down at the cooling bottles of white sitting in an ice bath and back up at him. "I'd planned to go."

"Good." His smile turned dirty, and he pitched his voice low. "Are you going to wear a skirt for me?"

I gulped just as Peter came back, carrying the wine in a gift bag. "Here you go. Cash or card?"

I pulled back without answering Hollin's dirty question. My mind filled with all the things we could do with me in a skirt again. Which was exactly what he'd wanted.

"Card," he said and handed it over to Peter.

After he paid, Hollin tipped his hat at us. "Thanks for this."

Then, he returned to his dad, who stood with Nora and August. They were eating burritos and drinking out of cold Coke cans. August held all of Nora's plastic bags of all the wares she'd acquired at the market. Nora waved when she saw me, and I waved back.

Peter leaned his hip into the booth and crossed his arms. "So, what's going on with you and Hollin?"

"Nothing," I said automatically.

"Uh-huh."

I tipped my head back and blew out a breath. "Is it that obvious?"

"Dude, yes."

"Well, fuck."

"Are you fucking?"

"I mean..."

Peter's eyes widened. "You and Hollin Abbey are sleeping together?"

"Shh," I gasped, putting my hand over his mouth.

"I'm so jealous."

My eyes bugged out. "Oh my God, Peter!"

"What? He's hot in that tall, muscular, cocky sort of way. He's not bi, is he?"

I covered my eyes and turned away from my brother. "We're not having this conversation."

"You could do a lot worse."

"That's reassuring," I said sarcastically.

Peter laughed. "Well, it's not that I was eavesdropping, but you'd better wear a skirt tonight for his party."

I smacked his arm. "Peter!"

"What? It was too delicious not to listen in!"

I shook my head at him. Even though he was being ridiculous, it made me happy that he seemed to...approve. He'd never gotten along with Bradley. It was like fitting a square piece in a round hole. It had been years since he'd encouraged me into any kind of relationship. And maybe I'd take his advice and actually wear that skirt.

19

PIPER

I wore the skirt.

He'd asked, and it was his birthday. It was silly but putting the skirt on, knowing he'd like it, made me feel pretty. God, I was just like every other girl. Doing stupid stuff for a stupid guy.

I didn't want to admit that maybe...just maybe...I was starting to like Hollin. We still fought like cats and dogs. But I was going to see him tonight, and my heart was skipping a staccato in my chest. I'd checked and double-checked my outfit. I'd put on my makeup meticulously.

Why? Why was I like this? Why *him*?

He was going to hurt me. Break my little frozen heart into shards. It should have been enough to keep me away from him. To reinforce the wall between us and never deal with what was inevitable. Yet the wall was crumbling. And I didn't know how to deal with this new me. The one that said maybe I should give him a chance to prove me wrong. Instead of assuming he'd hurt me.

Blaire, Jennifer, and I arrived at Wright Vineyard for the party. Already, the parking lot was packed full.

"Did Hollin invite everyone in the town?" I asked.

Jennifer shook her head. "That would be Julian."

"He was in charge of the party?"

"He's ridiculous. He doesn't think it's a party unless it's over the top."

Blaire shrugged. "Isn't he right?"

"I'd kill him if he threw me a party like this," Jen said.

I laughed. "He knows you better than that."

"Anyway, this is very Hollin," Blaire said. "He's larger than life, and everyone knows him."

It was Hollin. I hadn't put it together that it was going to be a birthday party for two hundred. Rather than just the lot of us.

Zach met us at the door. He was a giant of a man, who acted as security for most Wright events. He and Hollin rode motorcycles together. He wasn't exactly chatty.

He waved us inside. Nora must have had a hand in this because it wasn't the standard Wright Vineyard affair. Couches had been hauled in to fill the barn space. High-top tables littered the perimeter. There were actual disposable cameras on each of the tables and a few on the bar. That seemed dangerous when people got drunk. A massive blue, green, and white balloon arch with a gold number *30* in the center was in front of the stage. A few girls in dizzyingly small miniskirts were snapping Instagram pictures posed before it.

"This is...elaborate," I said.

"That's what happens when the birthday boy's sister is an event planner," Nora said, appearing out of the crowd. She drew each of us into a hug. "Do you like it?"

"It's incredible," Blaire said.

"The disposable cameras?" Jennifer asked with a wince. "That sounds like a recipe for disaster."

"It was Hollin's idea," she admitted. "I'll have someone wade through the number of dick and tit pics we'll get by the end of the night."

We all laughed because it was inevitable with this many drunk people in one room. I followed Nora through the crowd. Julian and Jordan were sprawled out on the couches. Annie leaned into Jordan with her diamond engagement ring glittering and on display. August was crushed in next to Tamara, hip to hip, with a space on his other side that Nora must have occupied before she got up to say hi to us. My gaze went to where the birthday boy was seated on a couch, regaling the crowd with some grand story about him and Campbell in LA.

His eyes snagged on me when I came into view. He stumbled on his story, missing his next cue as his eyes raked down my body. Apparently, all that care of getting ready had paid off.

He cleared his throat. "Where was I?"

Julian rolled his eyes. "Something about Campbell getting mobbed."

"Right. We couldn't get through, and I ended up shoving a paparazzi guy out of the way. He landed in the crowd, and we ran away as fast as we could. We barely made it upstairs into his hotel. It was a madhouse."

"Wild," Tamara said, fluttering her long eyelashes at him.

Nora groaned. "Are you telling that mob story again? Campbell should have known better."

"He knows better now," Hollin said.

Jennifer creeped in front of Hollin and settled into Julian's lap. "Hey."

Julian pressed a kiss to her lips. "I'm glad you're here."

Blaire nodded toward the bar. "Drinks?"

"Definitely," I said.

Hollin hopped up out of his seat and followed us to the bar. "Hey, glad y'all made it."

Blaire gave him a knowing look. "Both of us?"

I jabbed my elbow into her ribs. She laughed and waved at the bartender for the night.

Hollin grinned. "Of course." His eyes swept down my body again. "You look nice."

"Thank you."

"I like your skirt."

I glanced up at him, softening at the words. He'd just complimented me. Not been a total idiot, like normal.

"You look good, too. That looks like the shirt I borrowed," I said, running my hand along the collar.

His smile widened. "I never got that one back from you. What did you do with it?"

"It's somewhere in my room," I said dismissively. "Do you want it back?"

He leaned his elbow on the bar. "Not if you want to keep it."

I flushed at the words. They hadn't even been dirty or antagonizing or anything, and somehow, they still made me flush. "What would I do with a shirt that's three times too big?"

"You tell me."

Blaire covered her mouth to keep from laughing. She slid me a Bombay and lime. "Here you go."

"Hey, add these to my tab," Hollin said to the bartender.

"Sure thing, man," the guy said.

"You're the birthday boy," Blaire protested. "Aren't we supposed to buy you drinks?"

"Please, the Wrights are covering my tab."

I laughed. "Of course."

Blaire winked at me. "Have a good time."

Then, she disappeared back to our friends.

"Well, she's subtle, isn't she?" I said, taking a sip of my drink.

"She knows about us?"

"Don't your friends know what happened?"

"I told Julian. He thinks you're out of my league." Hollin rubbed the back of his head. "He's probably right."

I was stunned by the comment. That he'd even admit that. He wasn't self-deprecating. Normally, he was pure arrogance.

"That's not the Hollin I'm used to fencing with. I thought the sun shone out of your ass or whatever."

He grinned. "I mean, obviously, it does. I'm awesome."

I snorted. "There you are."

"I'm glad you made it, Piper."

I took another drink of my gin. "Me too."

We returned to the rest of the party. Everyone was carefully trying not to notice that we'd had an entire conversation without arguing. Or that Hollin kept looking at me as if he might eat me for dinner. And yet he hadn't made any of the crude remarks I'd anticipated. I'd anticipated at least one birthday-sex reference, but nothing. Not one sexual reference directed to me, not one push to get under my skin, not a single button pressed. I didn't know what to make of it.

"I can't believe we're almost to the first game of the season," Julian said.

I blinked and pulled myself back into the conversation. "For the soccer team?"

"Yep," Jordan said. "FC Lubbock opens the season for their first ever match. I'll get you all tickets if you want to go."

"And we'll all be at the gala," Hollin said.

"I've already given everyone tickets for that," Jordan said.

"I can't wait to see what Peyton has put together for the show," I added.

"She's performing?" Jennifer asked.

I nodded. "She's going to do a solo and a *pas de deux* from one of her New York City Ballet numbers."

"Oh, it'll be amazing," Blaire said. "She's so talented."

"Weston will be there, too," Julian said.

Weston Wright was the biggest shock that Lubbock had had in years. He was Jordan and Julian's half-brother. It'd turned out that their father had a secret family in Seattle while they grew up in Vancouver. Not just that, Weston was a twin, like me. He had a brother named Whitton *and* a much younger sister, Harley. Sometimes, I still couldn't wrap my head around the duplicity. I'd grown up with a strict family, but we all loved each other. I could never imagine someone from my family doing something that terrible to me.

The guys had gone to visit Weston and meet Whitton and Harley in the last year. But none of them had traveled to Lubbock again. This was a big deal.

"That's great!" Hollin said. "It'll be good to see him again."

Julian and Jordan exchanged a glance. There was something else they weren't telling us. But they nodded and changed the subject away from the gala.

The night continued, and Hollin and I didn't have one single argument. Was it because I wasn't fighting him on every little thing? Was it because he wasn't trying to push my buttons? Was it possible that the two of us could spend a whole night together in each other's company without me wanting to strangle him?

I'd known there was sexual tension between us. I

enjoyed that. I sometimes even enjoyed the fighting. But this was all new.

Later in the night, I used the restroom and reapplied my burgundy lipstick in the mirror. When I came back to the party, Hollin was missing.

I looked around, trying to locate him, and even asked Julian, "Hey, where did Hollin go?"

"I don't know. He was at the bar with Tamara."

I bit my lip. I didn't see Tamara either. She'd been flirting with him *all* night. Hollin had been mostly ignoring her attempts, but now, they were both missing. Coincidence? I didn't believe in them.

A knot formed in my stomach. Why the hell was I stressing out about this? If he wanted to hook up with someone else, he was well within his rights. We weren't exclusive by a long shot. We were nothing. Just two people who had hooked up...twice...sort of.

But I didn't like it. I suddenly didn't like the idea of Hollin hooking up with someone else. Let alone Tamara, who, one, worked at Wright and, two, was his sister's age.

I made some excuse and headed back toward the restrooms. People were making out in the alcove, but I didn't see Hollin. I didn't see Tamara either for that matter. I took a breath and released it. This was silly. I'd just go and stand outside. The grape fields were right off the edge of the barn. It'd help to be back in my happy place. It all came back to this dirt. And while Wright wasn't my winery, it had the same feeling to it.

I opened the back door and stepped out onto the chilly moonlit path that led down to the fields. I hugged myself against the cold. I only stopped walking when I found a figure standing on the edge of the field. Dirt crunched under my feet, and Hollin found me standing there.

"Hey," he said.

"What are you doing out here?"

"Escaping Tamara."

I arched an eyebrow. "Really?"

"Yeah. She keeps offering me birthday sex," he said, staring back out at the darkened field.

It was nearly a full moon. So, everything was vaguely lit up from overhead, but it was still dark enough to not be noticed from the back door.

"How nice of her."

"Not when I keep telling her I'm not interested. I'm her boss."

"That does border on harassment."

"I can handle it. Just needed...this." He gestured to the fields.

"It's like coming home."

He looked at me in surprise. "Yes. Grounding."

I breathed it in and released it. "That's how I feel, too. It's my favorite place."

"Mine, too." His shoulder knocked gently against mine. "I come out here and live it each morning. It reminds me why I do it. What I'm here for."

I could barely believe Hollin Abbey had just said that. Had echoed my own thoughts perfectly. As if when I was here with my feet in the dirt and the fields all around me, I was whole again. Nothing could take that away from me.

"That's it exactly," I whispered.

He smiled once at me. Not his cocky, ridiculous smile. But one of mutual understanding.

We stood side by side in the dark, breathing it all in. Until I was shivering from the cold breeze coming in from the north and he insisted we get me back into the heat.

It was getting harder and harder to remember that

Hollin and I were too different. Not when I had seen first-hand that he was just like me when it came to the winery. The Wrights were the businessmen, but Hollin had his feet in the dirt. He *loved* this place. And that was something I could understand.

Blaire kept dropping hints that I should stay at the party later than her. But Hollin was *drunk* by the end of the night. If anything happened, he wouldn't even remember. And I didn't want that. So, I said good night and headed back with Blaire. She side-eyed me but relented when I wouldn't say anything else.

I found Hollin's white shirt when I got home and brought it to my nose. It still smelled like him. Fuck.

I curled up with it, and the next thing I knew, I woke to the smell of Hollin pressed against me. I jumped up, bleary-eyed, but it was just the shirt. I laughed and glanced at my phone to check the time. I didn't have to be up for another hour. Though I had a text from an unknown number.

I clicked on it.

Piper! Long time since we've talked. It's Quinn. I hope all is well. I happened to notice that someone posted a picture of you with Hollin Abbey. Are you two dating? I couldn't even believe it when I saw it. It was a long time ago, but, girl, run! Run far away. I love you and don't want to see you get hurt. Come see me in Denver when you're next in town!

My stomach flipped at the unexpected message. Everything crashed back down. Quinn had seen me with Hollin?

I pulled up social and found the pictures she was talking about. A bunch of people from last night had added images into a shared album that was made public. And the very first image was of Hollin and me smiling for the camera.

I could deny it. We weren't dating. But Quinn's warning felt...fortuitous. As if I had let my guard down around him and let myself forget what he could do to me. How it could all fall apart. Quinn had moved to Denver to escape our living situation and Khloe. I didn't want to give him the power to hurt me that bad.

Hollin and I might be similar, but we weren't the same.

20

HOLLIN

I woke up on Easter Sunday with a hangover.

I'd already promised Dad that I'd show for the service, but I hadn't considered that my birthday would be the night before Easter. Or that I'd get quite so hammered.

After chugging a bottle of Gatorade, swallowing a pair of Tylenol, and taking a long shower, I was mildly human. The weather was nice enough that I could take the Harley out of the garage and drive in my Sunday best to church. My dad sighed when he watched me pull up, but Aunt Vail whooped as I cut the engine. August walked over, wide-eyed, to assess my baby, and Nora rolled her eyes.

"She's a beauty," August said.

"Fuck yeah, she is."

"Language," Aunt Lori groused. "We're at church."

"We're in a church parking lot," I corrected.

My dad shook his head. "Let's go inside."

I carried my helmet inside, and Vail sidled up to me. "Sure know how to rile your dad, don't you?"

"You're confusing me for the other son."

She laughed. "True. Campbell has that particular talent on lock. How was your birthday? Find yourself a girlfriend yet?"

This was a normal conversation with Vail. She asked me every other month if I'd found a girlfriend. I always shot her a side-eye, flexed, and acted like no one could handle these guns. It was a ridiculous tradition. But this time...it didn't feel quite right. I didn't have a girlfriend. For the first time in...years, there was someone I was interested in.

She noticed my hesitation. "Wait...did you find someone?"

I shrugged. "Sort of."

"What?" She gaped at me. "Look at you, growing up. Thirty looks good on you, kid."

"Yeah, yeah. Now, I have to get her to go out with me."

"What girl would even say no?" she asked with a wink.

Oh, she had no idea.

We entered the church and took our seats on the left side of the building. Piper's grandma was already seated on the other side of the church, but no Piper in sight. I hadn't seen her much at church before this. So, it wasn't a surprise. I'd just been hoping to see her.

The Wrights weren't yet seated at the front. Heidi and Julia were huddled together, holding Emery and Jensen's one-year-old daughter, Robin. Austin, Landon, Patrick, and Morgan looked sort of frantic. Sutton was pacing with Madison in her arms with her husband and son seated together on the pew. No Jensen or Emery in sight.

"Hey, what's going on?" I asked when I located Julian and Jordan.

"Emery went into labor," Julian said.

Jordan nodded. "I guess she wasn't due for another week, and her water broke in the church narthex."

"Jesus."

Julian shook his head. "Literally."

Jordan looked between us with a sigh. "Jensen rushed her to the hospital. They left Robin with family, and someone called to bring Colton in from New York."

"An Easter baby," I said.

The pastor stood to get everyone to their seats. Piper hustled down the side aisle in a knee-length white dress. She took the seat next to her parents and didn't even glance my way. Maybe she hadn't seen me come in. I'd have to stop her before she could leave.

The choir began sang, and the pastor spoke about new birth. Considering it was Easter, it was already an appropriate sermon. But with what was happening with Emery, right now, it hit even harder than normal. An actual new birth.

When the service ended, Piper didn't immediately run out. She stayed with her grandma as she chatted with all of her friends. I wanted to talk to her, but I didn't want to interrupt her time with her family either. Normally, I wouldn't care, but this was important.

Julian came back to stand by me. "So, are you and Piper dating yet?"

"You said I had no chance."

"Oh, I stand by that."

"But?"

"No but. I still think she's too good for you."

I snorted and jabbed him in the arm. "Thanks, man."

Julian grinned at me. "So, what is going on? You two were getting along last night."

"Yeah, I don't know. She runs scared every time I mention liking her."

Julian raised his eyebrows. "Do you like her?"

"Yeah, I do."

"And not just...in the way you treat all other women you're interested in?"

I side-eyed him. "I don't treat all women terrible."

"No, but you're not exactly...gentle either."

No, I wasn't. I never had been. Not for a very long time at least. But things with Piper were different. I didn't know how to explain it. I could barely explain it to myself. Last night, as we'd stood outside in the fields and stared at the sky, she'd understood me. We were together in that moment. The fields were her home as they'd always been mine. It was a turning point. And for the first time, I was considering that maybe it wouldn't be bad to *actually* date her.

"She's different."

"Because you're generally *meaner* to her?" Julian deadpanned.

"No, because she's like me."

Julian blinked at me. He was my cousin and closest friend, but I honestly had no way of making him understand. So, I strode away and followed Piper as she and her grandma left the chapel.

She was standing outside with the sun beating down on her shoulders when I came up beside her. She jumped slightly. "Hollin."

"Hey, Piper." I nodded at her grandma. "Nina."

"Hello again. Are you here to sweep me off my feet?" Nina asked with a twinkle in her eye.

"Always. Where shall I sweep you?"

"Alas, nowhere." She laughed and winked at Piper. "Have fun, *amorcita*."

"Can I help you get to where you're going?" I asked quickly.

"I can still make it on my own," she said with a smile. "*Gracias*."

Then, she released Piper's arm and walked hesitantly away. She still could manage on her own, but I wondered for how much longer.

"Had a good time at the party last night," I told her.

"I noticed. You got pretty drunk. I'm surprised you're even on your feet." The words weren't exactly flat, but there was none of the warmth in them from yesterday. As if she were bracing herself against me.

"It was touch and go," I said with a smile.

"Well, I should…" She gestured vaguely away.

I reached for her. "Wait, before you do." I took a deep breath. "Do you want to go out with me?"

She looked up at me as if she couldn't understand the words out of my mouth. "Why?"

"Why do most people date, Piper?"

"You don't date though."

"I want to date you," I told her with an easy smile.

"No."

I heard the word out of her mouth. I understood what it meant. And yet I didn't understand it at all. No? After the last couple of weeks together? After we'd connected all night?

"No?"

"That's what I said."

"But why?" I asked stubbornly.

"I don't owe you an explanation."

"I know," I said, breathing out. "I know you don't. I just don't understand. I thought we had something yesterday. We keep ending up right back here."

She shook her head. "This is a bad idea, Hollin."

"It doesn't have to be."

"You don't want to date me."

"Yes, I do. I'm telling you quite clearly that I do."

"We both know how this goes. Three dates, and then you get bored and move on."

I blew out a harsh breath. "Yes, I've gone on three dates with people and broken up with them. But the three-date rule doesn't actually exist. It's something the guys use to make fun of me. It's a joke, Piper."

"It's a joke because it's reality," she said, stepping backward. "I don't want you to hurt me. I don't want you to use me."

"*Use* you? That doesn't even make sense. I'm speaking plainly here. So, you're mad at me for sleeping around, and now, you're mad at me for wanting more? Which is it?"

"Both!" She crossed her arms. "It's both. Because I don't trust you."

"I'm not going to hurt you, Piper. Come on. At least give me a chance."

She stepped away. "I'm sorry. But no."

"You're scared," I said, pushing toward her as she walked away from me.

I should have let her go, but I couldn't. She wasn't even making sense. I'd hurt other people before. But that didn't mean I was going to hurt her. I'd never pursued a girl like this before. It was different. She had to realize.

"How do I change your mind?"

"You can't."

I pulled her to a stop again. "Look, do you think this is normal for me? That I have to pursue a girl like this? I'm not doing it because I want to see you hurt. I'm doing it because I like you, Piper. I like you, and I think you like me, too. So, why are you running away scared?"

"Because I've seen you over the last five years," she said,

yanking away from me. Her eyes were wide and guileless. Not angry, but sad. "I want someone who is serious, who cares about me, who wants me for more than a few dates. And you haven't proven that you're that person *ever*. Not ever. You don't know my favorite flower or what I like to eat for lunch or any of my favorite songs."

"We date to learn that, Piper."

"Do you know that information about *anyone* you've ever dated?"

I winced. There was one girl, but I wasn't ready to even mention her. And the ones since her...well, they were mostly a blur.

She huffed. "Exactly. You don't care about the girls that you date. And I won't be just another one of them. You don't know anything about me. So, how could you possibly like me?"

I ran a hand back through my hair in irritation. She was wrong. She was so wrong. I might not know stupid flowers or food or a song. But I *did* know her. I knew her way better than she thought I did.

"I know that you love the land like I do. You love your winery like I do. You love your people like I do. You're fiery and caring and smart and determined and not afraid to stand up for what you believe in. So, maybe I don't know the other stuff, but that's enough for me."

She gaped at me. Speechless from my outburst.

"I'm going to prove you wrong, Piper. I'm not the guy you think I am."

21

PIPER

I'd made a mistake.

Somewhere in all of my righteous anger, I'd screwed up. I'd made an assumption based off of past behavior and my own personal experience with Hollin that he was treating me like this to get back in my pants. He'd always been that guy. I hadn't thought he'd be any different with me. And after that text from Quinn, I'd been mad all over again for what he'd done to my friends and how it had impacted my own life.

But now that he was walking away, furious for my assumption and promising to prove me wrong, I realized it was all in error.

He didn't know me like I'd accused. But he'd hit the nail on the head. The fields, the winery, the people—*that* was my life. That was who I was and what I lived for. And he'd seen that without ever dating me.

Now, I didn't know how to backpedal. There wasn't a way to do it with my family leaving the service and Hollin returning to his family and the Wrights in disarray about Emery giving birth. This wasn't the time. It wasn't the place.

And Easter was a celebration for my family. Abuelita had said, in Mexico, the people would flood the streets, eat all the delicious foods that they hadn't had during Lent, and revel in a day of rest. The next week, they always drove down to the coast to eat fresh-caught seafood and relax now that the stone had been rolled away from the tomb.

We weren't going to the coast, and there was no feast outside of the service. But we were all returning to Abuelita's house for lunch. She'd made fish tacos, empanadas, shrimp patties with pipián, and heaps of ice cream in all of our favorite flavors. It was the way that it was always supposed to be.

I couldn't let my mistake hold.

"Hollin!" I called before he disappeared.

He stopped and faced me.

"Do you...have plans?"

He jerked his chin to the side. "What? Right now?"

I jogged back up to him despite people watching us. "We're going to Abuelita's for lunch. It's kind of a big deal in my family. Do you want to join us?"

He opened his mouth, still very confused, and then closed it. His head began to nod before he said, "Yes. Yes, I want to join you."

"Okay. Um...good. I'll text you the address."

"Do I need to bring something?"

"Oh, no. Abuelita will be glad to have another mouth to feed."

"What made you change your mind?"

I texted him the address. "You." Our eyes met again. "You were right."

He grinned, and it was the same wide, arrogant look I'd gotten from him for years. "Sorry, didn't hear you. Can you say that again?"

I swatted at him. "Don't push your luck, Abbey."

He laughed. "All right. I'll be there."

I watched him walk away with the weight lifted off of my shoulders. I had no idea what I was doing exactly. This could all crash and burn. But at least, I was giving it a chance. I didn't know what the future held. I didn't know where we'd end up even a month from now, but I wanted to see it through. I'd been trying to convince myself that I wasn't interested since long before that tour bus. I'd let Quinn scare me into pushing him away. Today, it would be different. And I'd take it one day at a time.

I parked my Jeep outside of the home Abuelita had owned since she'd arrived in Lubbock in the '70s. It wasn't much, but it had seen my mother grow up and all three of us kids as well. It held memories through pictures and food and dance. It was home as much as the winery.

As I hopped out of the car, I heard a rumbling coming down the road. And then I saw Hollin...on a fucking Harley.

I had known he had one. I'd seen him drive, but it had been a while. I always made fun of his obsession with his motorcycle, but, well, looking at him on it now, it was *hot*. Like really fucking hot. Especially because he was still in his suit from church. A suit and tattoos and a Harley...dear God.

He parked the bike behind my Jeep and jerked his helmet off. He caught me staring at him and grinned devilishly. "Want a ride, Medina?"

I gulped. "I've never been on one before."

"Oh, I could show you a good time."

I had zero doubts of that.

"You're making me consider skipping lunch."

He chuckled and strode over to me. "Well, we can't do that now, can we?"

"And why not?"

"Because I just got you to agree to go out with me."

I crossed my arms over my chest and lifted my chin. "Did you? I asked you out."

"Fine. It's mutual." He smirked at me. "Either way, I won."

"Are you able to be anything but insufferable?"

He stepped closer, pinching my ass. I yelped softly. "No. And you wouldn't want me any other way."

I rolled my eyes at him. "Maybe keep your hands to yourself in front of my family."

"Oh, I will do my best. I just had to get the ass grab out before I was around you for hours on end without being able to touch you."

"Ridiculous."

"What? You have a nice ass."

Despite myself, I laughed. He was wild and handsy and as insufferable as I'd said he was. But he was interested in *me*. Just me, apparently. Something I'd never expected from him. Actually from very few people. Even Bradley had dated other people in the midst of our off phase. He'd always looked up Instagram "models" and tried to convince me it was normal while rarely complimenting how I looked. So, I vowed to accept the fact that Hollin was attracted to me enough that he could barely keep his hands to himself. That felt like a good thing.

We took the walkway to Abuelita's house together.

"I feel like I should have brought something," Hollin insisted. "Wine at least."

"You're fine. Don't worry." I glanced over at him. "Also, I'll apologize in advance for what is about to happen."

"What is about to happen?"

The door swung open, and Peter stood in the doorframe. The little shit sure looked self-satisfied. "Piper, you brought a friend."

I rolled my eyes. "Peter, you remember Hollin."

"Hey," Hollin said, offering his hand. They shook even though they'd known each other for years.

I hadn't exactly warned Hollin, but he was about to endure the third degree. Even Bradley had gotten uncomfortable, and he'd been around my family for years. He usually didn't do a lot of my Mexican family traditions because he didn't—quote—"get it." Whatever that had meant.

But Hollin barreled inside with all the finesse of a bull in a china shop. He hugged Peyton and Abuelita, who was seated at the dining room table, shook hands with Isaac and my dad, and then swung Aly up into the sky and back down. She giggled dramatically. Hero worship was already there in her six-year-old face. Anyone who could throw her up like a rag doll was a friend of hers.

"What is going on in here?" my mom, Hannah, asked. She wiped her hands on her apron and put them on her hips.

"Mom, this is Hollin," I said.

"He's Piper's new boyfriend," Peter chimed in.

"It's about time," Peyton said. "We've all been wondering when this would happen."

"I thought he was flirting with me," Abuelita said.

She winked at me, and I shook my head.

My whole family was wonderful. I'd had a great upbringing. Better than most people that I knew. But sometimes, they were a little...much for new people. Not overbearing, but overtly friendly and always making little jabs at you. Not because they didn't like you, but because they *did* like you. If they treated you with quiet resolve, then that meant they weren't big fans. I'd know. That was how they'd treated Bradley.

"Why was I uninformed about all of this?" Mom asked.

"Me too, Hannah," my dad said, putting an arm around his wife. "Here I thought, she was going out with that Sinclair guy."

"Dad!" I grumbled.

"Boring," Peter said.

Peyton nodded. "Can't help but agree."

"Whoever is dating my Piper, I'm happy about it," my mom said. Hollin went to shake her hand, and she pulled him in for a hug. She kissed his cheek and smiled brightly. "Make her happy, or we'll run you out of town."

Hollin coughed out a laugh. "Yes, ma'am."

"There are your Southern manners. *Mira*, let's finish the cooking, so we can eat."

"Matthew," Abuelita said, gesturing to the kitchen. "Save *mija* from herself. We know she only belongs in the kitchen to make tamales."

"Mother," my mom groaned. "I can cook empanadas."

"Out of the way, Hannah," my dad said. "I'll get the rest."

My mom sighed. She had never been a great cook, except for the traditional meals that Abuelita had forced her to learn. My dad was the main cook. He loved spaghetti and fresh bread and random casseroles, of all things. He never cooked Mexican food. Just helped Abuelita as her sous chef. It was a perfect compromise.

"I'll help," Abuelita said, getting slowly to her feet.

"Mom," my dad said, "you should stay off your feet."

"I'll rest when I'm dead." She elbowed past him and into her kitchen.

"Well, have a seat, Hollin," my mom said. "Tell us all about yourself."

We entered the kitchen table, which was barely big enough for the lot of us. We squeezed in extra seats and had Aly in a booster. Normally, she'd complain that she wasn't a baby but not at Abuelita's. She had the ability to make us all feel young again.

Hollin told them about the winery, which was a conversation we knew all too well. And by the time my dad and Abuelita came out with lunch, my entire family was enamored with him. It wasn't hard. He was a people person to his core. Everyone loved him, except me...for the longest time. And now, even I'd been drawn in.

As we dug into the delicious food, Aly, still dressed in a tutu, as if she'd come straight from ballet class instead of Easter service, asked Hollin, "Are you going to marry my aunt Piper?"

Hollin laughed. "Uh..."

I choked on my sip of water. All eyes turned to the two of us. My face flamed.

Isaac laughed and slid an arm around his daughter. "Aly Cat, people don't get married after dating them for a few weeks."

Aly looked at him with wide, confused kid eyes. "But you and Miss Peyton did!"

"She has a point," Peyton said. "Didn't realize we were teaching her that."

"I think you should get married," Aly told him. "Then, I can be your flower girl. Do you know how pretty I look in my dress?"

"I don't," Hollin admitted, "but I'll be at the wedding for your dad, and you can show me."

"Okay!" she said, completely satisfied.

Hollin arched an eyebrow at me, and I shrugged. Kids. It was out of my control.

After lunch was finished, we all sat around outside, eating homemade ice cream. Hollin's phone dinged three times in a row. He'd been ignoring it, but the last one finally made him pull it out.

"Excuse me," he said and then got on the phone.

Peyton raised an eyebrow. "What's that about?"

Her guess was as good as mine.

"No idea."

But when Hollin came back, he was beaming. "Emery had her baby. A healthy boy named Logan Christopher."

"Oh, lovely!" my mom said.

"I'm so happy for them," Peyton added.

"Logan Christopher," I said. "It's a good name. And Emery is okay?"

"Totally fine."

"That's wonderful," Abuelita said. "An Easter baby."

We all celebrated the news, and after we ate more than our share of ice cream, I followed Hollin out the front door. We walked in silence to my Jeep, and I leaned back against it.

"So, that's my family."

"They're wonderful."

"Yeah?" I asked. "I mean, I think so, but...other people..."

"Don't matter," he said at once. "If anyone else has ever looked at your family and not thought they were incredible, they don't matter. You're so lucky to have been raised in a big family like that."

"Well, thanks. You have a big family here, too."

He shrugged. "Nah, not really. My mom died when I was in college. My aunt Lori only moved back and she married Vail. Campbell left after graduation. It's just been me and my dad and Nora. I only recently got my cousins and Campbell back."

I hadn't known that. He didn't exactly talk about his family, except how proud he was of Campbell and Nora. Almost as if he were their dad more than their older brother.

"Well, I'm glad you enjoyed your time."

"I did." He slowly threaded our fingers together. "Can I take you out on a real date now?"

"Right now?"

He grinned. "No. I'll make it a real date. I'll pick you up and everything. Your favorite flower is?" he prodded.

I shook my head. "Tulips."

"Got it," he said with a wink. He tugged me forward. "I'm going to kiss you now."

"Oh," I whispered.

Then, his lips were on mine, and all thoughts fled my mind. I'd kissed Hollin that day on the tour bus. But we'd been drunk and frantic. The entire purpose had been to get our clothes off. This was...not that. This was so much more. Sweet yet claiming, and soft yet unyielding. It was everything I wanted a first kiss to be and more.

And by the time he pulled back, I was breathless and leaning against him.

"I had a good time," he said against my lips.

"Me too."

"Friday?"

I nodded and met his baby-blue eyes. "Friday."

22

HOLLIN

*I*t had been years since I'd gone on a proper date. The kind that my dad had prepared me for as a kid. Not that I'd been a complete asshole, but flowers certainly hadn't been in my repertoire.

So, when I knocked on the door to Piper's place, holding a bouquet of tulips, I was definitely not prepared for Blaire and Jennifer to be standing there expectantly with wide, excited eyes.

"Oh my God, flowers," Jennifer said.

"Those are beautiful," Blaire said. "I didn't know you had it in you."

"Me neither," I admitted with a self-deprecating laugh. "Is...Piper here, or am I just seeing you two?"

"She's still getting ready," Jennifer said, opening the door wide so I could come inside.

Blaire took the flowers into the kitchen, where she arranged them in a vase.

"That doesn't sound like her."

Blaire grinned. "No, it doesn't. She might be talking herself out of it."

My eyes darted down the hall. "Uh, should I go say something?"

"No," Jennifer said quickly.

"We told her we'd kick her ass if she backed out," Blaire said.

"That's not promising."

Blaire winked at me from under her baseball cap. "She likes you. She's just stubborn."

"I like stubborn."

"We know," Blaire and Jennifer said at the same time and then broke down into giggles.

I waited patiently for Piper to come out of her room. I didn't know why she was nervous. We'd talked all week. I'd texted her while we were both at work and called her at night to talk. It was unlike anything I'd ever done before. Not for a long, long time at least. Normally, I got bored before this point. But not Piper. There was not a single thing about her that was boring.

Finally, the door cracked open, and Piper stepped out. My jaw nearly hit the floor as I took in her short black dress and flats. I'd told her we were going somewhere casual when she asked on the phone, but somehow, she made even a casual dress look incredible. It hugged her curves in all the right places. Her thick, dark hair was down in voluminous waves, and her makeup was subtle but smoky. Her lips were a cherry red that made me wonder exactly what they would look like, wrapped around my dick. I was still male after all.

I cleared my throat. "Wow. You look great."

She smiled almost shyly. "Thanks."

"I brought you flowers." I gestured to Blaire, who foisted the bouquet toward her.

"Oh, tulips." She smelled the blooms that I'd gotten in every color, and her eyes met mine again. "I love them."

"All right, you crazy kids," Blaire joked, "I'll hold down the fort. Have a good time."

Piper shot her a look. "Thanks, Mom."

Jennifer pulled Blaire back, and they both stifled laughs. They were enjoying this. All those times Piper and I had argued, had they known that it would lead here? I certainly hadn't. I'd enjoyed watching her squirm. And now, I wanted her to squirm in all sorts of other ways.

"Ready?"

Piper nodded, and we left her house. She stopped when she got to the bottom of the stairs. "What is that?"

I arched an eyebrow. "That is a motorcycle."

"You...drove your Harley here for our date?"

"Yeah. It's perfect weather for it."

"I'm wearing a dress," she protested.

"You'll be fine," I said with a smirk. "The dress is pretty long anyway, and you'll have your legs around me."

She met my gaze with a stubborn glint in her eyes. "You'd like that, wouldn't you?"

"Sure would."

"We could take my Jeep," she offered. "It has sides and four wheels, and if you want your hair to blow in the wind, I can make it topless."

I snorted. "Get on the bike, Medina. I even brought you an extra helmet."

I held it out for her, and she eyed it skeptically.

"Um, you know, maybe...maybe we shouldn't do this."

She was nervous. This wasn't me. This was the bike. "You said you've never been on a motorcycle. Are you...scared?"

"No," she blurted so fast and then cringed. "Well, maybe a little."

"Hey, look," I said, moving to her side. I tilted her chin up to look at me. "Would I do something that would endanger you?"

"No."

"Haven't I taken care of you and made sure you felt safe?"

"Well, yes."

I nodded. "That's right. So, this is going to be fine. Better than fine. It's fun. You're going to like it. And if you don't, we can come back and take your Jeep."

She swallowed hard, as if debating, and then nodded. "All right. Yeah. I'm being silly."

"It's not silly to express your feelings," I said automatically. "If you don't feel safe with me, then I don't want to do it."

"Okay," she said with a little more enthusiasm.

I handed her the helmet, and she fitted it onto her head. I buckled it for her and dropped my leg over the side of the bike. She took a fortifying breath. I heard her mutter under her breath, "I can't believe I'm doing this." And she hopped on behind me.

Having her weight against me on my bike felt fucking incredible. I had to shut down half of my brain as she settled in firmly against my back, wrapping her arms around my waist and drawing her thighs up to the sides of my legs.

"Ready?"

"Sure."

I turned on my baby, and the deep, vibrating rumble of her engine reverberated through my bones. This was the sound of fucking joy. Pure freedom. Just me and my Harley out on the road with nothing to do but drive. A smile came to my face, even as Piper gripped tighter. Then, we were off.

Riding my Harley through Lubbock was a specific sort of bliss. Having Piper with me to enjoy it was next level. I was almost sad when we arrived at our destination ten minutes later.

Piper clung to me for dear life even after I brought the bike to a stop in a parking spot and killed the engine.

"You okay, babe?"

Her limbs went to jelly. She jumped off and passed me the helmet. Her face was flushed and she had a wide smile.

"I thought it was...great," she admitted.

"Yeah?"

She bit her lip and ran her hands down her dress. "Mildly terrifying but exhilarating."

"You'd do it again?"

"Yes. Can we do it again?"

Her eagerness made me want to take her right then and there over my bike.

"After dinner."

She stuck out her bottom lip, and it took everything in me not to drag my teeth along it and suck it into my mouth. Ever since that kiss after Easter lunch, I'd wanted nothing more than to be physical with her. But if I was doing this right, then I was doing this right. We'd proven that sex was no issue. We were *fucking excellent* at that part. I'd never been great at *more*. So, here we were.

"Come on," I said with a laugh and dropped an arm over her shoulders.

"Where are we anyway?"

I pointed at the sign for Hill Barbecue. They were a local barbeque joint that had started as a downtown food truck. I'd loved their food and been happy for them when they opened their own restaurant. It meant business was good.

"Oh, Dad loved their food truck. He was sad when they closed. I had no idea they'd opened a restaurant."

"It's recent."

"My dad is going to be so happy. This is right down the street. I have a feeling we'll be eating here a lot for lunch."

I grinned. Good. Now, every time she showed up here, she'd think about our date.

We bypassed the large fence with *Hill Barbecue* scrawled in white paint on the side. The venue was entirely outdoors with picnic tables spread out around the area and their food truck relocated to a permanent locale. I'd checked the weather a dozen times before deciding on it. In a Lubbock spring, it was as likely to rain as for a dust storm to crop up, and we wouldn't have wanted to be caught outside with nothing but my motorcycle in either.

We crossed to the food truck and put in our orders. I got the brisket, and Piper went for ribs. I was impressed. They were the messiest thing on the menu. Not something I'd think most girls—any girl—would go for. She winked at me when I mentioned it and brought her Coke over to a picnic table.

I settled in across from her with my Topo Chico. "Bold choice, Medina."

"You've been inside of me. I don't think you're going to care if I have barbeque sauce on my face."

I nearly choked on my drink. "Point made."

"Tell me about those," she said, pointing to my sleeve. "What do they mean?"

"Ah, well, some have meaning, and some I think are cool as shit." I pushed up the sleeve of my shirt so that she could see the swirling shape of the dragon scales that traveled through the clouds and up into wings. Interspersed within the elaborate pattern were images for all of my family.

"This one is for Campbell." I showed her the music notes that scrawled up a row of clouds. "It's the chords for 'I See the Real You.' And this one is Nora." A rose in full bloom with deep, piercing thorns. "My dad. I got this one first and built the sleeve around it." It was an old-fashioned clock, almost steampunk, with the time set to the time I'd been born. I pointed out the cigarette smoke for Vail and the ribbon that twined with it to represent Lori. The cancer bow hidden in the clouds on my elbow was for Helene.

"And your mom?" she prompted, marveling at the stories I'd hidden inside the sleeve.

I froze at the words. I should have known they were coming. I rarely talked about her.

Her eyes swept up to mine at my silence. She must have read my unease. "You don't have to talk about it if you don't want."

I pulled my shirtsleeve back down and flipped my wrist over. A dove in flight was inked into my skin. "This is for her."

She traced her fingers over it. "It's beautiful."

"One of my last pieces. I don't talk much about her."

"How old were you when she died?"

"Twenty-two. Campbell was about to turn eighteen and Nora had just had her fifteenth birthday."

"I'm sorry. That's terrible."

I glanced down at the dove. It said so little about the person my mother actually was. "We had a...conflicted relationship."

"How so?"

"Well, Campbell and mom were really close. He was her favorite, even if she never explicitly said that. Dad and I always got along better. When I was around twelve, I guess, something happened. I'm still not sure what, but after that, my parents argued non-stop. I tried to shield the others from the constant bickering, but it never worked."

Piper listened but didn't make a face or anything. She waited patiently as I told the story.

"The fighting got worse and mom moved out. Campbell wanted to go live with her. He cried for a month straight because he couldn't see her. He'd called and begged her to let him go with her. So, she showed up one day to do just that. I'd never seen my dad so mad as when she tried to break us all up. He told her it was all or nothing. She couldn't show up, unannounced, and break us up for no reason. Mom went away empty-handed.

"Then one day, six months later, she came home, picked Campbell up, and took him away with her."

"Oh wow. Even after your dad said she couldn't do that?"

My jaw clenched. "Yep. Dad was furious. They fought more. He threatened to take her to the police for kidnapping." I shrugged. "Campbell was gone for two weeks, and then he was home. And Mom came with him, but the fighting never stopped. I thought they'd get a divorce. But they were trying to stay together for the kids."

"That doesn't sound like it worked."

My face was solemn. "It didn't."

"I'm so sorry."

"They stayed together all that time. Just fighting and miserable. Until one night, she stormed out in the middle of the night after a fight and was killed in a hit and run. Campbell blamed Dad for the fighting. It was all fucked up."

Luckily, our food arrived, breaking the tense conversation. She let the heavy topic lapse, for which I was grateful.

Instead, we laughed about her latest raunchy book obsession; my interest in early 2000s emo rock, which she found hysterical; and the large amount of sauce that had ended up all over her mouth, cheeks, and hands.

"Come on," I said, holding my hand out after she used a dozen wet wipes to clean herself up. "We have one more place to go."

"Oh?"

"Yeah. You'll like this."

23

PIPER

"*Y*ou brought me to my *own* winery on our date?" I asked skeptically.

Hollin grinned. "Hey, it's your favorite place."

That was true. Sinclair Cellars was and always had been my favorite place on the entire planet. And maybe, finally, I could show Hollin what was so great about it.

"All right, it is."

"I thought you could show me around. Tell me all the ways it's better than Wright Vineyard."

I snorted. "That's not going to be hard."

His smile was magnetic, and I wanted to lean into him. Nothing about this date was going as I'd expected. Though, technically, our first date had been with my entire family present and he'd passed that interaction with flying colors, I'd still been worried. I almost talked myself out of going a dozen times the last week. We talked on the phone, and he texted me all week. My friends were ecstatic. They said I looked happier than ever.

But trepidation had still almost won out.

Now, I had no idea why I'd been so worried. It was easy to be with Hollin if I stopped trying to fight him. If I didn't take everything he said as if it were an insult specifically designed for me.

The last thing I'd expected when I agreed to do this was that I'd feel *bad* for Hollin Abbey. I had known that his mom had died. I hadn't known about everything else that led to that moment. No wonder he had issues with dating. He clearly didn't trust women after his mom. Not that it justified how he'd treated people in the past, but I could see the invisible scars that had created that behavior.

"So, what do you want to see first?" I asked.

"Well, I did bring one thing with me."

"And what is that?"

He removed a bottle of wine from his bike.

I arched an eyebrow. "You brought *Wright* wine to *my* vineyard?"

He laughed. "I knew it'd get your hackles raised." He passed it to me, and I read the vintage on the front—*Abbey*. "It's the competition wine."

My cheeks heated. I remembered how he'd refused to let me drink any of it when he found out I'd also applied for the competition. I'd been embarrassed. He'd called me the enemy. That whole night was a blur of anger.

"You were such a jerk."

He nodded and slipped his hand into mine. "Yep. Kind of my MO, babe."

"And now, you think I want to drink that shit?"

"Was hoping you'd see it as an olive branch."

"Fine," I said, taking the bottle out of his hand. "I guess we'll do a little taste test then."

His smile only widened. "I was hoping you'd say that."

I directed him into the barn. Sinclair Cellars wasn't a

Friday night hot spot. The barn was mostly used for weddings, fall hay rides, and Christmas tours. That sort of thing. It was dark as I showed Hollin around to the back of the building and unlocked the door to the office space. I flipped the lights.

"Ah, this is where the magic happens," he said.

I grabbed a bottle of our wine and held it out to him. "Here we go."

"Where should we do this?"

I toed open the door that led into the barn and flicked on the twinkle lights overhead, which made it seem like we were really under the stars. I filched a pair of glasses from the bar and set them out. I tossed him the corkscrew. He caught it one-handed and pried open the cork on my wine and then his.

"You sure you want to do this? Sure you don't want to wait for the official tasting?" he joked.

"Pour the damn wine, Hollin," I said with a laugh.

Once the wine was poured, we each took a glass. I started with my wine. I knew exactly what it would taste like, but I wanted a baseline. He seemed to have the same thought, going for the *Abbey* vintage first.

"Why'd you name it that?" I asked.

Sinclair Cellars didn't have original, catchy names. We told you what the fuck you were drinking. And this was a beautiful, full-bodied merlot that was my go-to.

"I said that Wright could go on the sign, but Abbey was the blood of the vineyard. It was going on the wine."

I nodded, understanding. I'd always wanted Medina on the wine. I wanted to claim it for what it was. Mine. It had always been mine. And yet it had someone else's name on it. The Sinclairs had owned it before we did, and there was no reason to fix what wasn't broken.

"Cheers," I said.

I tipped back the glass and took a sip of my wine. Perfect. Exactly what I'd wanted. Hollin grinned and took another full drink of it. As if he couldn't get enough of the Abbey.

"Next?" he suggested.

I eyed him as I took the Wright wine in my hand. He cracked a smirk as he reached for my wine. We stood there for a matter of seconds. Each waiting for the other to make the move. It wouldn't change anything about the competition in a few weeks. But it felt momentous nonetheless.

"All right, Abbey," I said, and I took a drink.

Hollin mirrored me. His throat bobbed around the merlot as I took in the richness of his wine. Fuck. It was good. It was *really* good.

We looked at each other and then spoke at the same time.

"Yours is better," he said as I said, "Damn, that's amazing."

We both laughed.

"Well, fuck," he said. "I guess that doesn't prove anything."

"I guess it doesn't," I admitted. I took another sip of his wine. "But it is good."

"Yours is...perfection, Piper. You should be proud."

"This is your *first* official year, Hollin. How are y'all making this?"

He winked at me. "Can't tell you trade secrets."

"Course not. Now, pour me more." I held out my glass, and he added more *Abbey* vintage into the glass.

I didn't know what was going to happen to us at the competition. We were opponents. But maybe not quite enemies anymore.

"Want to walk the fields?" I asked.

His eyes landed on my lips. "Yes."

He slipped his arm around my shoulders, and we headed out through the vineyard. I knew the way like the back of my hand. The little circle of benches that we kept up all year even though they were only used during the fall and winter for our tours. But I breathed in the air and the darkening sky and being here, alone with Hollin.

"I'm glad we did this," I admitted when he took a seat on the bench.

He'd finished off his glass already and set it aside. "Yeah? Me too."

"I'm actually having a good time," I teased, setting my glass next to his and bending down to kiss him. Our lips were tinged slightly red, and he tasted like wine. I could have drowned in that taste.

He tugged me onto his lap. "You say that like you weren't expecting to."

"Well, no. It's not that."

"You going to tell me why you *really* didn't want to go on a date with me?"

I jolted slightly. "What do you mean?"

"You've been acting like I hurt you personally for weeks."

"You mean, besides you being a jerk to me for the entire time I've known you?"

He chortled. "Well, I suppose, yes. It felt like more than that. That didn't used to get to you."

"Ah, well…" I came to my feet. His hands slid across my ass before finally releasing me. "Do you remember two girls that you dated several years ago? Khloe and Quinn?"

He shook his head. "Doesn't ring a bell."

I breathed out heavily. All this time, it had completely wrecked my world, and he didn't even *remember* them.

"Well, they were my roommates." His brow furrowed,

and I pushed on, explaining what had happened. How he'd dated them both, led them on, and how it had decimated their relationship. The only reason I'd found a way to buy my own house was because of that horrid situation.

"Shit," he said, running a hand back through his hair. "No wonder you were mad at me."

"You always claimed that girls knew what was going on when you started, but I knew for a fact that neither of them had any idea."

"When was this again?" I told him the year that it had all gone down, and he looked far away, as if doing the math. "Ah."

"What?"

"That was before I got better about putting my expecta-tions out there." He sighed and looked down and then back up. "Don't go spreading this around, but I actually have had *one* real relationship."

I blinked at him. That was *not* what I'd expected from him. "*You* dated someone?"

"For two years," he admitted.

"What? How did I not know this?"

"I don't hang out with a single person who knew me at that time. Campbell was gone. Nora knew about her, but she was still in high school. She doesn't even remember. And after her...I cut everything out of my life related to her. Which meant I cut everything, except the winery and my family, out of my life."

"Jesus, what happened?"

"She...I don't know." He blew out a harsh breath. "It didn't work out. She left. I didn't hear from her for a couple months, and then she came back. Rinse and repeat for the next year. When she was finally gone, I decided I'd never deal with that again. So, I did a one-eighty."

He'd been hurt. He'd lashed out and been an idiot, but at least everything was starting to make sense about his behavior.

"I gave up on relationships." His hand came out and caressed my cheek. "Until you."

"This is only our first date," I whispered, staring down into those perfectly earnest eyes.

"Second. I'm counting lunch."

I laughed. "All right, second. I don't think we count as a relationship yet."

"Yet," he repeated, drawing me back into him.

His arms wrapped around my waist as I slung mine around his shoulders. We danced among the grapevines with nothing but the moonlight and stars glimmering down upon us. He'd said *yet*. As if he was here to prove to me that this was more than another one of his conquests.

When his mouth fitted onto mine under the lights of the Milky Way, I believed him.

24

PIPER

I wasn't in my bed. I rolled over and shielded my eyes. The sun slanted in at an odd angle from the windows. They were covered by blinds, but enough light came in to illuminate the room around me. No blackout curtains. A navy bedspread. A distinctly masculine design.

I was at Hollin's house.

The night rushed back in with perfect clarity. The kiss in the vineyard. The ride back to his house. The several bottles of wine we'd consumed before falling passionately into his sheets, drunk and delirious on the other. We'd passed out at some ungodly hour.

A smile crept onto my face as I shifted and my sore bottom rubbed against the sheets. Oh, right. Last night had been...perfect. Or as close to perfect as I'd ever gotten on a date. Never in a million years had I thought it would happen with Hollin Abbey. But it had.

"Morning," he growled low, pressing a kiss onto my shoulder.

I rolled over to face him and caught a glimpse of his sun-drenched face. The morning rays lightened his baby blues to nearly translucent. A five o'clock shadow graced his sharp jawline. His pouty lips continued their path up my shoulder and to my neck.

"Mmm, good morning," I purred, angling my head to the side to give him better access.

"I could get used to this."

"This?"

"You in my bed." His hand roamed freely across my bare stomach to my hip, drawing circles on my skin before reaching for my ass. I gasped as pain reared up from the night before. He pulled back with a lazy smirk on his lips. "Sore?"

"How could I not be?" I arched an eyebrow.

"Fair." He drew my lips toward him and planted a sensuous, long kiss on them. "Too sore for more?"

"Depends," I teased.

"I'll just have to take care of you," he said with that mischievous glint in his eye.

He rolled me onto my back and covered my body with his. My ass protested the sudden movement, but eventually, I was comfortable back against the soft sheets. But Hollin was kissing his way down the front of my body, and I forgot the pain entirely. He sucked one of my brown nipples into his mouth, kneading the other breast with his hand. I arched against him as he moved from one breast to the other, giving each ample attention.

"This doesn't hurt?"

I shook my head. "God, no."

His kisses ventured south across my stomach, down my navel. He swirled his tongue around my belly button before reaching the waistband of my thong.

"Don't need these," he said as he slid his thumbs under the material and dragged them down my legs.

He tossed them over the side of the bed and lifted one leg up to his mouth. He kissed the inside of my knee.

"This doesn't hurt?"

"No," I murmured.

He dropped it onto his shoulder and worshipped the skin up my inner thigh. I moaned softly as his lips touched the sensitive skin at the apex of my legs. When he stopped before reaching my pussy, I pushed upward, but he chuckled under his breath and stared on the other leg.

"I have to make sure the rest of you is okay, too, babe."

"That doesn't hurt either," I promised. Though the back of my thighs told a whole different story.

"What about here?" he asked as he pressed a kiss on top of my clit.

"Fuck," I breathed.

His tongue swirled around the nub, drawing it into his mouth and caressing it gently. He licked against the seam of my lips, dragging it up to my clit. I bucked at even the softest touches.

"Am I going to have to hold you down?" he asked.

"Please," I begged.

He grinned and set his hand against my abdomen, so there was nowhere else for me to go. With his arm strapped across me, I couldn't lift or escape. I had to lie there as he worked me into a frenzy.

"Don't move now. Be a good girl."

I groaned as he rubbed his hand back and forth across my lips without going inside. I wanted to rear up to try to escape, to get relief. Whatever he would give me. But I couldn't move, and he'd told me to stay still. So, I let loose vocally as his tongue swirled harder and more insistent against my clit, coaxing it to its peak.

Finally, mercifully, he slipped one finger inside of me.

My legs seized up on their own, drawing closed. He released my clit and used his hand to push me all the way back open for him.

"Hollin," I gasped as he returned to sucking on my clit.

Then, he thrust a finger all the way inside of me, and everything went molten. I wanted that to be his cock. I wanted him to stretch me and fill me. I might be sore from last night, but, fuck, I wanted it. The second followed the first, and he curled his fingers upward. I saw stars as he worked me to the point of no return.

"Close," I panted.

"Come for me," he commanded.

He thrust his fingers into me faster and faster. His tongue worked in perfect tempo with his hands. and I unleashed. My body tensing and shuddering under him.

I'd barely come down when he ripped open a condom and seated himself against my opening. He filled me with one long drive forward. I cried out as the last traces of my orgasm rocked through me, and he filled my still-sensitive body. He took both of my hands in his own and shoved them over my head as he pounded into me. My tits bounced. My body shook with the force of it. And all I did was want more.

"Going to come for me a second time?"

"Yes," I gasped. I could already feel the traces of another orgasm rising in me. "Touch me."

He switched my wrists into one of his hands as his other hand moved between my legs. He used my own wetness to draw circles around my clit.

"Oh fuck."

"Fuck yes," Hollin said. "Fuck."

Then, he grunted twice and stiffened, emptying himself deep inside me as he came hard and fast. My own orgasm was triggered by his, and I let loose. Stars swam in my vision, and as everything receded, the small triggers of pain returned. Welcome pain. Reminders of our escapades.

Hollin tossed the condom and drew me against his chest. "How are you feeling?"

"Mmm," I whispered, snuggling into him as sleep beckoned me all over again. "Nap time."

He laughed and kissed my neck. "What about breakfast?"

"What are you making me?"

"I thought...I'd take you out."

I slowly rolled over so that I was facing him. Was he asking me out again? "Really? Back-to-back dates?"

"If you don't mind wearing your dress again."

"I don't mind."

He kissed my nose. "I'm craving pancakes."

"I'm craving you."

He grinned. "I can oblige that."

Then he kissed me, and we both forgot about pancakes for another half hour.

Finally, we hauled ourselves out of bed. I did the best I could with my hair without anything to tame the wild mess. I swiped on some lipstick, and that was that.

The weather had turned murky overnight, and we took Hollin's truck instead of the Harley. I promised the bike that I'd be back on it later. Hollin beamed at my words. He liked how much I liked it. I'd never, ever thought I'd be a motorcycle kind of girl. But I completely understood the freedom with it. It was an adrenaline rush. And a powerful one at that.

Hollin parked in front of his favorite breakfast place, Stacked. It was a farmhouse design with wooden tables, country decorations, and cotton everywhere. Welcome to Lubbock.

Luckily, we were early enough that it wasn't that busy yet.

A hostess directed us to a table at the back, and on the way, a woman stopped us. "Hollin?"

She stood from her table, where she was seated across from an older gentleman. He was currently facing away from the table, on his cell phone.

"Eve, hey," Hollin said. They hugged briefly, and then he gestured to me. "Eve, this is my date, Piper."

"Breakfast date," Eve said with a smile. She was a knockout with almost black hair and green eyes, heavy makeup, low-cut top. "Cute. It's nice to meet you."

"You too," I said awkwardly.

"Eve used to play soccer with me back before The Tacos," Hollin explained.

"Ugh, I should have joined your team when you invited me. My team...sucks."

"We can always use another excellent striker. You and Blaire together would be a nightmare for every other team."

"I'll keep it in mind. It was good seeing you!"

Hollin waved, and we took our seat.

I arched an eyebrow at him. "Eve?"

He laughed. "Seriously, just soccer."

"And y'all didn't date?"

"Nah, she and Zach had a thing for a while."

My eyes darted back to the buxom woman. I imagined her and the giant bouncer at Wright together. "Good for him. Did you see who she was sitting with?"

"*Daddy* Sinclair," he said dryly.

I laughed at the outrageous nickname. "Daddy Sinclair?"

"Yeah. I don't know why but it seems fitting."

I snorted. "What is she doing here with him?"

"I don't know. She works for Sinclair Realty. She helped me buy my house."

"I find it hard to believe you never dated someone who looks like her."

"And why is that? You think she's hot?"

"She *is* hot," I told him.

"You want a threesome?"

I rolled my eyes. "Sometimes you make me forget that you're still Hollin Abbey."

He laughed. "Worth asking. I read that book you were reading, you know?"

"You *what*?"

"Yeah. So, I know that you like *reading* about threesomes."

I leaned my elbows on the table and met his smirk with one of my own. "I sure do. Two guys and one girl. You game?"

He winked. "If that's what you want."

I couldn't keep from laughing. "No way. I wouldn't think you'd be down."

"I'm not crossing swords or anything," he said quickly. "But if you wanted an Eiffel Tower."

"Oh my God," I said, my cheeks flaming. I looked pointedly at my menu. "We need to talk about something else."

"What can I get you?" the waitress asked, appearing out of nowhere and interrupting our perfectly outrageous conversation.

After we put in our orders, Hollin took my hand in his. Somehow, it was entirely natural.

"You know this is date three," I blurted out.

"Yeah?"

"If the guys are right, this means we've hit your limit."

He brought my hand to his lips and pressed a kiss to each of my fingers. "And what if I said that I wanted more?"

"Do you?"

"I want all of your dates. Every single one of them."

I swallowed the emotions clouding my throat. "You're serious?"

"Dead serious."

I was still skeptical. After all, I'd never seen Hollin date anyone. Even if he'd said that he'd done it before. It felt so removed from the present. Yet here he was, offering me the world. What kind of person would I be not to accept?

PART IV

LOVE STORY

25

PIPER

I'd been certain my skepticism going into this relationship was warranted. I thought I knew Hollin and the way he operated. That maybe our three dates wasn't real to him since one had happened with my family and the last had been a continuation of the night before.

Then, we had our fourth date at a bar downtown with live music. A fifth date at Fun Noodle Bar for ramen and dessert at Pie Bar. A sixth date, riding his motorcycle through Ransom Canyon and picnicking by the lake. Old movies at his place for the seventh date. Our eighth, we went trampolining, which was a sight to behold, watching someone as enormous as Hollin Abbey having the dexterity to do flips on a trampoline. We were both sore for three days straight after that. We spent the ninth date in with sushi and a bubble bath. The tenth date, we took my Jeep up to Palo Duro Canyon and hiked the two miles to the Lighthouse. We sat on the edge of the enormous rock, our feet dangling over the edge, and listened to the quiet of the universe.

At some point, I lost count.

There were more dates. More unofficial outings. Just us

being together, going out to get dinner, breaking for lunches, stealing kisses after work, nights in his sheets. And all the skepticism faded into nothing.

Hollin had been serious. He wanted this. And he proved it every day we huddled together and made more plans. More and more plans.

Suddenly, a whole new reality bloomed before me. I was doing this. I was actually dating Hollin Abbey. And I wanted more of everything he was offering. Not just the sex, which continued to be mind-blowing, but also the time together and all the silly moments. The fact that he *read* the books I liked so he could make conversation with me. That we liked the same music and binged the same movies. That I was kind of loving the Harley as much as he did.

"You're doing it again," Blaire accused with a laugh.

"Doing what?"

I stared out the front window of my Jeep as I drove me, Blaire, and her assistant, Honey, to The Tacos game.

"Getting that dopey smile on your face. You're thinking about Hollin."

"I was," I admitted.

"It's so cute!" Honey said from the backseat. She wore a Blaire Blush baseball hat over her shoulder-length blonde hair and lavender matching leggings and crop from a designer that Blaire loved.

Blaire agreed. "So cute. I'm happy for y'all. I knew there was a reason you two were always at each other's throats."

"Not sure that's stopped."

Buttons were pushed all the time. We were always challenging each other and seeing how far we could go. In and out of the bedroom. But it was the right kind of challenges. It wasn't anger for its own sake. It was different, better. Who knew I just needed a guy who didn't *bore* me?

She laughed. "True."

"And what about you? Any guy catching your eye lately?"

She wrinkled her little nose and drew her baseball cap lower on her head. "No."

"You were talking to that guy online," Honey said, waggling her eyebrows.

"What guy?" I gasped.

"No one," Blaire said with a huff. "You weren't supposed to see that, Honey."

"My bad." She got a sheepish look on her face. "I handle her messages, and sometimes, I answer fans and see personal stuff."

I arched an eyebrow at my best friend. "Spill."

"Fine," she said with a sigh. "There's this, like, TikTok star. He's real hot."

"He's a thirst trap," Honey volunteered.

I blinked. "A *thirst* trap?"

"Yeah. He's one of those guys who smiles sexy at the camera and takes his shirt off," Honey said. "Like a model."

"I see," I said with a laugh. "And y'all are talking?"

"He lives in Midland."

"A thirst trap in Midland, Texas. Now, I've heard everything."

Blaire shrugged. "I live in Lubbock. Anyway, that's how we started talking. Because he's only an hour and a half away."

"Have you met?"

"No. I'm sure it's not going to go anywhere."

Honey giggled. "Not the way he talks to you."

"And what is this guy's name?"

"Nate," she offered.

"Nate King," Honey volunteered. "You can look him up

@nateistheking. His family is into oil money. They run Dorset & King."

"Thank you, Honey," Blaire said sarcastically.

I'd look him up to see if he was everything Honey was going on about. It would be nice for Blaire to look at someone other than Campbell Abbey. She hadn't been in a relationship in a while. And look at me, suddenly happy and wanting my friends to have this ounce of freedom.

I parked the Jeep next to Hollin's truck and hopped out. Blaire grabbed her bag and fell into step beside me.

"Honey wants something to work out for me," Blaire muttered.

"So do I."

"Yeah, yeah. I'll find someone in this small town eventually."

I laughed. "You will."

"They're a bit close, aren't they?" Blaire asked, jutting her chin toward where Hollin stood on the sidelines next to Tamara. "I can kick her ass if you'd like?"

When needed, Blaire could flip to *defensive best friend* mode in the blink of an eye. And I didn't doubt for a second that she'd get into it with Tamara for touching Hollin. Not that it was necessary. I already knew that Tamara made Hollin uncomfortable.

"I can handle it."

Blaire nodded and jogged off toward the field.

I walked right up to where Hollin stood. His smile brightened at the sight of me. I grabbed Tamara's hand and removed it from Hollin's arm.

"No," I said flatly.

Tamara's cheeks flamed . "Uh...I...we were just talking."

"Of course."

Tamara bit her lip and then scurried away over to

August and Nora.

Hollin's smile only grew. "Jealous?"

"I am not jealous of the child."

He dropped a kiss on my lips. "Yes, you were, and it was hot."

"No. She just can't touch what's mine."

"So, I'm yours?"

I blinked at the words. I hadn't even considered them before saying it out loud. I hadn't liked the idea of someone else touching him. We hadn't had a conversation about what we were, but considering we were spending every minute of our free time together, it was pretty clear—at least to me.

"Are you mine?" I challenged right back.

He pushed my hair back out of my face. "Yes."

"Oh," I said, turning to mush at the way he'd said that one simple word.

"Well then, yes," I agreed. "You're mine."

"That sounds damn good out of your mouth, Medina." He brushed his nose against mine. "Maybe I can have a taste of what is mine later."

"You're filthy."

"No, I'll be filthy later. Maybe we should take a shower." He winked at me.

"Get out here, Abbey!" Isaac called from the field.

"Yeah, Hollin," Julian shouted. "Get your head in the game."

"My head is somewhere else entirely," he said, planting one more kiss on my lips.

The guys called out to him as he kissed me. He winked at me and ran out onto the field.

"Yeah, yeah, fuckers. I'm coming."

I watched him go with a shake of my head. He was mine. *Mine.*

"*Y*ou're whipped," Julian said when I stopped by his office to tell him I was going to lunch with Piper...again.

"Pot, meet kettle."

"Yeah, but Jennifer is my girlfriend. What is Piper?"

"She's...well, we're dating."

"Exclusively?"

I scratched the back of my head. "Yeah."

Julian leaned back in his chair and tapped a pen against his seat. "You've shot to hell the three-date rule."

I snorted. "True."

"So, girlfriend?"

"She's mine. We haven't defined it beyond that," I said with a shrug. "Right now, I'm enjoying the fucking ride."

"Are you bringing her to the gala?"

"I'm asking her today. She was shaky the first couple dates. Maybe the first dozen dates."

"Can't blame her. Considering your history."

"No. It's fair." And it really was. She had every reason to be skeptical because of my history. Especially considering what she'd told me about her friends. I'd been such a dick back then. I'd thought I'd gotten better, but until Piper, no one else had mattered. "I didn't want to get ahead of myself. Make sure she understood what I wanted before I dropped a black-tie event on her."

"And what *do* you want from her?"

"Dude, I feel stupid for even saying it, but...everything."

"Who are you, and what have you done with my cousin?" Julian laughed. "Are there wedding bells in your future after all?"

"Shut up. I just mean, I want to see where this goes. I'm not pumping the brakes."

Julian stood and held his hand out with a wide grin. I shook his hand.

"Good. That's what I wanted to hear." When he released my hand, he slapped a letter into my palm.

"What's this?" I asked, turning the letter over to read the header—*IWAA Texas Wine Award Competition*.

"See for yourself."

I tore into the envelope and pulled out the letter. I read it in a daze. My eyes shot to Julian's. "We're in?"

He nodded. "We're in."

"Holy shit. We're finalists for the wine award." My eyes bulged as I scanned the letter a second time. "This is the official invite to Austin for the finals."

"Yep."

"Fuck, man. I wasn't sure it'd happen. I hoped, but..."

"I get it," Julian said automatically. "But if anything was going to work, it was the *Abbey* vintage."

I hugged my cousin tight for a second. "Guess I'd better go find out if Piper made it in, too."

Julian laughed. "Good luck with that."

"No kidding."

I pocketed the letter and headed to my truck. I drove to Sinclair Cellars to pick up Piper for lunch. I was thinking something more celebratory than our usual. Or maybe we could celebrate tonight with a fancy dinner. Something I wouldn't normally go for, but it wasn't every day this sort of thing happened.

I barged through the back door and knocked on her closed office door.

"Come in," Piper called.

She looked up from her desk when I entered.

"Hey, babe."

"Hey," she said with a smile. "Just finishing some paperwork. Where are we going for lunch?"

"Depends."

"On what?"

I withdrew the letter. "Did you get one of these?"

Her eyes widened. "Is that what I think it is?"

"Wright Vineyard is in the finals," I declared.

"I haven't looked through the mail." She reached for the stack that someone had apparently deposited on her desk. She rifled through it all until, miraculously, her own golden ticket dropped into her lap.

Her eyes were wary yet excited as she sliced the top open with a letter opener. She reverently took out the letter and read the contents.

"Oh my God," she gasped. "We made it!" She jumped up. "We made it!"

"Congratulations!"

"We're real enemies now, Abbey."

I laughed as I scooped her up into my arms. I twirled her around in a circle before dropping her back down on her feet. She drew my lips down to meet hers.

"Maybe we should...drive down together," I offered.

"Really?"

I nodded. "No point in both of us driving to Austin."

She considered it. "Might be fun. Like a getaway."

"I'm into it, if you are."

"I am," she said with a small smile.

"Good. And...about the gala this weekend," I said, brushing my hand across the back of my neck. Might as well get this over with. "Do you want to go with me?"

Her eyes lit up. "As your date? To a black-tie event?"

"Well, yeah. I know you were already planning to go to see Peyton perform and..."

"Yes," she said, taking my hand in hers. "I want to go with you."

I smirked down at her and captured another kiss. "Yeah?"

She nodded. "I was hoping you'd ask."

"Yeah? What number date is that?"

She slung her arms around my neck and leaned into me. "You know, I've completely lost track."

My smile widened. I liked that. At first, she'd been counting religiously, as if waiting for the bottom to fall out. Now, I felt none of that from her at all. I'd had no real reason to worry about the gala.

"Does that make you my girlfriend?" I was teasing but also serious. The words stuck to the roof of my mouth like peanut butter. God, it had been years since I'd ever thought that word out loud without a joke behind it.

"I don't know." She arched an eyebrow at me. Always defiant. Always pushing. Just how I liked her. "Does that make you my boyfriend?"

I pressed my mouth to hers until she sighed against me. "What do you think?"

"Yes," she all but panted. "Yes to everything."

"Good girl," I purred.

She laughed and kissed me again. "So, celebratory lunch?"

"Or I could take you out somewhere nice for dinner."

"Or both."

"Both," I agreed easily. "Whatever my girlfriend wants."

She squeezed my hand. "I like that."

"Me too."

Her brows knitted together. She lifted her nose into the air. "Huh."

"What?"

"Do you smell that?"

"Smell what?"

She shook her head. "I don't know. Smoke?"

"I don't smell anything."

But I stopped thinking and scented the air. She was right. There was a hint of smoke. I hadn't seen any on the horizon when I drove in. But I wasn't exactly paying attention. I'd been buzzing from the news and too excited to see her. I couldn't even remember the drive.

"No, I do smell it," I told her.

"Maybe someone burned popcorn or something," she said. But there was doubt on her face. It didn't smell like popcorn. "I should check it out."

"I'll come with you."

"It'll only be a minute."

"If there's smoke, there could be fire. No way I'm letting you investigate that alone."

She huffed in that *I am woman, hear me roar* way of hers but eventually relented when it was clear I wasn't letting my fucking woman walk off into a potential *fire* alone.

"Fine."

I followed behind her out of the office. As soon as we

were out of the safety of her office, I could see that the hallway was hazy with smoke. I couldn't believe we hadn't noticed the smell before. I pulled my T-shirt up to cover my mouth and nose and gestured for Piper to do the same.

"We should get out of here," I told her.

"In a minute," she said, rushing faster forward.

The deeper we veered through the maze of offices, the thicker the smoke got. We didn't see anyone else. Either everyone had left or they were all gone for lunch already.

We reached the door that opened to the barn. The door was cracked, and smoke billowed out of it. I coughed and crouched down to escape the worst of it. It was getting hotter, too.

"Piper!" I cried. "We have to go. It's not safe."

"Peyton's wedding dress," she gasped.

"What?"

"She was...she was keeping it here." Tears formed in her eyes from the smoke. "It's just in the closet. I can get it!"

"No, that's crazy," I said, grabbing her arm.

"It's from a New York designer. She had it made for her. I need to rescue it."

"It's a goddamn dress. You're not going in there."

"I'll be quick."

A stubborn look of determination crossed her face. She was going to go into a burning building to save her sister's wedding dress. It would have been funny if it wasn't so goddamn dangerous. Who knew what the next room looked like? It could be engulfed in flames. The ceiling could collapse. The smoke could suffocate her.

She was going to do it anyway.

I saw the moment when she made up her mind. And it was the same moment that I made up mine that we were fucking done here.

I grabbed her around the waist. She screamed as I tossed her over my shoulder and stepped away from the billowing smoke. She hit her fists against my chest and coughed harder as she tried to speak. The smoke was getting thicker. We needed to leave. We never should have come this way. It was way past time for us to be able to do anything to fix this. And I didn't care if she beat me to a pulp; I was going to get her out of there.

The door I'd come in from earlier was standing ajar. I kicked it open and inhaled my first gasping breath of fresh air. I carried Piper a dozen feet away from the building before dropping her on her feet.

She collapsed to her knees and hacked up a lung. "Hollin! I could have gotten it."

"Look!" I snapped, pointing back to where we'd come.

She gasped. Her hands flew to her mouth as she stared at the barn she'd grown up in, the barn she loved, go up in flames. The fire was primarily on the opposite side of the building from where we'd been, but it was spreading fast. The building was old, and it went up like tinder.

Tears streamed down her face. "Oh my God."

"I know."

"What are we going to do?"

I dropped onto the ground next to her. "We wait."

And then we both heard the sirens in the distance.

27

PIPER

*M*y home was burning to the ground. And my heart shattered into a million pieces as I watched the flames engulf it. I'd grown up in that building. I'd worked in it for years. It was as much a part of me as the vines and fields.

At least they were safe. The fire hadn't jumped to any of the fields. Our entire crop could have been destroyed in a matter of hours if that had happened. I had no idea how we would have come back from that. A whole year of wine would have been gone.

Luckily that hadn't happened. That was what people were saying.

We were *lucky*.

I didn't feel lucky.

I felt empty.

The firefighters had shown up and were trying to control the raging fire within. We still had no idea what had caused it. Everyone was speculating it was an electrical fire. The building was old and could have used some maintenance, but I hadn't thought anything like this could happen.

My dad rushed up to me. "*Mija*, you're all right."

"I'm fine, Papa," I said, letting his warm presence envelop me.

He brushed back my hair. "I was so worried. I was down at the cellar when it started. You're not hurt?"

I shook my head. "Shaken up. Some smoke inhalation. I'm fine."

Hollin stood next to me with his arms crossed over his chest, watching the fire consume my entire life. More tears came to my eyes as I glanced at him. I was okay because of him. He'd saved me. He'd carried me out of the smoke and flames when I was too stubborn and stupid to listen to reason.

"Thanks to Hollin," I told my dad. "He carried me out."

My dad held his hand out to Hollin. "Thank you, Hollin. Thank you for saving my daughter's life."

Hollin balked at the words but shook my dad's hand. "Yes, sir. I acted on instinct."

"Mine disappeared," I said. Tears came to my eyes again, and my dad wrapped me in a hug. "Peyton's dress."

I was being irrational. It was just a stupid dress. But in the midst of the inferno, when I should have backed off, all that I could feel was panic. This was Peyton's day. This was something I could do. I hadn't known how bad the fire was. I'd thought I'd had time. Thank God that Hollin had seen reason when mine had flown from my head.

"Shh, *mija*. All that matters is that you are well. We can all live without a dress but not without you." He kissed the top of my head. "I'm going to check on the other employees who got out. Stay with Hollin." He smiled at my boyfriend and hugged me again. "*Te amo.*"

"*Y yo a ti*, Papa."

He released me and walked around to the employees

scattered around the outside of the burning building.

"I'm sorry," I blurted out.

Hollin looked at me as if I'd lost my mind. "You have nothing to apologize for."

"I was an idiot."

"Hey," he said, wrapping an arm around my shoulders. "You didn't know how bad it was. You're not an idiot."

"Thank you for getting me out."

"I'm here to take care of you," he said, pressing a firm kiss to my lips.

I nodded and snuggled up against him.

We waited for the next hour as the firefighters did all they could to put out the flames within. My mom and Peter showed up sometime in the middle of that, hugging me and watching the damage.

"I can't fucking believe it," Peter said with a shake of his head.

"Peter," Mom hissed.

"He's right," I said. "It's terrible."

"We're glad you and your dad are all right."

"Me too."

And then Peyton rushed in. It was the person I most and least wanted to see. Even though I'd told Hollin that I'd been stupid, I still felt unbelievably guilty about what had happened. And what I was about to have to tell Peyton.

She sprinted across the open field toward where we'd congregated. Even at a full run, she looked like the graceful ballerina she was.

She crashed into me, hugging me hard. "Pipes, you're okay."

"Hi, seester."

"I can't believe this happened. Do you have any idea what started it?"

I shook my head. "Electrical fire? But it's just a guess. They'll figure it out."

"It doesn't matter anyway. Nothing we can do to fix it."

"Your dress, Peyton. It was still inside."

She blinked. "Oh." Then, she deflated. "Well, I guess I'll find another one."

"In less than two weeks?" I asked skeptically. "And where are we going to have the wedding? It was supposed to be in the barn."

"That's what you're worried about?" Peyton asked. She was wide-eyed, and her crazy curls were up in a slightly relaxed ballet bun. But she still looked frazzled. Just as frazzled as the rest of us. "You were *inside a burning building*, Piper. I care about you and Dad and Hollin."

Hollin smiled at her. "That's what I've been saying."

"I know. I know," I said, tears coming on strong again.

"We'll figure it out," Peyton said. She pulled me into another hug. "It's going to be okay."

"Honestly, *mija*, the wedding is going to be wonderful, no matter where it's held," Mom said. "No matter what our beautiful ballerina is wearing. It will be perfect because it is the joining of two people, who were made for each other, in front of their families. It is not about the place or the dress. Just the family and love."

I nodded, swiping at my tears. "You're right. But what are we going to do?"

"You can have it at Wright Vineyard," Hollin piped up automatically.

My entire family looked at him with dropped jaws.

"Really?" Peter asked.

"Are you sure?" Peyton asked.

"Oh, but that's so sweet," my mom said, melting at his words.

"We can't...I don't know if we could afford it," I blurted out.

Hollin gave me the dreamiest smile and took my hand. "I wouldn't expect you to pay for it."

"Oh, Hollin, that's...wow." Peyton stifled her own sob. Tears came to her big brown eyes. And then she hugged my boyfriend. "I don't know how Piper got this lucky."

He laughed and tapped Peyton's back. "We don't have any events that weekend. You're already working with Nora. It shouldn't be too hard to move everything across town."

"Thank you," I whispered.

"Of course."

"I'll get on the phone with Nora," Peyton said, going into planning mode. "See what she thinks and if she needs me to do anything."

Peyton took out her phone and walked away from the group. My mom and brother went to talk to my dad. Chase Sinclair had arrived at some point, and he was in deep conversation with him. Right, a lawyer—probably a good idea. I was too shell-shocked to have even gotten to that point of processing.

I turned back to Hollin. "Thank you for doing this."

"Hey, it's not a problem. I know that you wanted it here. I get how much it means to you, but if I can help, I will."

I stood on my tiptoes and pressed a kiss to his lips. "How *did* I get this lucky?"

He snorted. "I'm the lucky one. Who else would get a girlfriend stubborn enough to walk through a burning building for a wedding dress?"

I covered my face and laughed. "Oh my God, I'll never live it down. What was I thinking?"

"You love your sister. You were concerned about her wedding."

"Yeah. True."

He passed me the water bottle that the paramedics had given us when they arrived with the firefighters. "Drink some more water. Your voice is all scratchy."

I took the water from him and downed half of it. We sat in the grass until all was said and done. The longer the adrenaline wore off, the worse I felt. Not that I was sick or anything, but I felt like I'd been hit by a bus.

"Come on," Hollin said, offering me a hand. "Let's get you home."

"Ugh," I groaned. The last thing I wanted was to go home and have to talk about this more with Blaire and Jennifer. I'd texted my friends to tell them what had happened. But I didn't feel ready to discuss it. "Can we...go to your place instead?"

He raised an eyebrow. "If you want. I thought you'd want your own bed."

"I just...want to be alone."

"I'll be there," he reminded me.

"Alone together."

He nodded, as if understanding. He'd carried me out of a burning building. I wouldn't have to say a word to him about it. So, I followed him to our cars. My hands were shaky, but I shook off Hollin's concern about me driving myself. I parked out on the driveway before dropping onto the ground below and walking in through the front door.

"Shower," Hollin said, gently pushing me toward his bedroom.

"What? Why? I was thinking alcohol and nap."

He laughed. "Have you smelled your shirt lately? Your hair?"

I brought the front of my shirt to my nose and immediately started coughing. "Oh Jesus. Smoke."

"Yeah. So, shower."

"Does my hair smell like it too?"

He shot me a look. He knew how sensitive I was about my hair. It took *forever* to clean and doubly forever to dry. I hated washing it and hated blowing it out. But letting it air dry was worse. It meant it would be five times the size I wanted it to be with frizz for days. Who knew if or when I'd get all the smoke smell out of it?

I grumbled under my breath and followed him into the bathroom. He put the water on its hottest setting as I stripped. When he turned back around, I was topless, and he gaped at me.

"I feel like we've been here before," he said with an arched eyebrow.

"I wasn't topless that time outside Wright."

"No, but I thought you were." His hands slid around my sides and pulled me into him. "Your bra was nude, and at first, my brain didn't process it. And that was when I knew."

"What?"

"How much I wanted you."

"Because I was almost topless?"

"Well, yes, but we found the ring."

He unbuttoned my jeans and slid them down my legs. I stepped out of them, cringing at the memory.

"Oh yeah. I try to block that out."

"I was irrationally angry that he'd think about proposing to you."

"But you didn't even like me."

"Sure I did. I liked pushing your buttons. And when I thought about you with someone else, I got pissed off." He hefted his own shirt over his head. I ran my hands down his bare chest, taking in his words. "I wanted you to myself."

"And now you have me."

His smile was blinding. "Every stubborn inch of you."

He slid out of the rest of his clothes and dragged me into the shower under the spray. I laughed as the water hit my back, soaking through my smoky hair. He drew us both under the jets. He kissed me hard, stealing my breath and all conscious thought.

My back hit the white tiles, and I lifted a leg around his hip, drawing him in closer. Today had been harrowing and exhausting. The adrenaline had dissipated, and with it had come a hollow emptiness that I didn't want to touch.

But *this*...

This I still wanted.

Hollin Abbey had saved my life. He had been an actual hero today. And more than that...he was now my official boyfriend. And I wanted him to make me forget the last terrible hours and remember the bliss I'd been in when we put a label on our relationship.

He grasped my ass in his hands, digging his fingers hard into me before lifting me into the air. I wrapped both legs around his waist as he leveraged me against the shower wall. Steam fogged the shower window. It clung wet and warm against our bare skin. My breathing was ragged and my throat raw from the smoke.

I dragged his bottom lip between my teeth, biting down just hard enough for him to pinion me against the tiles.

"Fuck," he ground out.

His cock jutted up between us, long and throbbing.

"Please," I gasped.

He obliged, lining us up and thrusting hard upward. I gasped and cracked my head on the tile. My vision was blurry at the edges as he plunged inside of me. I shook with the exertion of holding myself up. Even Hollin's massive legs quivered as the slick surface threatened to undo us.

I was close when he finally dropped me to my feet, spun me around, and pushed my body forward. I braced myself on the bench, and he drove back into me. His hands returned to my hips. With better leverage, he used all his momentum to jerk into me. I met every thrust with my own push backward against him.

It was only a matter of minutes before I was crying out into the shower. My orgasm forced his, and then he held me fast against him as he finished. I dropped onto my knees. My head was light, and everything felt woozy.

I looked up at him from heavily lidded eyes. "Hi."

He chuckled and bent down to kiss me. "Hey you."

He helped me to my feet, and on shaky legs, he soaped up my body and then his. He lathered up my hair with his shampoo, running his hands through the thick, long tresses, and repeated it with the conditioner. I'd never been taken care of like this before. And all of the tension from the day swirled away down the drain.

When he finished, he wrapped me up in a towel and carried me to his bed. I laughed, but it felt nice to have him tuck me in. He pulled on boxers and snuggled in tight behind me. He pressed a kiss to my shoulder.

"How are you feeling?"

"Sleepy," I said, pushing my back against his hard chest.

"Good. That's what I wanted."

"You planned this?" I only half-accused, my voice already drifting into dreams.

"Planned to take care of you? Yes."

I couldn't even argue. It had worked. It was what I'd needed. Now, I could finally relax enough to sleep. I'd process what had happened tomorrow. Today, I needed this...just him.

28

PIPER

*T*hankfully, my dad dealt with most of the fallout with the barn. It had been caused by an electrical fire that swarmed swiftly through the space. Because it had taken so long for the fire to be put out, the barn was unsalvageable. The entire thing would have to be torn down and rebuilt. We had insurance, but it was disheartening, to say the least.

I had no idea what we'd do until that point. Almost all of the offices had been in there. Most of the wine had been in the cellar, but years and years of work had been lost in the fire. In the interim, we'd given most of the staff time off and moved me and my dad down to the cellar until we figured out what to do.

By the time the weekend came around, I desperately needed the break. The gala for the DII soccer team was tonight. If I hadn't agreed to go with Hollin, I might have skipped the entire thing. Peyton had assured me it was just what I needed and that I couldn't miss seeing her perform. Which was true. I loved to watch her dance.

So, I put aside my aching heart and got ready for the

event. In years past, the three grandkids had always gone to Abuelita's house, dressed in our prom attire. Abuelita always wanted to be the first person to see us in our outfits. And even though prom was long past, the three of us had agreed to show off for Abuelita one more time.

Peter stood in his tuxedo as Abuelita, seated at the dining room table, circled her finger in the air. "Do a little twirl."

He sighed. "I don't twirl."

"You took ballet for a few years, like the rest of us," Peyton said. "You know how to turn."

He shot her a look and did a perfectly executed pirouette. Peter had been better at the grace of it all than I ever had. If he'd stuck with it like Peyton, maybe he would have ended up in New York, too.

"Lovely," Abuelita said. "Now, slower. These old eyes don't see like they used to."

He obliged, turning in a slow circle as Peyton went into the bedroom to change. "I do look pretty sharp, don't I?"

I wrinkled my nose. "You're all right."

"Hey! Chess will like it."

"That young man is very dreamy himself," Abuelita said.

Peter laughed. "What would Grandpa think about that?"

"He's been in the grave for a dozen years. And when he was here, he knew I had eyeballs."

I cracked up. Leave it to Abuelita to be checking out guys fifty years younger than her.

Peyton came out next, not in a ballgown, but her tutu for the ballet *Serenade*. She was performing the solo and *pas de deux* at the event tonight. It was a stunning display of tulle, perfectly fit to her measurements.

"Oh, *mi amorcita*," Abuelita said. "*Perfecto*."

"Thank you," Peyton said, stepping up and pressing a kiss to her cheek.

"I always loved that one," I told her.

"Me too," Peyton said wistfully.

Giving up her life in New York City and ceasing performing had been difficult for Peyton. She had a life and a career here as the artistic director that she loved, but sometimes, it was hard. How could it not be? Ballet had been the only thing she cared about for years.

Then, it was my turn. I carried the black dress bag into the room. Blaire and I had picked it out online from a designer that she partnered with. We'd had the thing tailored to my build once it came in.

"Need help?" Peyton called.

"Please."

Peyton entered the room and buttoned up the tiny buttons at the back.

"I'll be doing this for you next weekend."

She laughed. "If I can find a dress."

We'd gone dress shopping at all of the local places, but nothing had fit her that would be ready by next weekend. I'd promised to go look for her in Dallas or New York, if need be, to find something. Someone *somewhere* could make this happen.

With the dress securely in place, I drew on my black heels and walked into the living room. Abuelita's breath caught.

"Piper," she breathed softly. "Where did my little girl go?"

I smiled and spun in a careful circle, letting the light catch the soft shimmer to the black-and-silver dress. It gave her a perfect view of the square neckline, ruched middle, and nearly completely open back. The waist tapered in before falling to the floor in a swirl of beautiful fabric. When I twirled, everything flared up like I was an actual princess. It was better than anything I'd ever worn to prom, and I felt perfect in it.

"I love this tradition," Peyton said. "You look gorgeous, Piper."

"Hollin won't be able to keep his hands off you," Peter said with a laugh.

Abuelita shook her head. "She won't be able to keep her hands off of him."

I rolled my eyes. "Abuelita can't keep her hands off of him."

Abuelita arched an eyebrow. "He's very charming."

We all chuckled at her. Then, the doorbell rang.

Peter rushed to answer it, and there stood Hollin Abbey in a black tuxedo, carrying a bouquet of roses.

"Abbey," Peter said, pulling back to let him inside.

My eyes ran down the length of him. My mouth went dry. Abuelita was right. I wasn't going to be able to keep my hands off of him. My hands, my mouth, my body. Maybe we shouldn't even go to this thing, and I could stand here and objectify him forever.

His eyes were on mine as he equally gaped. I was the girl who loved blue jeans and boots. I wore skirts and dresses sometimes but nothing fancy. This was next level, and he was admiring me in the same way that I was admiring him.

When I didn't move, Peyton smiled and took the flowers. "They're beautiful."

He cleared his throat. "They're actually for Nina."

My grandma put a hand to her chest. "For me?"

"Yes. I thought you deserved them," Hollin said with a wink.

I grinned at him slyly. The little charmer. "That's nice of you."

"Well, thank you, Hollin," Abuelita said. She tried to stand, but Peyton stopped her.

"I'll put them in water for you."

"Come give me a hug before you go."

I hugged Abuelita. She felt smaller than before. I pressed a kiss to her cheek and told her that I loved her.

"Have fun," she told me sincerely.

"We will."

I waved good-bye to the rest of my family and followed Hollin out to his truck. "What? No motorcycle?"

He slid an arm around my waist and dragged me tight against him. "God, you're beautiful."

I laughed. "Me or the fact that I suggested your Harley?"

"Both." He kissed me long and hard, and I forgot the entire world existed in that kiss. "But mostly, I was worried about your hair."

I touched the perfect updo that Peyton had worked into my hair. He was probably right. It had taken forever to get my hair to cooperate. But maybe it would have been worth it. "Fair."

Hollin opened the passenger side door for me and helped me and all the layers of my dress into the truck. It was an effort in a million layers of tulle and satin and four-inch-high heels, but we managed. He got into the driver's side and turned for downtown and the new Buddy Holly Hall.

"Have you been inside the new building yet?"

He nodded. "I went once with Jordan and Julian, but it was during the day. You?"

"Just the ballet studio."

Peyton's company had their own studio space inside the

building. It was stunning and reminded me so much of the space she'd had in New York. I was sure that made her feel more at home.

"You're in for a treat."

Hollin parked out front, and as we headed inside the building, I saw how absolutely right he was. The hall was beyond impressive. Everything was mile-high ceilings with a giant, circular glass staircase and tiered balconies. A long bar had been set up on either end of the hall. And a string quartet was playing from a small stage, filling the room with music. It was modern, sleek, and stunning. I loved everything about it.

I found Annie, Blaire, and Jennifer as soon as we entered.

Blaire squealed at the sight of my dress and flung her arms around me. "Look at you!"

I laughed. "Thanks. It's all your doing."

"Psh, I found the perfect dress. You're the one wearing it."

All of my friends looked incredible. From Blaire in a powder-blue dress that clung to her with a thigh-high slit, to Jennifer in a more modest pale pink number with a full skirt, to Annie, ever daring, in a sleek forest-green dress that had cutouts on both sides.

Hollin kissed my temple and then went to get drinks.

"Y'all seem happy," Annie said.

"We are."

"I love to see it," Jennifer said.

"We all do," Blaire chimed in.

"Where are the guys?" I asked to take the focus off of me.

"Jordan and Julian went to schmooze the team owner," Annie said with an eye roll.

"Sounds like them."

"They're up there with Jensen and Morgan," Jennifer said, pointing to the front of the room, where the CEOs of Wright Construction and Wright Architecture stood with the owners of Wright Vineyard. It was a big Wright-fest.

The rest of the Wrights were scattered around the room. Austin and Julia stood with Landon and Heidi, laughing at each other. Morgan's fiancé, Patrick, walked up to his best friend, Austin, and punched him in the arm. They leaned in to talk to one another. I didn't see Emery, but that was unsurprising. It had only been six weeks since Easter. She was probably home with baby Logan. I'd never been involved with the Wrights until Jordan and Julian moved into town. Now, I felt like part of their royal circle in some way. They'd even invited all of us to Jensen's lake house out at Ransom Canyon for Memorial Day weekend. I didn't think Hollin and I would make it back from the award ceremony in time, but it was a nice gesture all the same.

The team owner stood up to make a speech, thanking everyone for coming and for their support. Hollin came back with my drink—a Bombay and lime. He handed one off to Blaire, too, and she thanked him profusely.

"This is the stuff," she said, taking a sip.

Afterward, we relocated to the auditorium for a special performance by the Lubbock Ballet Company. Peyton was effervescent. It had been a while since I'd seen her onstage. She reprised her role as the Sugar Plum Fairy during *The Nutcracker* each year, but that had been months ago. Watching her dance brought me right back to my childhood. I'd spent more hours watching my own sister take flight than I'd put into any kind of sport or event that I was interested in. Well, besides the winery...and that had ended well for me.

"I'm going to sneak backstage to see her," I told Hollin. "I'll be right back."

"Give her my regards. That was great, and I know nothing about ballet."

I laughed. "It's amazing what happens when she lets her knee rest."

He roughly kissed me. "Don't be gone too long."

"Oh, boo. You'll have to make friends with the soccer team."

He laughed. "Yeah, what a hardship."

I grinned and disentangled myself from him. I found the stage door and entered backstage. I recognized the rest of the artistic staff, who waved at me. Then, I found Isaac and Aly watching from the wings. Aly was in a tutu, as if we could get the girl out of the damn thing.

"Hey," Isaac said. "What did you think?"

"She was perfect."

"Isn't she always?" he asked, practically glowing for his fiancée. He'd helped construct this building and the soccer complex, and he was prouder of Peyton's fifteen minutes onstage.

"Miss Peyton promised to teach me this role," Aly said very seriously. "She said that I just need to work on my pirouettes."

"Absolutely," I agreed. "You can do anything you put your mind to."

Tori trotted over. "Hey, Piper!" We hugged like lifelong friends. "Oh my God, I heard about the winery. That's terrifying."

"It was."

"I'm glad you're okay and that y'all were able to move the wedding to a different location. Peyton has been talking about it nonstop at work."

"I bet she has. Luckily, the wedding planner is handling everything."

"Thank God for her!"

Aly took ahold of Tori's dress and yanked twice. "Excuse me. Where is Miss Peyton?"

Tori dropped to Aly's height. "That is an excellent question. She was changing. She should be here any minute. Do you want to have your turn on the stage? If we're quiet as mice, we can dance out there."

Aly's eyes widened to saucers. "Yes, yes, yes!"

Tori looked to Isaac. "Is it all right?"

"She'd hate me forever if I didn't let her. Go ahead."

Tori took Aly's hand, and they crept like mice onto the stage. Then, they did jumps and turns and pranced around the stage. I laughed with Isaac at the sight, and Peyton showed up in a long yellow dress.

"Oh my goodness," she said. "How adorable."

"Seester, you were brilliant," I said, hugging her tight.

Peyton squeezed me back just as hard. "Thanks. Not my best, but—"

"Hey," Isaac said with a sharp look at her. "You're still a principal to me."

"I love you," she said, falling into his arms.

I couldn't wait for them to be married next weekend. What could be more perfect than high school sweethearts reunited? They'd finally gotten it all to work out, and their love transcended. And I realized...for the first time...that I wasn't overwhelmingly jealous of what they had.

My heart fluttered. I *had* what they had.

Was I falling in love with Hollin Abbey?

29

HOLLIN

*W*hen the performance was over, the party returned to the atrium. The string quartet was replaced with a local DJ, and everyone took to the dance floor. Jordan introduced me to the owners and one of the players from the MLS team FC Dallas, who was on loan to our team for the opening season. Levi Branson was only eighteen years old and already one of the best up-and-coming players in the MLS. It was crazy to think I'd be able to watch him from home all season.

"Hard to believe the whole team rests on one eighteen-year-old," Jordan said as we stepped away.

"Agreed. Pretty wild."

"Ah, there they are."

I looked in the direction he pointed and saw Julian and the unmistakably related Weston Wright. Jordan and Julian were my cousins on their mom's side, but their half-brother wasn't related to me at all. It was weird. But either way, I was just glad to see him.

"Weston, you remember Hollin?" Julian said.

"Yeah. We met last summer briefly."

I shook his hand. "Good to see you back in town."

"Didn't plan to make my reappearance at a black-tie event." He tugged on his suit. "But my band dissolved in the middle of Eastern Europe this spring. I said *fuck it* and flew back to the States."

"How exactly does a band dissolve in the middle of another country?"

Weston rolled his eyes. "It's a long story. Drugs, an arrest, and a deportation. I decided I was over it. I like to play the keys, but I'm not here for the rest of it."

I laughed. It was a rough life out on the road, and Weston only played backup, not like Campbell.

"That sounds wild. So, what are you doing now? Going to try to get into another band in Seattle?"

Jordan and Julian exchanged a look. The same one they'd given each other the last time Weston was brought up. As if they had a secret and they weren't sharing with the class.

"Actually," Weston said, "I'm moving here."

My jaw dropped. "Really?"

"Yeah. There's a local music studio where I could work part-time. Worst-case scenario, I find a job in IT again." He glowered at that thought. "Not what I want to be doing, but whatever pays the bills. And it'd be good to get to know my brothers."

"We're glad you're moving here," Julian said automatically.

Jordan shoved his hands into his pockets. "Just wish we could have convinced Whitton, too."

"Whitt," Weston said with a sigh. "He's...I don't know. Hopefully, he'll come around when Harley graduates."

"Why is that?" I asked, confused.

Weston glanced over at me and smiled. "She got into

Texas Tech. Mom was furious that she wanted to move halfway across the country, but she's a National Merit Scholar, and she's going for free. She'll be here in August."

"Wow. Smart girl."

"She always has been," Weston said. "Let's hope Whitt comes with her."

"Dance with me," Annie said, shimmying up to Jordan with a grin.

He sighed, as if suffering. "No two-stepping."

"Oh, but you do it so well," she joked with a wink.

"I believe that is my cue," Jordan said as he disappeared onto the dance floor.

Julian followed with Jennifer. And Blaire even grabbed Weston's hand. He looked baffled by her beauty and stumbled out onto the floor. Turned out, he had moves though. Under that shaggy hair and rockstar broodiness was a good dancer.

My date was still absent.

I found Nora also standing alone and leaned back against the table next to her. "Where's August?"

She shrugged. "He said he was going to the restroom. Haven't seen him since."

"Piper has been gone forever, too."

I wanted to be out there on the dance floor with my girlfriend. I'd never wanted that before. This was all surprisingly new territory for me. To want to spend all my time with Piper was a marvel.

"Restroom?" Nora asked.

"Peyton."

"Ah, yeah, well, that makes sense. She looked stunning tonight."

"She floated," I said, crossing my arms.

"I can get you backstage," Nora said. "If you miss your girlfriend that much. You're pouting."

"I am not pouting," I said, glaring at my little sister.

She laughed. "I'm glad you're happy. Here, let me show you."

I followed her out of the main atrium. "How do you know how to get backstage anyway?"

"Event planner," she said, pointing at herself, "remember?"

"Right."

Nora opened a side door that I hadn't even known existed. We slipped into a service hallway, and Nora gestured to move to the right.

"The backstage of the theater is around this corner and down the next hall," she said.

But when we turned the corner, she froze. I nearly stumbled right into her. Then, I saw what had stalled her feet. August had another girl pressed up against a wall in an alcove. The pale skin of her leg was visible as she had it currently wrapped around his hip. Her other hand was in his hair, and they were kissing. Actually, they were going to town. One step away from fucking in this darkened corner.

"Motherfucker," I growled.

I launched myself at August, grabbing him by the collar of his tux and yanking him backward. I threw a punch without even thinking about it. The bastard fucking deserved it. The satisfying sound of my fist crunching into his face made it all worth it.

"Fuck," August cried. He covered his nose, which was now bleeding, spattering blood onto his white shirt.

"Hollin, stop," Nora cried.

I released the asshole with a hard shove. He stumbled backward a step, his hand coming up to his nose to stop the bleeding. The girl rushed forward, as if to help him, and it was then that we both caught sight of who August had been kissing.

"Tamara?" Nora squeaked.

Her best friend stood there, flushed and disheveled, and had the audacity to look concerned. "Oh my God, Nor."

August gaped at the lot of us. "It's not what it looks like."

"What does it look like?" I snapped.

Nora's eyes lurched between August and Tamara.

Her boyfriend. Her best friend.

Her boyfriend. Her best friend.

August and Tamara had dated in high school, but it was a brief thing. When they went to college, August and Nora got together. Tamara had gone to school in Dallas and only moved back in the last year. Nora and August had been dating for years, and Tamara hadn't even been a blip on the radar. In fact, all she'd done the last six months was hit on *me*.

"It looks like you were making out with my best friend," Nora snarled. Despite how strong she sounded, there were tears in her eyes, and her hands were clenched into fists. She must be falling apart inside.

"I can explain," August said. "Please, Nora."

He reached for her. Nora shied back in fear, and I came to stand between them.

"Don't fucking touch her."

August shrank back at the sight of me.

"How can you explain?" Nora asked. "How?"

"We were going to tell you," Tamara said, bursting into rehearsed tears.

Nora froze at those words. "Tell me what? This wasn't...spontaneous?"

August shot Tamara a look that could kill. Which told

me all that I needed to know. This definitely had not been the first time.

"How long has this been going on?" Nora demanded.

"It's...new," August said.

But Tamara had no gumption. "Since the concert."

"The Cosmere concert?" Nora gaped at them. "When I went to see my brother and both of you conveniently had to stay behind?"

I did the math. We'd gone to see Campbell two months ago. Fuck.

"Shut up, Tamara," August said.

"She deserves to know the truth," Tamara cried. "I was flirting with Hollin all this time to make August see that he needed to break up with you."

Nora's jaw dropped. My eyes widened. Well, I hadn't expected that.

"You've been flirting with me since you got the job at Wright Vineyard. Don't try to twist this," I roared at her.

Tamara pulled into herself, away from my anger. She turned back to her best friend. "I'm sorry, Nora. But we're in love. We were always meant to be. He didn't know how to tell you."

"What the fuck?" I growled.

Nora shook her head, taking another step back. I needed to get her out of here. This had gone too far. Tamara was being purposefully cruel now, and Nora didn't deserve that. She didn't deserve any of it.

"What's going on, y'all?" Piper said as she traipsed down the hallway. "I heard your voices."

Her feet stalled as she took in the sight before her. Me standing between Nora and August. Tamara's disheveled appearance. August's broken nose.

"Is everything okay?"

I shook my head and put my arm around my little sister. "We were just leaving."

"Nora, wait," August said.

"I don't think so," I spat. "You did all your explaining with your tongue down someone else's throat."

Piper stepped up next to me. There was fire in her eyes as well. "We're leaving. And you should, too."

I herded Nora back the way that we'd come. She didn't make a single sound until we were out of the hallway, across the atrium, and back in the fresh air.

"Are you okay?" Piper asked, reaching for Nora.

She sniffled and then burst into tears. Piper took her in her arms. I felt murderous at the sight. That douche bag had made my sister cry. I was going to kill him. I was going to fucking wreck his life.

And Tamara. I seethed. The way she had acted around me got on my nerves, but I hadn't realized she was capable of such deception. And I still had to work with her. It wasn't like I could fire her for hurting my sister.

"Let's get you home," Piper encouraged.

"No," Nora said with a sniffle. "I can...I can get an Uber. I don't want y'all to miss the party."

"Hey, it's okay."

"We don't mind at all. You shouldn't have to take an Uber or be home alone."

Nora wiped at her eyes. "Are you sure? I don't want to be a bother."

"Shush now," Piper said, holding her close again. "You're not a bother to anyone." She looked up at me. "Go get the truck."

I nodded and jogged across the parking lot to my truck and drove at illegal speeds to get back up to the front of the building. Together, we helped Nora into the backseat, and then I took off across town.

Piper sat in the back with Nora with her arm around her for support. What I'd felt before for Piper was one thing, but as I looked at her taking care of my sister, my heart swelled almost uncomfortably.

I'd never felt like this before. Like I'd do anything for this girl. To see her give up her night out in that beautiful dress for someone else, someone I cared about...I didn't even have words for that.

Okay, I had one word.

But I'd never said it out loud to anyone who wasn't family. I didn't know if I was ready to say it right now either. Didn't stop me from feeling it.

30

PIPER

"*A*re you sure you want to go home?" Hollin asked from the front seat. "You should stay in my guest room."

Nora shook her head. "I want to crawl into my own bed."

He met my gaze and frowned. "Don't you live with Tamara?"

She froze. As if the thought hadn't hit her before that moment. "Fuck."

I gritted my teeth. I knew exactly what she was going through. I'd lost two friends and roommates to a terrible situation like this. It had been Hollin's fault all those years ago, and it was certainly August's fault now. Though much of the blame rested with Tamara as well.

"I'm going to need to move out," she muttered. "Where am I going to live? What about my lease?" She hit her head on the back of the seat. "Fuck, what am I going to do?"

"You can stay with me for now," Hollin said. "After that, we'll figure it out. One day at a time."

"It's best not to go back tonight," I told her. "You don't

want to deal with her if she comes home...or wonder where she is if she doesn't."

Nora ground her teeth together and nodded. "Fine."

Hollin pulled off the loop to head to his house instead of Nora's apartment. Nora was silent the rest of the way home. I wasn't sure if she was seething or trying to hold herself together. Either way, I was glad that she wouldn't be alone tonight. Hollin parked in his garage.

"Do you need anything?" I asked as we entered the house. "Ice cream?"

"No," she said with a sniffle, rubbing the back of her hand across her eyes. "I'm going to get into bed. Maybe take a shower. Thanks for doing this. Really."

I crossed my arms and watched her with concern as she disappeared into the spare bedroom. A minute later, I heard the shower turn on.

"Fuck, this sucks," Hollin ground out.

"Yeah. Poor Nora."

"What a fucking idiot! He should be glad Campbell wasn't here. If you think I overreacted for punching him, wait and see what happens when Campbell finds out."

"I don't think you overreacted."

"Yeah?"

"I wanted to punch him, too," I admitted. "It makes no sense. They were so happy. They were together all the time. I remember him dropping by the winery when she was meeting with Peyton just to bring her Starbucks. How do you go from that to kissing her best friend?"

"I don't know, but they've been doing a lot more than kissing."

I cringed. "I agree."

"Fuck."

Hollin kicked the baseboard in frustration. "This isn't how I wanted the night to go."

He walked into the kitchen and pulled out a bottle of wine.

"We need something stronger."

He glanced up at me, and a flicker of a smile hit his lips. "You're probably right."

He replaced the bottle and grabbed whiskey instead. I strode over to the kitchen, sinking into a seat at the island. He poured us each a knuckle's worth of the stuff and slid the glass into my hand.

I took a sip and flinched slightly. It was good whiskey. I only drank the stuff under extreme circumstances. Gin and wine were more my preference. But tonight had been hard, and we needed hard stuff to go with it.

Hollin chuckled at my expression. "Well, at least there's some alcohol that makes you pull a face."

"There's plenty of alcohol that does that."

"I've watched you toss back tequila shots like it was nothing."

"It was nothing."

He shook his head. "You're some woman."

"Whiskey has its own particular burn."

"Tequila gets me naked," Hollin said.

I arched an eyebrow and swirled the drink. "That so? You were mostly clothed on that tour bus."

He met my gaze. "That's true. Maybe it makes me want to fuck."

"Mission accomplished. Should we switch to tequila?" I winked at him.

It was enough to bring out that cocky smile that I'd somehow come to adore. I didn't know when it had happened.

One minute, that smile had made me want to fight him at every turn, and now, it made me wonder if he was going to take my clothes off right then and there. Had it always been a sexual look and I'd made it seem like this terrible thing?

"I need tequila to get your clothes off anymore," he teased.

I shot him a challenging look back. "If you're lucky."

"Babe, it's not about luck."

I laughed at the arrogant way he'd delivered the line. It would have bothered me before, and now, I found it endearing.

I tossed back the rest of my whiskey. He refilled the glass, unprompted, nursing his own drink.

I read the lines of him. The muscular shoulders that fell into the tapered waist. The tuxedo elongated his square build and took him from cowboy to billionaire in the change of fabric. I liked the duality. That he could pull off a suit just as well as his Wranglers and Stetson. The truck just as well as riding around on his Harley. He wasn't one thing; he was everything.

"How did you want the night to go?"

"Hmm?" he asked, peeping up at me from where he'd been staring into his whiskey.

"You said this wasn't how you wanted the night to go."

"Oh." A soft blush came to his cheeks, and somehow, that was even hotter. "I guess I had this idea that we were going to dance all night. I wanted to show off my girlfriend to the rest of the world. And now, we're back here. No dance. No showing off. And my sister is heartbroken."

I finished the whiskey and set it back down on the counter. "Well, I can fix one of those things."

I offered him my hand. He looked down at it for a

second before putting his into mine. I directed him out of the kitchen and opened the back door.

"What are you..."

"Trust me," I told him.

We stepped out onto the back deck and under the pergola. The May night was warm, but Lubbock was more desert than not. So, the nights were cool, and the wind blew in, making the heat more bearable. It was a perfect night. The stars bright and twinkling overhead. And the moon just a crescent sliver in the sky.

I wrapped my arms around Hollin's shoulders and adjusted his hands to my waist. The back of my dress was incredibly low, and with the way he held me with his hands, his fingers brushed against the bare skin. I shivered slightly at the touch. So intimate.

Then, we swayed side to side. No music. No people. No big, beautiful gala.

Just the two of us, cocooned by the night sky. Wrapped in all her glory. The swelling depths of affection drew us together until there was nothing left.

I rested my head on his shoulder, and he pulled me even closer against him.

"This was what I wanted," I said with a soft sigh of pleasure. "This was *all* I wanted."

"Me too." Hollin kissed the top of my head and held me close, repeating, "Me too."

31

PIPER

*W*ith Peyton's wedding coming up so quickly, I spent all of my free time helping her prepare. And there was a lot more to do now that the wedding had to be moved to Wright Vineyard on such short notice. Nora was taking on the bulk of the change, but it was clear that after what had happened with August, she was only a shell of herself.

She wasn't crying like she had been that night at the gala. But she wasn't...happy either. In fact, the poor girl was in mourning. She hadn't just lost her boyfriend. She'd lost her best friend, too. I tried to be there for her, as did the other girls, but it wasn't the same. She'd known Tamara all her life. And the two people she would normally turn to with her heartbreak were the ones who had sundered her heart.

She'd even ditched her high heels for most of the week. I rarely saw her in flats off of the soccer pitch and sometimes forgot that she was only five feet tall. It was as if they had even stolen her extra height.

But the biggest problem of them all was still the wedding dress.

We'd found a few dresses in town that fit, but none of them were what Peyton wanted. Especially not compared to the designer dress that had been destroyed in the fire. Even though there was nothing I could do about it, I still felt deeply responsible.

"It's not your fault," Peyton said the morning before the wedding. "And anyway, we're going to get this fixed. Katherine said she could handle the mission."

Katherine Van Pelt was a friend of Peyton's from her time in New York City. Her and her husband, Camden Percy, were flying down for the wedding. Katherine had once been a model and was in the know with designers. She'd reached out to a few with Peyton's measurements and promised to fly in with what she found. She'd landed in Lubbock, and she would be coming straight to the hotel suite Peyton had gotten for the weekend.

"I know," I said. "I feel like I put unnecessary stress on you."

"You *caused* the fire in the barn?"

"No."

"And you purposefully put the dress somewhere you couldn't reach it?"

I rolled my eyes. "No."

"Then shut up," my sister said with a laugh. "It's not your fault that my dress was burned to a crisp and that the venue was destroyed. It was a fluke. A one in a million chance. We're here now. We're making the best of it. I don't want my maid of honor to feel guilty."

I nodded. "Okay."

I'd braved a burning building to try to rescue that dress. There was nothing else I could do at this point. I was just anxious to have the dress problem rectified. It would feel like tomorrow could go off without a hitch.

Finally, an hour later, a knock sounded on the door. I rushed to open it, and there stood Katherine Van Pelt in all her glory. She was tall with cascading brown hair and the kind of figure people would kill for. She was Helen of Troy or Aphrodite. Songs had been sung about her. Wars had been waged for her. Just a tilt of her full lips sent men falling to their knees.

"Well, your fairy godmother has arrived," she said with an arch of one eyebrow. Her designer bag hung from one arm, and she was in a red dress that clung to her narrow frame with black stilettos.

She strode into the suite as if she owned it. Considering her husband was the CEO and majority shareholder of Percy Hotels, it was entirely possible that she did. Behind her, she enlisted the staff to wheel in racks of white dresses, all carefully hidden behind a variety of designer bags.

"Thank you," she said, tipping each of them generously, as if money grew on trees. "Camden sends his regards. He has business to attend to, and then he's going golfing all day. Apparently, he befriended a PGA golfer here. Who knew you had a PGA golfer in Lubbock?"

I grinned. "Landon Wright?"

"Oh, you know him?" she asked.

Peyton laughed and stood to embrace Katherine. "He's kind of royalty around these parts. The vineyard we're getting married at belongs to his cousin."

"Charming," she said. "Well, let's get to it. You're going to like one of these gowns. I just know it."

"I can't thank you enough for doing this," Peyton said. "You're a lifesaver."

"Fashion is my specialty. Honestly, watching all the

designers fall over themselves to get me what I wanted was pure entertainment in itself," she said with a grin. "Now, where is the champagne?"

I popped open the bubbly and passed out drinks. We sipped from a rosé Moët & Chandon while Peyton worked her way into the dresses. I helped with buttons and zippers and clasps. There were *so* many of them on each and every dress.

Despite Katherine's assurances that they were all to Peyton's measurements, they didn't all fit. One dress was all smooth edges, except for a pooch at the waist. One fit her waist, but the lace at the underarms was strangely long. One was just an inch too long, even in her wedding heels.

Katherine hissed at that and offered to shred the designer a new one. Height wasn't going to change regardless.

Peyton laughed it all off. "There's going to be the perfect one in here. Don't worry about it."

As someone who had spent most of her life being fitted for tutus of every style and variety, Peyton was having the time of her life. Trying on all of these dresses made her smile and preen and twirl. As if each one were a new costume she was putting on for a performance.

Finally, we fitted her into one. I finished buttoning up the dozen buttons on the back, and then I stepped aside. She stood before the full-length mirror with an awed expression before facing us.

Katherine clapped softly. "That's it. That's the one."

"I love it," I gasped.

Peyton covered her mouth as tears came to her eyes. "It's perfect."

It was even better than the one that had been *made* for her. The one at the bottom of a fiery grave. Somehow, this fit her lithe ballet figure to perfection. The bust was all lace in an almost balconette structure with visible boning that gave the top a corseted look. An airy tulle skirt reminiscent of all the past ballets Peyton had danced in fell to the floor with an embroidered floral design starting at the top and tapering off. The entire thing shimmered slightly when it caught the light. And to her delight, it had two of her favorite things—a hidden slit to reveal her baby-blue heels and, best of all, pockets.

"Who designed this?" Peyton asked. "I must write to the designer to thank them."

"Of all people, Harmony Cunningham," Katherine said, standing and fingering the skirt. "Her mother handed over most of the reins to Cunningham Couture to her, and it is *blooming*. Who knew that taking the girl out of the spotlight would revitalize the brand?"

"I used to always want to wear Elizabeth Cunningham's vision," Peyton admitted.

"She designed my wedding dress," Katherine said. "Well, that's the one. I'll tell Harmony. She'll be pleased. You'll probably even have your wedding in magazines."

Peyton laughed. "That was already going to happen. Ex-prima and her new beau." She rolled her eyes. "Magazines have been hounding me for the last year."

"And in that dress, you'll be the highlight of the season."

"Thank you, Katherine," Peyton said, drawing her into a hug. She turned to me next. "See? Nothing to worry about."

"You were right," I told her. "Now, let's get you married."

"I'll say, 'I now pronounce you man and wife,' " the pastor said.

"Then we kiss," Isaac said with a wink.

Peyton flushed.

The pastor laughed. "Exactly," he said.

I stood off to the side of Peyton, holding her fake bouquet during the rehearsal. Peter was on my other side. Jordan and Annie stood for Isaac across from me and my brother. I liked that they'd gone nontraditional and had their people on either side rather than separating guys and girls. At the end, Jordan and Annie would walk down the aisle together, a precursor to their impending wedding. And I'd walk with my twin. It was going to be perfect.

"And that's that," the pastor said. He gestured to Nora. "All yours."

Nora nodded solemnly. She was back in her heels, trying so hard to regain the bounce in her step. But she didn't quite manage it. She was professional but not enthusiastic.

"Excellent. Let's do the walk out. Each aisle will go one at a time, starting with Peyton's family and then Isaac's," Nora said, directing everyone. "Afterward, we'll take family pictures. While that is going on, we'll move everyone inside to the barn. Any questions?"

The parents all crowded around poor Nora. Isaac and Peyton were speaking with the pastor about the wording and such. I stood with my brother, Jordan, and Annie.

"It's hot as hell," Peter grumbled.

"Supposed to be worse tomorrow," I told him.

"Great."

Annie laughed. "This isn't even a bad May day."

Jordan shook his head. "At least you aren't in a three-piece suit."

"Exactly," Peter added.

Annie and I exchanged a conspiratorial smile. We'd gotten lucky. Peyton didn't care one lick about what we were wearing as long as it was in the champagne, rose gold, or blush family. We'd gone shopping together this winter and picked something out that didn't cost either of us a fortune and ended up with these gorgeous, shimmery dresses. They weren't exactly the same, as we were different builds, but they complemented each other. In fact, they worked out even better with Peyton's new dress. I couldn't wait to see the entire vision come to life.

Jordan had just gotten on the phone for business when another truck pulled into the parking lot. My smile lit up when I recognized it. I traipsed across the lawn of Wright Vineyard and rapped on the window.

Hollin rolled it down and hung slightly out the side. "Can I help you, ma'am?" he drawled, low and country.

I laughed. "That is quite some twang you have on you."

He tipped his cowboy hat at me. "Ma'am."

"You're ridiculous. I didn't think you were coming up here for the rehearsal."

"I wasn't," he said as he popped the door of his truck. "But I wanted to see you."

"Oh good."

He wrapped an arm around my waist and kissed me. He'd been letting a beard grow out the last week, and the whiskers scratched against my face. I hadn't minded them scratchy elsewhere.

"You keeping this?" I asked, pulling gently on the beard.

"You like it?"

"I am yet undecided. You look good either way."

"Well, it'll be gone soon. We all agreed not to shave until the wedding. Julian hates it," he said with a laugh. "So, it's half the fun."

"Ah, I see. No wonder Jordan and Isaac both have beards. Why did you even decide this?"

Hollin shrugged. "We're guys. I don't know."

I rolled my eyes. Typical.

He took my hand in his as we returned to the rehearsal. Everyone had moved out of the baking sun and into the air-conditioned barn. Thankfully, the reception would be indoors even if the wedding was out in the sun.

Jordan and Isaac both shook hands with Hollin.

"Just think, you're next," Isaac told Jordan.

"Patrick first," he said with a laugh.

"Sure. Patrick and then us," Annie said with a smile. Her eyes darted down to her ring. She hadn't stopped messing with it since he'd proposed.

"And who's after that?" Isaac asked. "Julian?"

Jordan quirked a self-satisfied smile. "Maybe Hollin."

I laughed at the suggestion. We'd only been dating since Easter. Julian and Jennifer had been dating a year. There was no way that was in our future yet.

Hollin pulled a ridiculous face. "Yeah, right. We all know Julian is next."

I frowned slightly at the way he'd said it. The way he'd scrunched up his face. The immediate denial. It wasn't like I was looking to get married. Far from it. But I'd stopped to consider it. I'd said *yet* in my head. That was a huge step forward, but eventually, I wanted to get married. Maybe even to Hollin.

Hollin frowned. "What?"

I laughed, brushing it off. It was stupid. A month ago, I hadn't even wanted to date him. "Awfully quick about that Abbey."

He pressed a kiss to my lips. "It is Julian next. That's all I'm saying."

"Someday, dude," Jordan said, clapping him on the shoulder. "Someday, you'll have to grow up."

"That day is not today," Hollin said. "Marriage is a trap."

That sounded more like his issue with his mom. Marriage had to seem that way to him after what he'd gone through. Maybe it had nothing to do with me at all, and I was reading into it. I didn't need to read into anything with Hollin. He always said exactly what he was thinking with me.

Annie caught my attention and rolled her eyes. She mouthed, *Men*.

We both laughed.

She sidled up next to me. "Jordan was the same way, I swear. And then, bam, he couldn't live without me."

"Sounds right."

I pushed it from my brain. One day, I'd get there, just like everyone else.

And when he glanced back at me and smiled, I knew I was far past gone. I wanted it to be with Hollin. I wanted everything with him.

32

HOLLIN

*T*oday was the wedding, but that wasn't what I was excited for. It was in second place to my brother coming home. The tour was officially over, and he was off until he had to get back into the studio and work on a new album. Normally, he'd hole up in LA, but things were different. Now, he was coming back home.

Nora had wanted to come with me to pick him up from the airport, but she was too busy with the wedding. She was still furious with August and Tamara. Not that I could blame her. I'd gotten a bunch of boxes and helped her pack up her apartment. She was currently living in my guest room. Dad had offered for her to stay with him, but she hadn't wanted to. Moving back home would have felt like a defeat. I didn't know how she was putting on a happy face. She was a professional—that was for sure.

Having Campbell home was going to help her, too.

Campbell had given me directions to pick him up from the private terminal where he had his own suite. He was driven straight to the airplane, and all of his baggage was handled exclusively. Lubbock was a small airport, but it still had all the luxury for when celebrities came through.

He'd argued that I didn't need to pick him up at all. They had BMWs to cart him around as part of the service. But I'd called him a pretentious prick, and he'd agreed to let me pick him up.

I pulled up in front of the private entrance, and a second later, he exited, looking like the rockstar he was—Ray-Bans, leather jacket, and all. Campbell had always had his own style and never cared what anyone thought. But since he'd gotten famous and had designers working with him, he'd grown from a little punk kid into what he was now. And as ridiculous as it was, he could even pull off leather pants.

"Hey, fucker," I said as he opened the door.

He shot me a look. "At least you keep me down-to-earth."

"That's what I'm here for."

He slung his leather duffel and rolling suitcase into the back and dropped into the passenger seat. "Fuck, it's good to be out of the airport. The last leg across Asia was rough. I'm going to be jet-lagged for days."

"You up for this wedding?"

Campbell ran a hand back through his hair. "Yeah, sure. Why not? If I fall asleep on my feet, it's not my fault."

"I'll be sure to let Peyton and Isaac know."

Campbell yawned. "Wake me when we get there."

"You're going to want to be awake to hear this."

He tipped his head at me. "Hear what?"

I explained to him what had happened with Nora, August, and Tamara. His expression went from puzzled to furious in a matter of minutes.

"Are you fucking kidding me?"

"Nope. I saw it myself."

Campbell's face darkened further. "Where does he live?"

"Plotting an arson?"

"Ah, good call, brother," he said. "I was thinking we beat the shit out of him, but sure, let's burn his house down."

I laughed sardonically. But Campbell looked serious. I'd told Piper that I was glad Campbell hadn't been there. He had a temper. It always ignited around our dad. They'd almost come to blows a few times when he was in high school. I worried about his image out on the road if he ever lost it like that in public. But so far, I hadn't seen anything. I hoped August wasn't stupid enough to show his face. It would take a lot of effort to not let Campbell cave his face in.

"Nah, we're not going to do anything else."

Campbell ground his teeth together. "He deserves to pay."

"Yeah, he does. But it's not up to us."

"How is she?"

"A mess."

"Fuck," Campbell said. "Well, I guess I won't sleep then."

I nodded at him. He understood in the way that only my brother could. Nora was a total wreck. She might try to play it off at work, but I was there when she came home at night and cried herself to sleep. It wasn't healthy, and I didn't know what to do other than be there for her.

"It'll help to have you around. When are you going back to LA?"

He shrugged. "I don't know. The rest of the band went home. Michael was up my ass to get back to his wife and kid. As if it was my fault. We'll see how long the record label will let me have downtime before demanding a new album."

"You have any material for it?"

"Yeah. I wrote about a hundred songs on the tour, but they all suck."

I laughed. "You say that about them all."

"Because it's true."

"Whatever. Everyone loves your music."

"Yeah. Just takes a lot more than my lyrics for it to become music. The group together makes it not suck."

"No plans to go solo?"

Campbell shot me a look. "Ask me how often I get asked that in interviews."

"Bet the band loves that."

"Yeah, they fucking love it," he said sarcastically. "And no, I have no plans for a solo career."

He was on top of the world. I was glad that he wasn't going to leave everyone else behind now that he'd gotten there.

I let him rest as I drove us to the winery. The wedding wasn't until this afternoon, so I'd let him get a power nap to combat the jet lag, but I wanted Nora to see him first. When I parked, Campbell woke groggily and all but fell out of the door.

Nora was running around frantically, directing the event. But when she caught sight of Campbell, she dropped everything and darted forward in her crazy high heels. They collided, and he hugged our sister tight.

"Hey, shrimp," he said with a laugh.

"I'm so glad you're here."

"Me too. Good to be on this side of the planet."

"You look like shit," she said.

He ran a hand back through his hair. "Thanks."

"And leather pants?" She cringed. "Seriously?"

"Thank God I have siblings," he said with a shake of his head.

"You're not wearing them to the wedding, right?"

He snorted. "No. Hollin's got me covered. I will be perfectly presentable."

"No guyliner?" Nora asked with a smirk. It was the first real smile I'd seen from her in a week.

"You two are the worst," Campbell said.

"Obviously." I faced Nora. "What's the schedule looking like?"

"Peyton is in hair and makeup. Piper, Peter, and Annie agreed to help with setup. They'll be leaving here any minute for hair and makeup. I have a long list of last-minute things that need to be done."

"Tell me what to do."

Campbell groaned. "Direct me somewhere to nap."

"Baby," Nora said affectionately.

I pointed Campbell in the direction of the offices. There was a couch that his long limbs wouldn't fit on, but it would be better than nothing. Nora listed off everything that she wanted me to do, and I followed her through the barn, which was decorated beyond comprehension, and out back to where the ceremony was being held.

The chairs were in place, but much of the remaining decor hadn't been put up yet. Except for a large wooden altar that was currently being installed. My eyes narrowed as I recognized the two figures in front of it.

"Is that Bradley?" I asked, grinding my teeth together.

"Yeah. He made the altar. He'd agreed to do it for Piper before they broke up. I've been the main contact though."

"What is she doing over there?"

Nora huffed. "Flowers."

Piper was attaching a cascade of flowers to the wooden archway. She and Bradley were talking, and she kept tilting her head back and laughing. They looked a little too comfy for my taste.

"I'm going to go say hi."

"Hollin," she said softly. "I have a lot of shit to do."

"Then do it. I'll be right back."

"Try not to be an ass."

"No promises."

She rolled her eyes, but she was staring past me to where my girlfriend stood with her ex. She swallowed at the sight. Nothing was happening with Piper and Bradley, but it was reminiscent enough of August and Tamara. She quickly turned away.

I stomped down the aisle toward Piper. She had her back to me and was laughing at something Bradley had said. I grabbed her around the waist, and she shrieked in surprise. Then, my lips were on her. And, yeah, I was being an ass, but she was mine.

Piper pushed me away with a laugh. "Hollin, stop it."

I arched an eyebrow. "No chance in hell."

She shoved me again and lowered her voice. "Be nice."

Nice? Yeah, no, I had no interest in nice. I wanted Bradley to know exactly where he stood right now. And that was not at Piper's side. They'd dated on and off for years. *Years.* How was I to compete with that? She'd always ended up going back to him. Time and time again. Obviously, this time was different because we were together. But I didn't want him to get any ideas.

"Hey, Hollin," Bradley said, offering me his hand.

I stood taller and shook it—hard. "Bradley."

"I was...just finishing up here." He glanced at Piper, and something passed between them. She frowned. "Have fun at the wedding."

He brushed past us and stormed away from the altar he'd built for the wedding.

"Hollin, Jesus," Piper said with a huff.

"What?"

"You don't have to be like that. You won. Isn't that enough?"

I balked at her anger. "So, I'm supposed to stand around and let you two reconnect?"

She rolled her eyes. "We weren't reconnecting. We're friends. I have no interest in him, and you know that. You didn't have to rub it in."

"Why not? It's fun."

But she pulled away from me as I reached for her again. "I should go apologize. I don't want him to think poorly of us. It's mean."

My eyes rounded. "You're going to go apologize to *him*?"

"Yeah, I am. Just because he wasn't right for me doesn't mean he's a bad guy." She pressed a kiss to my lips. Her expression softened. "You already have me. Isn't that enough?"

I tugged her against me again and stole another kiss.

She laughed. "I'll be right back."

She slipped through my fingers and disappeared after her ex-boyfriend. I glowered at his back. It might have been mean, but I was unaware I was supposed to care about his feelings. I didn't want to upset Piper, but she was mine to kiss whenever I wanted. Was it so bad to want Bradley to know it, too?

33

PIPER

"Bradley, wait," I called as I rushed off after him.

But he kept trudging across the open field, back to his truck. I jogged to keep up with him, glad that I hadn't had hair or makeup done yet.

"Wait."

He slowed to let me fall into step beside him. "What are you doing, Piper?"

"Trying to apologize."

Bradley raised his eyebrow. "Why? You got what you wanted, didn't you?"

"Don't be like that."

"Like what?" he asked. He jerked his head again, facing forward. "It's fine."

"It's not. I didn't want to rub it in or anything. We've been friends a long time."

"You're not rubbing it in," he ground out.

I shot him a look. "I know you're pissed."

Bradley stopped abruptly in the grass and faced me. "Fine. I'm pissed. Are you happy? Is that what you wanted to hear? Seeing you with him makes me want to set something on fire."

I winced at the analogy. "I don't joke about setting things on fire anymore."

He sighed and put a hand on my shoulder. "I'm sorry. I didn't mean it like that. I hate what happened to the winery, but I hated even more that I couldn't be there for you that day. And just...*Hollin*?" he asked in exasperation. "Hollin fucking Abbey, Piper?"

"I know. I didn't think it'd ever be him either."

"Did it start before or after we broke up?" Bradley demanded.

"After!" I said quickly. "Of course it was after. We didn't even like each other."

"You were wearing his shirt," he reminded me.

"I swear, that was unrelated."

Though...I had been attracted to him then. It had been the start of it all. Even if it hadn't been the day that we hooked up. Not that I planned to tell Bradley that.

"I can't believe *you* would pick *him*. You hated him for years. He's a player, and you know it."

I sighed. I was never going to be able to make this okay with Bradley. Maybe it was stupid to even try. "I don't want to discuss Hollin. I came here to apologize. That's it."

"Whatever. If you want to date the guy that every other person in town has dated, then by all means," he said, looking off in the distance, as if the thought pained him. "I didn't take you as a girl who would enjoy being second or third or fourth choice. Hell, a hundredth choice. He literally picked every girl in town over you. And I...I picked you over everyone else."

I wanted to respond, but what could I say? He wasn't wrong. And it wouldn't be enough either way.

Bradley realized I wasn't going to say anything else, shook his head, and stomped the rest of the way to his truck. I didn't follow him. I'd said what I had come to say. It was understandable that he was upset, but it didn't change how I felt about Hollin.

I headed back toward the altar, but Nora had already sent someone else to finish putting up flowers. She flagged me down.

"You're up for hair and makeup."

"Where did your brother go?" I asked her.

"I put him to work."

I sighed. Well, that talk would have to happen later. Hopefully, he wasn't mad that I'd gone after Bradley. But there wasn't anything I could do about it now. I needed to get ready.

The rest of the day went at lightning speed. We finished hair and makeup, and Jennifer showed up to take hundreds of pictures. Peyton and Isaac had a first look, and we took *more* pictures. Seeing Isaac's face when he got a glimpse of Peyton in that Cunningham Couture dress was the sweetest moment. I loved it so much for them. Aly pranced around through the pictures in her white-and-pink tulle dress. She made everyone laugh, and Jennifer insisted that the pictures were all the better for the natural smiles.

The wedding itself was short and sweet, just as it should be. Lots of laughter as they read their own vows. Tears as they choked up in the middle. Applause when they kissed. Isaac scooped up Aly and carried her out of the ceremony with her on one hip and Peyton on his other side. It was exactly what I'd always wanted for my sister.

We stayed behind for *more* pictures. This time with our entire family. Dad helped Abuelita into the shot. She'd been unsteady on her feet, and I'd been glad that an usher had escorted her into the venue.

After we stood for family pictures with both sets of families, we finally migrated into the barn. Isaac and Peyton initiated their first dance and encouraged everyone to get on their feet and join them.

I hadn't talked to Hollin again since the problem with Bradley this morning. I'd been too busy with all the wedding stuff. But he walked right up to me as soon as the DJ called for everyone to dance.

He swept me up into his arms. "You look beautiful."

My lips tilted up into a smile. "Thank you. I like this suit." My hand ran down the front of his charcoal suit. "Are you still mad about earlier?"

"Mad?" he asked with a furrowed brow. "Of course not. I was the ass. Nora reminded me multiple times that I was the ass."

I laughed. "That sounds like her."

"Yeah. She keeps Campbell and me on the straight and narrow."

"I'm glad. Because you know the thing with Bradley was nothing. He was jealous, and I should have let it go."

"It's all right, Piper." His gaze shifted behind me for a few seconds and back to my face. "We all have exes. It's all complicated."

"Yeah," I said with a shrug and then leaned my head against his chest.

"So...who is Blaire's date?"

I followed his gaze and found Blaire in a mint dress, dancing with a guy that I'd only seen from social media videos. "Ah, Nate King. Mr. Thirst Trap."

"Excuse me?" he asked.

"Yeah, he takes videos of himself, like pulling up his shirt and winking at the camera."

Hollin gave me an incredulous look. "Porn?"

I snorted. "No. Just like TikTok and Instagram and such. They met online. He lives in Midland, and they went on a date this week. She asked him to the wedding as a joke, and he said yes."

"My brother sure doesn't look pleased," Hollin noted.

Campbell sure as hell didn't look happy. He looked hot as hell though. I'd only seen him in his regular attire, which usually meant ripped jeans and leather jackets. But today, he was in a crisp black suit and tie. It had his own flair of eccentricity with gold trim and a shimmery gold pocket square. But still, it was the most put together I'd ever seen him.

He was currently glaring at my best friend's back. As if she'd purposely decided to bring a date to thwart him. Though...maybe she had.

"Do you know what happened with them?" I asked Hollin.

He shook his head. "He blows me off when I ask him."

"Blaire is the same way. She insists that Campbell didn't even know who she was in high school."

"Yeah, right. Not with that look."

"I know. Maybe it'll come to blows tonight, and we can finally find out."

Hollin snorted. "He's already on edge after what happened with Nora."

"Yeah, fuck August."

"No, thank you," he said, pulling me away from Blaire and Nate and Campbell.

The first dance ended, and we applauded. The rest of

the party went off without a hitch. The food was incredible, and the cake even better. I stood next to Hollin as the party did the Electric Slide.

"You're not going to join?" he asked.

"I have limits, and a wedding line dance is it."

He chuckled as he slid his phone out of his pocket and checked his messages. "That sounds right."

I watched Blaire, Annie, and Sutton shimmying to the dance. Peyton was at the center of it all, teaching the dance to Aly, who picked it up like clockwork. Jennifer stood nearby, taking pictures as everyone got down.

"Piper, come on!" Annie called.

"Get out here!" Blaire said.

"Right now," Peyton agreed.

Aly stomped her foot. "That's an order."

I snorted and shook my head. A second later, they all barreled off the dance floor toward me. "Oh God, save me."

Hollin laughed. "Have a good time."

"Ugh," I groaned.

"I'm going to go down to the cellar. I'll be back in a few minutes."

My friends grabbed my arms and dragged me out on the dance floor.

"Save me when you get back."

He shook his head as they ordered me into the Electric Slide. I went along with the words with disdain as Hollin somehow got out of the entire thing. Typical.

Once the music ended, I hustled off the dance floor. Peyton waved but let me retreat. She could only pull that off once and get away with it.

Blaire plopped into a chair next to me and kicked up her feet. "Thanks for joining us."

"It didn't look like I had much choice."

"What do you think about Nate?"

"He's hot," I told her. Nate was currently at the bar, talking to Jordan and Julian. "Seems to get along with everyone."

"Yeah."

"Pisses off Campbell."

"What?" she peeped.

"You haven't felt his gaze on you like a hot brand all night?"

Blaire rolled her eyes. "No way."

"Are you ever going to tell me what happened with y'all?"

"Nothing," she said automatically.

"Riiight," I drawled.

"I'm here with Nate, and that's all that matters."

"If you say so."

Blaire pinched her lips together. One day, I'd get the story out of her. One damn day.

Nate strode across the room and handed a drink to Blaire. "Bombay and lime."

"Excellent." She gestured to me. "Nate, this is my best friend, Piper."

Nate King was tall, dark, and handsome. I'd stalked his social media videos after Honey had confessed that Blaire was talking to him. He was drop-dead gorgeous. It was no wonder he had a million followers, who liked to watch him dance and sing and wink at the camera. He and Blaire had done a few videos together and the results were staggering. Apparently, their joint audiences liked them together, too.

I shook his hand. "Nice to meet you."

"You too," he said with a disarming smile.

I could see why he got millions of likes and follows. The charisma oozed out of his pores.

A slow song came on the speakers, and Nate held his hand out. "Dance?"

She grinned excitedly and put her hand in his. He dragged her out on the floor and whirled her around the room. I was happy for her. It had been a long time since I'd seen my friend even consider dating.

"What a party," a voice said, sliding into Blaire's unoccupied chair.

I found Chase Sinclair seated next to me. I'd seen him in the crowd, but the wedding was upward of four hundred people, and it had slipped my mind that he was even here. Small-town weddings were enormous. And since Peyton had had so many friends coming in from New York, it had swelled nearly out of control.

"Hey. Yeah, it's great, right?"

"I suppose." But he was watching Annie and Jordan out on the dance floor.

"Did you want to dance?" I asked. "Hollin left to take care of something. Work, I guess."

"I'll just sit, if you don't mind."

"Sure. I didn't realize that you were invited."

He arched an eyebrow. "I wasn't. I came here with a date. Tori. Do you know her?"

"Oh, Tori. Yeah. She works with Peyton."

"That's right. We met online," he said with a shrug. "Tinder."

"I'm happy for you," I told him honestly.

And after things hadn't worked out with him and Annie, I wanted him to be happy. We'd had one date, but it hadn't been anything special. Dating someone new was a good start for him.

"Thanks," he said with a self-deprecating smile. "It's nice to kick back. I've been working with my dad day and night.

The insurance company for the barn has been such a headache."

"What do you mean?" I asked in confusion.

"Well, you know," he said casually, "because he bought back Sinclair Cellars."

PART V

A LOVE LIKE WAR

34

PIPER

*M*y stomach dropped out of my body as we both came to our feet. "What are you talking about?"

Chase paled and straightened. "You *do* know, don't you?"

Every nerve in my body went numb at the same time. It couldn't be true. It just couldn't. No, Chase must be wrong.

"That's not possible."

He frowned. "I swore that you already knew."

"No. Why would you say something like that? The winery is my entire life. There is no way in a million years that my dad would sell to your family again. Never, ever, ever."

"Piper, I'm sorry."

I scrambled away from him. I couldn't deal with this right now. It wasn't true. It absolutely wasn't true. And my dad would confirm it. That was the only scenario that I would consider. Chase had wrong information. That was it.

I scoured the room for my dad. He was currently standing in a corner, talking with some people I only had vague recollections of. Some of Peyton's friends and a guy he golfed with. They were all laughing, as if my entire world wasn't imploding.

"Piper," Chase said, reaching for me again.

But I was well past whatever he was going to say. I needed to hear it straight from the source.

I hiked up my shimmery dress to march across the room. Someone tried to stop to talk to me, but I just kept going. My dad saw me coming, and his smile ignited.

"Piper!" he cheered. "You remember my friends—"

I interrupted him, "We need to talk."

He balked at my tone. If I'd used that voice with Abuelita or my mom, either one of them would have been cussing me out in Spanish for ten straight minutes until I got my attitude in order. My dad looked half-ready to start in on it, but I didn't have the energy for any of that today.

"Now," I barked.

He seemed shocked. "If you'll excuse me, I need to speak with my daughter."

The men all looked at me with wide eyes and raised eyebrows before hustling away. Let them talk. I didn't fucking care.

"What is it, *mija*?" my dad asked. "You were very disrespectful."

"Tell me it isn't true."

"What isn't true?" He conciliatorily held his hands out in front of him.

"Tell me," I ground out, "that you didn't sell the winery to the Sinclairs."

My dad opened his mouth and then closed it. "I, uh...I was going to tell you."

"Oh my God," I whispered, covering my mouth in horror.

Everything I'd felt earlier when Chase said the most

asinine thing I'd ever heard came back to me fresh and new. My stomach dropped hard, and at the same time, it felt as if it were in my throat. Everything tingled and ached as if I'd been hit by a bus. I was numb and empty and on fire and bleeding out, all at the same time. This couldn't be real.

"No," I whispered.

"Let's step outside," he said, gesturing to the open door at his back.

I rushed through the door and took in deep, heaving breaths. I couldn't get enough air in. I was hyperventilating. "How could you do this?"

He hurriedly closed the door. "It isn't what you think."

"What isn't what I think, Dad?" I demanded. "You sold us *out* to the Sinclairs. You sold the winery that *we* run. The winery that *we* have made what it is. I was always upset that you wanted to keep the name, but I understood. It made sense because it was an established brand. But now? I can't fathom what you were thinking."

"Listen, *mija*, we were in trouble."

"Trouble?" I asked. "What sort of trouble?"

He shook his head and paced away from me. "The IRS performed an audit on the company. Remember that last year?"

"Yes. Of course. We handed over all of our documents, and then all was well."

My dad shook his head. "No. We handed the documents over, and it turned out, the accountant we'd worked with for the last decade had been pocketing our tax payments and forging our paperwork."

"What?" I cried. "How could this have happened?"

"I had no idea. I trusted him with my life. But we weren't the only company that he did this to. We would have lost everything. We owed over a million in back payments. Plus fines and fees. There was no way I could afford that. There were only two options: bankruptcy or selling."

I shook my head. Desperation was taking over. This was too much. Far too much. "So, you sold."

"Bankruptcy would have been on our records for seven years. We never could have gotten anywhere. The winery would have been all but defunct. I took the only viable option."

"You reached out to Mr. Sinclair."

He nodded. "Arnold had been contacting me periodically over the last decade, as he'd resumed interest in the winery. I never took him seriously. I never had any intention of selling. But we needed the money."

"And you never told me," I hissed. "We could have done this together, Dad. You took it all on yourself."

"I did what needed to be done."

"That's why Chase has been coming around the winery. Why he was there when the barn burned down."

"Yes," my dad said. "I got Arnold to agree that we would continue to manage day-to-day operations. It's no different than before."

"No different?" I gasped. "Are you crazy? Everything has changed."

"Nothing has changed."

I stepped away from him. He had no idea of the absurdity of what he was saying, the enormity of how this affected us all. He might have gotten Mr. Sinclair to agree to treat it like normal, but for how long? Was it written into the contract? How did we know that we wouldn't all be fired tomorrow and put out on the street?

The bottom line was that the winery was no longer *mine*. I'd grown up there. It was the one constant in my life. The one thing I'd always loved and turned to. And now, it didn't even belong to me.

"You're wrong. This changes everything."

"Piper," my dad said earnestly.

I kicked off my uncomfortable heels and carried them as I walked away from my dad. I didn't want to cry in front of him. Didn't want to have to process all of this information in front of the person who had created this catastrophe.

And it was already done. Finalized and signed away. There was nothing I could do to fix it. I was fucked.

I couldn't go back to the party either. As much as I wanted to be in there, celebrating with my sister on her big day, there was no way I was going to be able to keep it together. Not now.

All I needed was my boyfriend. I needed Hollin to hold me and tell me that it was going to be all right. He'd gone through West Texas Winery falling apart and gotten Wright Vineyard out of it. There was hope, and only he could give it to me.

Tears streaked down my cheeks as I hurried down the walkway toward the cellar. I sure hoped that he was still down here and hadn't come back to the barn when I went outside to talk to my dad. I didn't even have my phone on me to text him and ask where he was. So, I kept walking far, far away from Peyton's happily ever after.

I opened the cellar, dropped my heels at the entrance, and headed down the worn wooden hallway toward Hollin's office. I choked back a sob and cracked the door.

"Hollin, I need to talk to you."

I froze.

Because Hollin wasn't alone.

He was standing in his office with his hands gripping Tori's shoulders.

35

PIPER

A vacuum opened in my mind, and all the air rushed out. There was nothing inside but a sense of depthless unknown. Because what I was seeing made no sense. I couldn't even process what they were doing together. Not after the last couple months. Not after finding August and Tamara together. Not after the way Hollin had reacted to seeing me just *talking* with Bradley.

I wanted to be the bold, stubborn, tough-as-nails Piper. I wanted to rip into him right then and there. To tear him apart for having the audacity to make me think he had changed and throwing it all back in my face.

But I'd been hurt too much today. I could barely stand after finding out about the winery. I'd yanked all of my walls down, hand over fist, to let Hollin into my heart. And then this? This was too much.

"What...what's going on?" I asked, my voice breaking on the words.

Hollin pushed Tori back a step. "Piper..."

My eyes tracked between the two as Tori slowly turned

to face me standing in the doorway. She bit her bottom lip and took another step away from Hollin.

"I don't understand."

"This isn't...it isn't what you think," Hollin said.

I almost laughed, but it came out as a muffled sob. "Isn't that what August said?"

The blow landed, and he winced. "I'm not anything like that fucking idiot. Nothing was happening here."

"You're alone with another girl."

"I'm just going to..." She gestured to pass by me.

But I blocked her path. She wasn't going to get to just leave.

"Aren't you here with Chase Sinclair?"

Hollin wrinkled his nose. "Seriously, Tori?"

She shrugged at Hollin. "I thought it'd piss you off the most."

I looked between them. My confusion deepened. They seemed to know each other. And here I'd thought, he was stupid enough to go back to his old ways. Give up on our relationship and fall for some other vapid girl. But it was more than that. Like I was missing the key to open the vault that explained how any of this made sense.

"I don't give a fuck who you're here with," Hollin growled.

And he looked angry. I'd seen him look like that before when dealing with August. It didn't absolve him of what the fuck was happening right now.

"Then, why are you down here with me?" Tori asked.

"I'd like to know that, too."

Hollin looked up at me helplessly. I didn't like that expression on him. He'd been caught, and now, he was acting the part of the prey. When I'd only ever seen him as the predator.

Tori sighed. "Just tell her."

"Tell me what?" I asked, hugging my arms to my chest.

"Tori is my...ex," Hollin finally said.

"So? Aren't there a hundred of them?"

"No," he said softly. "There's...just Tori."

I looked between them one more time, and it all fell into place. The ex-girlfriend who had wrecked his life. The one who had abandoned him after years of bullshit and left him in shambles. The very *reason* he'd been an asshole to my friends. The reason he hadn't dated since. Until me.

Lucky me.

"Okay," I said slowly. "The one who ruined your life?"

Tori huffed and stared at the ground. "Really, Hollin?"

"Shut up," he snapped.

Tori looked up at me and frowned. "I didn't mean to hurt you, Piper. I really did like you."

I blinked at her. "It sure doesn't seem like it."

"Wait...how do you even know each other?" Hollin asked.

"She works with Peyton," I said. "We've been getting lunch and stuff for a while. I'm going to guess that you knew the whole time that I was with Hollin."

"I figured it out after you told me about the concert."

I winced as I remembered divulging to her about the tour bus sex. It had been fine because I was talking to a stranger. Not realizing I was talking to his ex-girlfriend, who apparently still had designs on him.

God, I felt like an idiot.

"I don't deserve this."

"Please," Hollin said, reaching for me.

"Don't touch me!" I yelled at him. "Don't you dare touch me. I don't know why you're down here or what you're doing with her. But it all feels like a cosmic joke at my expense."

Hollin sighed heavily. "It's complicated."

"Complicated," I repeated. The word tasted like cyanide —acrid and bitter. Suddenly, that empty feeling evaporated, and all that was left was a burning, seething rage. "Complicated is *bullshit*. You're a hypocrite. You were jealous and angry that I was even talking to Bradley out in the open, where anyone could see, obviously doing nothing nefarious. And now, you're here in your office with *her* instead of at the wedding. You didn't tell me what you were doing or who you were doing it with. So, forgive me if I don't give a single fuck about your complicated situation. The fact of the matter is, you hid this from me."

Tori reeled back at my anger, but I was still blocking the exit. There was nowhere for her to go.

"I did, and it was stupid. Tori has been texting and emailing me for months, and I wanted to make her fucking stop," Hollin said, gaining his own anger back.

But at those words, I stumbled back a step. "What? *Months*?"

"She emailed when she moved back into town around Christmas and more aggressively since the concert," Hollin said. "I didn't know why, but I guess I do now. She's trying to come between us."

"You know why I did that," Tori gasped. "I did it because we were supposed to be together."

Hollin rounded on her. "Shut your mouth."

"You could have told me," I yelled back at him. "You could have told me that your ex was reaching out to you, but you didn't. Think about why that is."

"It's because she didn't matter!"

"If she didn't matter, you wouldn't be down here, alone with her."

"She has a point, Hollin," Tori muttered.

Hollin didn't even acknowledge her this time. He only had eyes for me.

"She messaged me at the wedding, asking me to meet her. I only came here to tell her to leave me alone. That is the only reason I came here."

My horror dawned brighter and more lethal. "Let me get this straight. She messaged you at my sister's wedding. You opened the message while you were *standing next to me*. And instead of telling me about it, you went to meet her?"

Hollin opened his mouth as I laid out the facts. Then shut it quickly.

"I don't care if she manipulated the shit out of you," I told him. "I trusted you, and you broke that trust."

My voice wavered again, and I realized I was shaking. My entire body trembled from head to toe. Hollin looked like he wanted to take me in his arms, but there was no turning back from this shit.

"I'm sorry," he said earnestly. "I should have told you. I thought I could handle it myself. That if I ignored her, she'd go away. And if I could end it here and now, we wouldn't have to worry about her anymore."

"That's the thing, Hollin—*we* weren't worrying about anything. You had this one all to yourself." I shook my head. "Fuck, I can't deal with this right now."

"Piper, please," he said, stepping toward me again.

"Just...leave me alone."

Then, I turned and fled the office. I picked up my heels on the way out and just kept running. I couldn't go back to the party. I couldn't fake it enough for Peyton, and the last thing I wanted was to ruin her wedding day. And I didn't want to face my dad or Chase or anyone about what had happened with the winery. If Hollin came looking for me, I didn't want him to find me. I didn't want anyone to find me.

There was only one place that could envelop me entirely —the vineyard. This wasn't *my* winery, but my winery wasn't mine anymore either. It never would be again. Just like Hollin. Everything I'd worked for, everything I'd opened myself up for, was gone.

So, I darted into the maze of grapevines. I lost myself in the earth. The sun setting big and orange on the horizon. I ran until I couldn't run anymore and then dropped to my knees in the dirt, panting and breathless. I cracked wide open. My hands clawed into the ground, tears watering the holes I dug, and all the primal fire released until I had nothing left.

36

HOLLIN

"Fuck," I raged, throwing all the paperwork off of my desk.

Tori edged past me now that Piper had left, but I'd known her long enough to see that she was pleased. Her lips tilted slightly upward. She'd gotten everything she'd wanted. I'd thought that she'd go away if I ignored her. When that didn't work, I thought I could finally tell her to stop contacting me, stop interfering, stop trying to weasel her way in, like she always had before. And now, I'd spectacularly fucked everything up.

"Why can't you leave me alone?" I roared at her.

Tori blinked, tears coming to her eyes, like flipping a light switch. "Don't yell at me, Hollin."

"All I wanted was to be free of you."

"Well, I didn't want to be free of *you*," she shouted back. "Can't you see that?"

"No," I said, shaking my head.

"If you wanted to be free, then you wouldn't be here."

"I came to tell you to leave me alone. I told you multiple times to *stop contacting me*."

"But it doesn't work! It doesn't work for us," she said, reaching for my hands.

I yanked away from her. "It's over, Tori. It's over. I love someone else."

"You think you love her?" Tori sneered. Her expression was of pure horror. "You don't *love* her!"

"Stop."

"You can't love her. That's not possible, Hollin. You still love me. You'll always love me."

I wrenched away from her and stormed toward the door. "I don't love you, Tori. And you don't love me. You just need me to crawl after you. That's all you've ever wanted."

"Hollin," she gasped, following me out the door.

But I was done with this conversation. It had been stupid to think that I could make Tori leave me alone. That I could make her stop. That she wouldn't twist everything up until my insides were a pretzel that I didn't know how to disentangle. That was all she'd ever known how to do—hurt me.

"Hollin, stop," she yelled. "Why are you doing this to us?"

I ground my teeth at the question and whirled on her. "Just stop. I spent a lot of time fucking other women to forget all the immeasurable ways you hurt me, Tori. I decided I'd never date again. That I would never put myself through what you did to me again. And then I finally —*finally*—found someone worth it all, and you started your same narcissistic, gaslighting behavior. Like the idiot you'd created, I fell for it...*again*. Fuck." I ran a hand back through my hair.

I wanted to hurt her the way she'd always hurt me. But all it would do was make her twist me up even more. She wasn't worth it.

"I'll be damned if I let you ruin this thing with me and

Piper. She's the best goddamn thing that has ever happened to me. And you...you're nothing."

I left her standing in the hallway of the cellar and ran out after my girlfriend.

"Piper!" I called into the night.

The barn was brightly lit as the sun reached toward the horizon. She could have gone back to the party, but I doubted it. She was as stubborn as ever. She wouldn't want anyone to see her upset. Let alone to hurt her sister on her wedding day. But where the fuck would she have gone?

"Piper!"

I glanced up the hill and found her blue Jeep standing out bright in the parking lot. So, she hadn't left, which meant one thing. My eyes landed on the fields. She had to have gone into the vineyard. It was her happy place in the same way it was mine. But if she was already inside, how the fuck was I going to find her?

I didn't give it another thought. I pushed through the vines and into my fields. My heart raced as I called her name and raced down the rows. The fields were several acres big. She could be anywhere. Still, I jogged on the soft dirt in my stupid suit, ruining the fancy shoes Julian had convinced me to get for the occasion.

It wasn't until the sun dipped completely behind the horizon and only the last dying rays still shone over the fields that I gave up. She was gone. She was just fucking gone. She was out there somewhere, thinking that I wanted Tori more than her. I'd been stupid enough to come when Tori called, and I didn't even have a good enough reason for it all. It was...years of being fucked up that had driven me back into her stupidity. And I wanted out of it. I wanted it to be done and over.

I wished that I could explain it all to Piper. But what

explanation would be good enough? She deserved better. That was for damn sure.

With a frustrated sigh, I left the vines, making it out into the open before I lost all the light. If Piper was out there still, I hoped she could find her way through the dark. I didn't know what else to do. It wasn't like I could get a search party out for her. How would I even explain?

"Fuck," I said again as I trudged up to the barn once more.

I came in the back way and looked around for Campbell and Julian. I didn't know if it was luck, but they were standing together, drinking whiskey and laughing. If my situation wasn't entirely shit, I'd be happy to see them getting along like this. My two closest friends. But all I felt right now was despair.

They looked up as I approached them. Julian took in the wreck of my suit. Campbell's eyes were on my face.

"What did you do to your suit?" Julian asked. Our little fashion guru.

"What happened?" he asked, always the intuitive one.

"Same problem," I grumbled.

Campbell passed me his drink. "You look like you need this more than I do."

I downed the entire contents in one long swallow. "Yeah."

"Seriously," Julian said. "Those are Dior."

I snorted. "Remind me not to let you convince me to buy designer shoes again."

"Remind me that you should only ever be in cowboy boots."

"Yeah." I snatched his drink out of his hand, too, and downed the contents. "So, I might have fucked up."

"We can see that," Campbell said.

"What did you do?" Julian asked.

With a final sigh, I explained the situation that had gone down. Both guys frowned as they listened. Julian crossed his arms over his chest. Campbell looked incredulous, at best.

The worst of it was that...neither of them even knew about Tori. Everyone I'd known during her years of misery had basically been purged from my life. I wasn't still friends with anyone from that time, except maybe Zach, but we'd only become close afterward. I hadn't exactly had friends when we were dating. She was the kind of possessive and jealous girl who didn't like me to even talk to other people. My brother had been in LA. Nora had been in high school. Julian hadn't moved here yet. The two closest people in my life, and neither of them had any idea.

"Fuck," Campbell said when I finished. "Why didn't you tell me?"

I shrugged. "What would I have said?"

"That your girlfriend was abusing you," Julian said flatly.

My mind immediately rejected that thought. It wasn't a thing *done* to guys. Certainly not anyone else I knew. It was something you saw in TV and movies when the guy was beating his girlfriend. It wasn't like what I had gone through. Was it?

"It wasn't like that."

"The fact that you can't see it says you're still fucked up," Julian said, his voice laced with sympathy. "This happened to a friend of mine back in Vancouver. She fucking disappeared because her boyfriend went crazy anytime she talked to anyone else. He could do whatever he wanted without consequence, but he had her so warped that she didn't even see it. She cut us all out because she said she loved him. It was only years later when she got her and her daughter out and was in loads of therapy that she came back to us. It's emotional and psychological abuse, Hollin."

I shuddered. It made me sound so...weak. That I'd let her rule my life for so long because of everything we'd gone through. That I still wasn't over it. That she could still wind me up. Fuck, fuck, fuck.

Campbell put a hand on my shoulder. "Which means, it isn't your fault."

"Maybe not," I said. "But hurting Piper was."

"To an extent. Abuse fucks you up though, man," Julian said. "I can't defend what you did to Piper. I'm not saying what you did was smart. It wasn't. It was fucking stupid, and Piper has every right to be mad at you. But you're not coming at it from a good place to start."

"And you definitely need therapy," Campbell said. "It helps."

"*You're* in therapy?" I asked with raised eyebrows.

"If I wasn't, do you think I'd have my anger in check the way it's been on tour?" Campbell shot me a look. "I had a problem, and I got help. The only real triggers now are people hurting my family."

"August," I said.

He nodded.

"Jennifer has been in therapy for years, too," Julian said. "I went once we started dating. She thought it would help me deal with my dad. Literally every person on the planet should be in therapy. We're all fucking traumatized by our childhood."

I snorted. "True." It helped, hearing that the other guys were in therapy. That this kind of thing happened to other people. I wasn't alone. It wasn't just me. "I'll...I'll think about it."

"Good," Campbell said with a smile.

Julian clapped me on the back. "That's what we like to hear."

"But what do I do about Piper?"

Campbell and Julian exchanged a bleak look.

"Give her time," Julian said. "She's the most stubborn woman I've ever met. Do you think she's going to forget that you abandoned her at her sister's wedding to talk to your ex without telling her?"

I grimaced. "No, but I'm not going to stop fighting for her."

"That's my brother," Campbell said, punching me on the arm. "May I recommend a bottle of Maker's for your broken heart?"

The three of us commandeered a bottle or two, and I drowned in my own misery. They were there to try to pick me up. Jordan appeared at some point and tried to convince us to stop. The guys filled him in on the situation, and then Jordan took a seat across from me and poured us both another glass. I was that thoroughly screwed that even Jordan didn't see another solution. I was well and truly fucked.

37

PIPER

I didn't go into work on Monday.

My dad called to find out where I was and when I was coming in. I didn't answer. Blaire finally picked up after he called seven times in a half hour and explained that I wasn't feeling well. It wasn't a lie. I felt terrible. I was wrapped up on the couch, watching mindless television.

The problem with having roommates who worked from home meant that they spent most of the day babying me. When, in reality, I wanted to be left alone. My heart was shattered in a million pieces. The two things I cared about most in my life were gone.

There was no way that I was going in to work at that place that held all of my memories and all of my joy. Knowing now what had happened and how it had been stolen from us by our accountant's stupidity and then the sale of the property. I didn't even know all the specifics about how it had happened, but I found I couldn't care.

And Hollin...he was just as bad. He'd sent a number of texts that I deleted without reading. He'd called until Blaire, once again to the rescue, answered and told him to leave me alone.

"You're going to be okay," she said, brushing my hair back from my face. "You'll get through this."

"How do you know?"

"You're too stubborn to do anything else."

Over the next couple days, Blaire and Jennifer made me tea and fed me through my misery. After I told them what had gone down, they didn't ask too many questions. Jennifer had already known. Hollin must have told Julian. Great. Everyone would know soon enough. I was glad at least that Jennifer did the majority of filling in for Blaire, who was personally offended on my behalf.

"If he shows up, I'm going to kick his ass," she said.

"That would be a sight."

She grinned and then dropped it. She picked at her fresh manicure with a sigh. "We have a game tonight. I assume...you're not coming?"

"No."

"It'll be our first game without August. We got a new player to replace him, Eve Houston."

I flopped backward. "I know her."

"Really?"

"I met her with Hollin," I said, my voice raw as I said his name.

"Yeah? Well, I hope she's good."

"Have fun."

"What are you going to do?"

I gestured to the couch, where I'd taken up residence.

She sighed and nodded. "All right. Maybe you should talk to someone."

"I don't want to talk to anyone."

"Abuelita?" she suggested.

I met her gaze and saw the fear in them for the first time. She was worried about me. Worried that I wouldn't get off of the couch again, except to use the bathroom and sleep. Worried that I was broken. And I felt broken. I didn't want to do anything, but I didn't want to hurt the one person I had left.

I nodded. "Okay. I'll go see Abuelita."

Blaire's face lit up. "Excellent. Do you want me to drive you?"

"No, I can do it. Have fun at the game."

Blaire nodded uneasily. "Will do."

I got up when she left to change and went straight for the shower. When I came out, freshly washed, I pulled my hair into a messy bun on the top of my head. I changed into jean shorts and a tank top, grabbed my keys, and headed over to Abuelita's.

She couldn't possibly say anything that would make me feel better about the catastrophe that was my life. But maybe she'd make me her secret family recipe pozole, and that would help.

I parked out front and rang the doorbell. I waited a minute for her to answer and then tried the door. "Abuelita?"

"*Mi amorcita,*" Abuelita said as she stepped out of the kitchen. "*Lo siento.* These legs don't move quite as fast as they used to."

"No need to apologize." I kissed her cheek.

"I'm pleased that you're here." She affectionately tapped my cheek twice. "Come. What can I make you? You must be hungry. We'll get some meat on those bones."

I laughed softly and followed her into the kitchen. "I was thinking pozole."

"In the summer?"

"I need the comfort food," I admitted.

"*Sí*, pozole it is."

She directed me to the pantry to gather ingredients. The recipe wasn't even written down. She had it in her head. It was all three of us grandkids' favorite dish. We were fond of all of her food, but the pozole was her best. As I cut up an onion and crushed garlic, Abuelita told me stories about Mexico and her parents and the love they'd had. She spoke softly the entire time as the stew came together in a boiling pot that smelled like home.

She dished us up each a bowl, and we sat at the small table in the kitchen instead of the larger dining room table.

"Now," Abuelita said, "tell me what is troubling you."

That was when the tears sprang free again. "I don't know what to do."

"About the winery or this boy of yours?"

Of course she already knew. She hadn't been surprised that I'd shown up out of the blue, asking for comfort food. She had been waiting for the right moment to address it.

"Both. I'm supposed to drive down to Austin for the wine awards with Hollin. And now, I don't think I should even go."

"Because of what your father did?"

"Yes. He...sold the entire thing out from under me. He never even consulted me. I dedicated my life to that place. I thought, one day, it would be mine, as it had been his."

Abuelita nodded. "It was not the right decision to leave you out. But believe me when I say that, sometimes, parents do things that they believe are best for their children and do not consider how it will harm them in the process. He was trying to protect you."

"By keeping me in the dark?" I asked with a shake of my head. "I would have found out eventually and then what?"

"You'd have dealt with it. As you are now."

I sighed and shook my head. "I guess. But I don't forgive him, and I don't know how."

"*Mira*, give it time. This is all too important. *No te rindas.*"

"I'm not giving up," I told her. "I just feel defeated. And Hollin...he lied and hid things, and then...he wasn't even there for me when I found out about the winery."

"Are you mad because he hid things or because you were alone when you found out?"

I squeezed my eyes shut. "Both. He was my person. He was supposed to be there. And when I came to him in distress, I found him with someone else. They weren't... doing anything, but does it matter?" I searched Abuelita's face. "He said he went to see her to get her to stop talking to him, but I don't know how to trust him anymore."

"Before this, he seemed a good man," Abuelita said.

"He was."

"He cared for your family. He cared for you. He made you happy. *Lo amas?*"

Did I love him?

That was the question, wasn't it?

"I thought I did," I admitted. "But now, I don't know. I'm just so mad. Everything was stolen."

"You have time," Abuelita said, taking my hand in hers and squeezing. "You do not have to decide today. Go to this award ceremony. See what the world says about this wine you have worked so hard on. See how you feel about this man. Decide if it's worth living without him."

When I returned home, Blaire was still gone, but there was a familiar truck in the driveway. I tipped my head back and groaned. Just what I needed to deal with.

Hollin hopped out of his truck as soon as I got out and followed me toward the door. "Piper, please, can we talk?"

"I'm not up for talking."

"I found out about the winery."

I ground my teeth together. "Okay."

"I can't believe that your dad sold it out from under you."

"Yep," I snapped.

"The guys found out at the game, and I raced over here to talk to you. When did you find out? Why didn't you tell me?"

I laughed, a sharp, bitter note. "Why didn't I tell you? Because you were occupied with Tori. That's why."

"Fuck."

"Chase blurted it out at the wedding. He thought I already knew. And when I was hyperventilating and needed you most, where did I find you?"

He cursed under his breath again. "I fucked up. I really fucked up, Piper. I need to apologize...again...for what happened. Blaire told me that you hadn't left the house, and—"

"Stop," I said, holding up my hand. "Blaire did not tell you that so you would come grovel."

"No. She chewed me a new one at the game."

"Yeah. You're lucky she needed you at the game. She was threatening violence."

"I deserve it. Piper, I'm sorry."

I finally faced him when I reached the door, but I didn't go inside. God, he was handsome. Even though he looked about as good as I felt. He was sweaty from the soccer game and still in his red Tacos uniform. His blond hair was a wreck. There were bags under his eyes from sleepless nights. But his blue eyes were so sincere, so heartfelt. I wanted to melt into that look. To get lost in the Hollin Abbey who had been my wonderful boyfriend these past months. But I remembered too viscerally how he'd hurt me the way I'd always expected that he would.

And I remembered what it was to put up walls against his charms. I'd been so good at deflecting Hollin that it was basically my superpower. I needed that resolve more than ever to live through this.

"I don't want to hear it."

"It was my mistake. Tori manipulated me for years. And she was still able to do it now. I should have seen what she was doing, and still, somehow, I was all fucked up with it. I can't do things right when it comes to her. Which is why I cut her and everyone else who knew me when I was with her out of my life. It was the only way I knew how to move forward. Even Julian and Campbell had no clue we'd dated. Only you even had any idea that I had an ex-girlfriend."

I bit the inside of my cheek to keep from sympathizing with him. Tori sounded like a total headache. She'd wormed her way into my life so seamlessly, too, without ever mentioning that she'd dated my boyfriend. And betrayed me just as quickly.

"I'm going to get better. Julian recommended a therapist to help me recover from her emotional abuse. I feel stupid that I even have to go, but he said she's the real deal." He ran a hand back through his hair. "And I'm not just saying this to get you back."

"No?" I asked, my voice wobbling.

"I'm going either way. Apparently, how I've been coping with the trauma is...problematic." He met my gaze with a frown. "To say the least."

"Good. I'm glad you're going," I told him honestly. I crossed my arms across my chest and held tight to my anger. "But it doesn't change the fact that you hid her contacting you from me, or that you went to see her, or that when I needed you, you weren't there. I can't switch off the betrayal, Hollin."

"I know. I know. Fuck." He stepped away from me and back. "I wish I could take it all back. Have a do-over."

"Yeah, me too," I whispered. "But...you can't."

"Are you still going to Austin?" he asked.

I could see that he barely restrained himself from asking if I was going with him. Because that was too much to ask for.

"Yeah. I'll be there."

He nodded, a yearning smile touching his lips. "Good. Good. I was worried that you might not go because of the winery situation."

"No, I'm not giving up," I said, repeating the words Abuelita had ingrained in me. "That wine was my hard work. I won't give up just because of what my dad did."

"I can't imagine how you're feeling about it, but I'm glad that you're still going."

"That doesn't mean that I'll see you there," I warned him.

He held his hands up. "Right. I just...wanted to see you. I know I can't make this all go away, but I'm not going to walk away from this, Piper. I fucked up. I get it. And I see every step where I went wrong. But you're the best thing that's ever happened to me, and I'm going to try to fix this."

I swallowed hard at those words. I wanted all of that, too. But something had broken between us. I didn't trust him anymore. I didn't know if I could believe his words. As much as I wanted to. And now, the fragile, cracked heart inside my still-beating chest recoiled from more damage. He'd done that, and I didn't think he could undo it.

I reached for the handle. "I wish you'd thought about all of this before Tori happened."

"Me too."

He took another step toward me as I entered my house. His hands came to either side of the door, taking up the entire expanse with his incredible bulk. He looked like a sad puppy but a determined one.

"Hollin, I can't do this," I whispered as tears came to my eyes again.

He brushed the tear from my cheek with his thumb. "You're my good girl, but I didn't realize that you'd changed this bad boy until it was too late."

38

PIPER

"So, you just sent him home?" Blaire asked. She leaned on her elbows and looked at me with wide eyes.

"I did."

Jennifer sat similarly on my bed as I packed my bag for my trip to Austin. "Good for you, Piper. He has a problem, and he's working to fix it, but it doesn't change the damage he did."

"Exactly."

"Okay," Blaire said with an eye roll at Jennifer. "As much as I hate what Hollin did, he feels real remorse."

"I think so, too," I admitted.

"But..." Jennifer added for me.

"But I'm still mad."

"Understandable," Blaire said. "Are you going to see him when you're in Austin?"

"Not if I can help it." I held up a black dress for my friends, and they both put two thumbs down. I returned to the closet to find something else acceptable to wear to the ceremony. "I'm going to try to have a good time. Mingle with other people at the event. Hopefully come home with an award and decide what to do from there."

"Wait," Blaire said, and then she dashed into her room.

Blaire and I could fit into the same size, but she was significantly shorter than me. So, we didn't share clothes much. It wasn't often she went rummaging through her walk-in closet to find something for me.

"It's smart to wait it out. Maybe it'll work out with Hollin, but you shouldn't give in because he apologized. Sometimes, *I'm sorry* isn't enough," Jennifer said.

"Speaking from experience?"

Her cheeks heated, and she laughed. "I guess so."

"This!" Blaire passed a maroon dress into my hand. "It's too long on me, but I've been meaning to have it hemmed and not gotten around to it. Plus, where am I going to wear it anyway? It was meant for you."

I tried to give it back to her. "Blaire, I can't."

"Yes, you can." Blaire handed the dress back to me. "Have a spectacular time. Don't worry about Hollin at all. We love you and want you to do your best. You'll be the highlight of the evening in that."

"Thank you," I told her as I gently packed it into the bag.

I had no idea what I was in for this weekend, but at least I'd look smoking hot while I did it.

The drive to Austin was boring and desolate. Six hours to a separate destination in Texas, and I'd barely seen another inhabited town. I couldn't help thinking that the drive would have been much better with Hollin. He would have played music and told ridiculous jokes and made outlandish sexual innuendos. I would have laughed a lot.

I cleared my head. It didn't matter. Because I wasn't talking to Hollin, and I didn't want to see him when I got there. It was pretty much guaranteed that we'd run into each other at the ceremony, but I hoped it wouldn't happen before then.

The IWAA Texas Wine Award Competition was held annually at the Austin Convention Center downtown. They'd booked out three of the largest nearby hotels, and I'd gotten a place at the Four Seasons downtown off the Colorado River. I was glad I hadn't canceled my room when Hollin invited me to go with him. Otherwise, I'd be screwed right about now.

I parked my Jeep and rolled my suitcase into the glossy and extravagant interior of the hotel. I checked in at the front desk, and despite the luxury downstairs, the rooms were relatively standard. A package from the competition committee awaited me, including a bottle of champagne, chocolate-covered strawberries, and a bunch of IWAA paraphernalia. I popped one of the strawberries into my mouth. I could get used to this.

After changing out of my travel gear, I put on a pair of black cigarette pants and a blue blouse. I spent the rest of the afternoon checking in at the convention center; wandering the event space, where hundreds of vendors had set up to sell their wares; and going through the book of all the things I could do tomorrow before the award ceremony.

I met a handful of people who were also competing in different categories. We all agreed to meet at the bar downstairs after dinner. I didn't have dinner plans. So, I ordered room service, then dressed with care and headed down to the bar.

But instead of finding my new friends, I found Mr.

Sinclair and Eve seated on circular high-tops. Mr. Sinclair flagged me down.

Fuck, I didn't want to talk to him. I didn't even know what the fuck he was doing here. Had he always planned to come to this thing? Was he here to torment me?

And another thought...what exactly was Eve doing here with him? Sure, they worked together. She was one of his real estate agents. But that had nothing to do with Sinclair Cellars.

She wore a dark blue dress with a slit nearly up to her hip and Louboutins. I only recognized them by the red backs. I didn't know how well real estate agents were paid, but I didn't think they could regularly afford a thousand-dollar pair of shoes.

"Miss Medina," Mr. Sinclair said with a wide smile. "I'd hoped that I'd see you here."

"Hello," I said politely. I nodded at Eve. "Hi."

"Hey there," she said with a smile, twirling a cherry around in her glass.

"Sit. Have a drink with us."

"I'm actually meeting some people." I looked around the bar, hoping to find my new friends but none of them were in attendance. I glanced down at my phone for a quick getaway, but all that was there was a message from my new friend, Yani, letting me know that dinner was running late. Great.

"Just one. I'm sure they can wait." He gestured to a seat, and reluctantly, I sank into it. "Now, what are you drinking? Amaretto sour, like Eve here?"

"No, thank you. Bombay and lime."

He flagged down the waiter and put in my order. "Now, Miss Medina..."

"Piper," I said easily. "You can call me Piper."

He shot me a Cheshire smile. I could see how he'd be charming if I didn't already hate his guts. "Of course. You can call me Arnold."

I had no intention of calling him anything.

"I feel like we've gotten off on the wrong foot," he said once my drink arrived.

"Is that so?"

"Yes, your father mentioned that you were upset when you found out about the vineyard situation."

I boiled at the thought of my father mentioning my emotional state to this man. I shot him a perfectly blank look. Silence worked better for me than speaking sometimes. I didn't want him to know the full extent of my rage. In fact, I didn't want to have this conversation at all.

"It's understandable. You were running the company, and, without your knowledge, the business changed hands."

I gritted my teeth and considered stabbing him in the eye with my straw.

"I want to reassure you that it's going to be no different than before," he said with that same smile. "I don't intend to interfere in day-to-day operations. You and your father have the full run of the place. I'm simply going to be bankrolling the winery."

"I see."

I tried to find relief in that. He wasn't going to interfere and ruin the thing that I loved. But somehow, I didn't. I wasn't even sure I believed him. I didn't have a good relationship with the Sinclairs. Not after what they'd done to Wright Vineyard and then their daughter, Ashleigh's, train wreck. They were gluttonous. Anything they could scoop up, they did. This was another one of their conquests.

"I want us to be partners," he said smoothly.

"Partners," I reiterated.

"Of course. The circumstances of it ending up in your father's hands were a mark on my family name." My eyebrows rose. He held his hands up quickly. "I respect your father. What he's done for the place is above and beyond. But for us, for *me*, my father wanted me to run the winery, and I was more interested in real estate development. I didn't realize until it was too late that he was going to divest himself of the winery. He took my success elsewhere as disinterest. I have always coveted the property and wanted it to succeed. It brings me no joy to hurt you, but this was a long time coming."

My hand clenched the glass. If I'd had any more strength, it would have shattered. How dare he! He acted as if my father had had no part in all of this. As if it had just been given to my father and not earned. And as if he had been entitled to the property all along. As if he'd been *waiting* for this to happen. What an absolute asshole!

"Must we discuss business?" Eve asked. She seemed to be the only one at the table who realized how angry I was.

Mr. Sinclair turned his full attention to Eve with a smile that showed quite clearly why she was here. He was enamored. Oh fuck. Wasn't he married?

"Of course. We're here to celebrate." He raised his glass, and I followed with Eve clinking her glass against mine. "To *our* award tomorrow."

I saw red all at once. *Our* award? *OUR?*

That was too far.

It was too damn far.

He might have gotten us out of financial problems. He might have purchased the winery that was my home. But he hadn't done *shit* with the wine.

I was the one who was there day in and day out. I was the one who worked in the fields and dealt with the on-site problems and who had produced the wine that was currently a finalist for this award. In no way, shape, or form was this award *ours*. It was only ever *mine*.

Before I could open my mouth, a hand smacked down on the table. "Mr. Sinclair," Hollin said, suddenly at my side.

I jumped. I'd been so distracted by my increasing fury that I hadn't even seen him enter or approach us.

"Hollin," Mr. Sinclair said with a smile. "Good to see you."

He stuck his hand out, and they shook.

"I was toasting to our success. I hope you don't mind. Since we have every intention of beating Wright Vineyard tomorrow."

"Healthy competition is always appreciated." He nodded his head at Eve. "Hey, Eve."

She smiled, but it didn't quite reach her eyes. "Hey."

"How'd you like The Tacos?"

Mr. Sinclair faced her. "Tacos?"

"It's a soccer team," she told him. "Hollin asked me to sub the rest of the season because they lost a player."

"Yeah, see, we found my sister's boyfriend making out with someone else," he said, leaning forward dangerously. "I broke his nose and kicked him off of the team."

Mr. Sinclair met Hollin's eyes square on. The implied threat was bright and vibrant. Even Eve didn't respond.

"Eve was nice enough to help us out. She's good like that."

Mr. Sinclair nodded. "How nice of her."

Finally, Hollin turned to me. He looked hot in dark jeans and a white button-up, just like the one I'd borrowed from him all those months ago. He'd shaved, and his hair was done. But his blue eyes were storm clouds, dark with intent.

"Can I borrow you, Piper?"

I gulped, and despite myself, I nodded. I wanted—*needed* —the out. "Sure." I pushed my drink across the table toward Mr. Sinclair and Eve. "Thanks for the drink."

Hollin directed me across the bar and back out into the lobby until Mr. Sinclair and Eve were no longer visible. I sagged back against a wall. I crossed my arms over my chest, closed my eyes, and released a deep breath.

"You looked ready to murder him," Hollin said. "Thought you could use the out."

"Yeah," I said hollowly. "He kept going on about how the award tomorrow would be *our* award. Ours. As if he'd had *anything* to do with it."

"Fuck. What an ass."

"I thought you were going to hit him."

He cracked a smile. "Nah. He's the kind of douche who would press charges. I said all he needed to know."

"You think he and Eve..."

"Don't you?"

I nodded. "Yeah. She's wearing Louboutins. I doubt she bought those shoes."

"Sugar daddy central from Daddy Sinclair."

I cracked up at the name. He'd said it before at breakfast, but it fit even better now. When I met his eyes, the ice had melted, and it was just him. Everything felt so... normal. As if we were meant to be here together. Just like this.

But reality rushed back in.

He must have seen the moment that I realized that we were standing together alone. Because he took a half-step back, giving me breathing room. We were on precarious ground.

He'd been there when I needed him against Daddy Sinclair. When he hadn't been there when I found out about the sale to begin with. It meant something, and I appreciated it. But I needed more time.

"I should go upstairs and get some rest."

His eyes flickered to my lips and then back up. "I could... walk you."

My mind reeled with all the things that would happen if I said yes. The elevator doors would slide closed, and he'd push me back against them, kissing me breathless. We'd break long enough to make it to my room. He'd kick the door down, and we'd try to rip each other's clothes off. He'd get annoyed with how long it was taking and get his hands and his cock under my skirt as fast as possible. Bury himself inside of me.

I blinked as the daydream popped. I flushed red and backed up a step. It would be so easy. But sex was not our problem. We'd had great sex before we ever had a relationship. Sex would only complicate things more now. We couldn't go back to who we had been on that tour bus.

I shook my head. "Good night, Hollin."

Then, I walked away.

And he let me.

I was still focused on the bullshit that Daddy Sinclair had been spouting to me. My anger, curbed slightly by Hollin's interruption, rekindled. *Our* award. Fucker.

I pressed the button for the elevator, and as I entered, I froze as an idea hit me. It was outrageous. Completely crazy.

But I was going to do it.

39

HOLLIN

*W*atching Piper walk away was one of the hardest things I'd ever done.

She'd wanted me to come back to her room. I could see that in her eyes. The way she disappeared inside her head. She'd looked as if she were imagining what the night would entail. And I wanted that.

But I let her go. I could have pushed. She would have let me push. It had been on her face. But if we'd fallen into bed like I wanted to, she'd have hated me in the morning. That was the opposite of what I wanted. Not when she'd dropped her guard enough to let me rescue her from Daddy Sinclair. She'd stayed and talked to me for a few minutes, as if everything was going to be all right.

It meant I had a chance.

Any chance was worth it with her.

I'd had plans to wait in the bar for her all night. Now, I had no plans. She wasn't going to come back down after that. I didn't blame her, but I still needed a drink.

I returned to the bar and ordered a Jack and Coke. I was sipping on it when Eve Houston took the seat next to me.

"Hey there," she said, waving the bartender down for another drink.

"Eve," I said. "Where's your sugar daddy?"

She lifted one perfectly arched eyebrow. "He had to take a call."

"Ah, the wife?"

Eve smiled at me and ordered another Amaretto sour. "I have no idea. I try not to pay that close of attention to that kind of thing."

I snorted. "Like whether or not the guy is married."

"Are you going to kick me off of the team?"

I laughed softly. "Did you hurt my sister?"

"No."

"Piper?"

"No."

"Then no. What you're doing is stupid and dangerous. If his wife found out, he'd lose half of everything. And you'd be fucked since you work for them."

"Well, until this moment, no one else knew." She glanced over at me, and I saw the first hint of fear from her. She didn't want to lose everything for this guy. She'd gotten caught up in it. Power dynamics and all.

"But now, I know," I said.

She took the drink from the bartender. She had it put on Daddy Sinclair's tab. Cheeky. "You do. So, I guess I'm trying to figure out what you're going to do with the information."

"Did he send you to ask?"

She shook her head with a laugh. Eve had always been beautiful in a way that said she knew it. But young. Almost as young as Nora. We'd only crossed paths because of soccer. I might have been interested once...if she hadn't been into Zach. Never a more drastic change in relationship had I seen.

"No way. He isn't even thinking about it. But I like contingency plans."

"Trying to figure out if it's time to bail?"

Eve tapped her glass against mine with a wink. "Maybe."

"Don't worry. I don't plan to do anything with the information."

"Cool," she said, taking me at my word. "Well, see you tomorrow at the ceremony."

I waved her off and downed the rest of my glass. I had a second and third until a buzz hit me in the face. Then, I returned to my room and crashed. All I wanted was to be in bed next to Piper. Instead, I was here. Alone.

This fucking sucked.

The award ceremony wasn't until seven tonight. So, I spent the day wandering the convention center, keeping an eye out for Piper. It was a huge place, so I didn't see her, but I was still frustrated that it never happened. I tasted a decent amount of wine, made some connections for Wright Vineyard, and played the part that Jordan and Julian had been grooming me to take over.

With a frustrated sigh, I went back to the Four Seasons, changed into a black suit, and left for the award ceremony. I was offered a glass of champagne as I entered the enormous ballroom. A large stage was at the front of the room. A banner hung behind it with the IWCC logo on it. The logo was also represented on two projection screens on either side of the stage.

Hundreds of tables filled the space, and as a finalist, I was shown to my table near the front. I took the one seat for

Wright Vineyard and was seated next to the three corresponding seats for Sinclair Cellars. Interesting.

One for Piper, of course.

And then Daddy Sinclair and Eve appeared at the table, making it clear that they were also representing the winery. Piper was going to throw a fit if she found out. Christ.

I shot her a quick text, in case she wasn't aware.

Heads up. Daddy Sinclair and Eve are seated at the Sinclair Cellars table. Didn't want you to be blindsided.

But though my message appeared as Read, she didn't respond to it.

I ordered a drink as I waited and tuned out the conversation. I should have brought Julian or something. He'd had plans with Jennifer already and offered to break them, but I hadn't let him. Now, I was regretting that.

The lights flickered overhead, and a speaker stepped up to the podium, asking everyone to take their seats, as they were about to begin. Piper's place was still empty. What the hell? Where was she?

I sent another text.

Everything is about to start. Where are you? Did you decide to sit somewhere else?

Again, straight to Read.

"What the fuck?" I muttered under my breath.

Eve leaned across Piper's empty seat and whispered, "Where's Piper?"

I shrugged. "I have no idea. I never in a million years thought that she would miss this."

"Maybe she's late."

But I doubted it. Piper was never late. She'd been messed up last night. I'd let her go back to her room. Maybe I should have pushed after all and tried to be there for her more. Had she decided to bail on the entire thing?

Finally, the lights dimmed, and I had to put my phone away. Piper wasn't here.

She wasn't late.

She just wasn't coming.

"And the winner of the IWCC award for Best in Class goes to..." The commentator opened a sealed envelope. He read the results and broke into a smile. "Wright Vineyard, *Abbey* Vintage."

My jaw dropped as the award was called out. I was struck perfectly still. I couldn't believe it. Was this real life?

Eve nudged me. "That's you! Go up there!"

After two hours of awards, I'd been essentially numb to the winners. Wines were awarded medals—bronze, silver, gold, and double gold. Each one was a blind taste by a panel of judges. They weren't judged against one another, but as the quality of the wine as a whole. But at the end of each category, *one* wine was chosen as Best of Class. And that was essentially the *winner* of the entire ceremony.

And that was *me*.

I stumbled out of my seat and ascended the stairs to the podium. A trophy was thrust into my hand with a muffled, "Congratulations."

I stared out at the audience from under the bright white lights. The crowd applauded my success. Cameras flashed. People were cheering. I'd never experienced this in my life, and I was momentarily dumbstruck.

I retrieved the acceptance speech I'd written from my suit coat pocket. Julian and Jordan had insisted I have one just in case. I'd thought there was no chance in the world that I'd get here, but now, I was, and thank fuck they'd pressured me into writing something.

The words came out like I was speaking with marshmallows in my mouth as I thanked my family and friends and the vineyard. It all happened in a flash, and then I was ushered backstage. I took a handful of pictures for the photographers. I downed three large glasses of water all in a row to stop my body from shaking from disbelief and mild stage fright.

When I got a second to myself, I took out my phone and video-called Julian and Jordan. Their faces filled my small screen, and I held up the award.

"We fucking did it!" I said.

"Holy shit!" Julian said.

"I knew we'd win," Jordan said.

"You didn't know," Julian said with an eye roll.

"I suspected."

"Well, it happened."

"Congratulations. So well deserved," Jordan said.

"We're going to have to find a prominent place to display the trophy," Julian said.

I nodded. "Definitely."

Julian cleared his throat. "How'd Sinclair Cellars do?"

"Piper didn't show."

"What?" Jordan asked sharply.

"That makes no sense," Julian said.

"I know. And then they didn't even medal. I'm so fucking confused. Their wine was as good or, as much as this pains me to say, better than ours. I don't know what the fuck happened."

"Huh," Jordan said. "That's confusing."

Julian frowned. "Well, if you figure it out, let us know."

"Will do. Next year, you fuckers are coming with me."

They laughed and agreed. I cut the line and took an offered drink. There was a big gala event after the award ceremony. I was close enough to the end of the thing that they weren't allowing us to go back to our seats. I thought about calling Piper, but if she hadn't answered my texts, I doubted she'd answer a phone call.

Finally, the ceremony ended with a huge round of applause. The lights came back up all the way, and everyone entered the next ballroom for the dance portion. I should go mingle, but I was more confused than anything.

So, I took my trophy with me as I made my way toward the judging panel. A few people stood around, discussing the different medal placements. I wanted to know where Piper had ended up. And how it was that she hadn't even placed.

But Daddy Sinclair beat me to it.

I interrupted his ranting. "What's going on?"

Daddy Sinclair whirled on me. He looked ready to rail at me, too. "They said I *withdrew*."

I blinked. "What?"

"Sinclair Cellars withdrew from the competition," the poor stone-faced woman at the judging table said.

"That's absurd."

"Precisely!" Daddy Sinclair snapped. "I would never withdraw from the competition. I had it under good authority that we were going to place highly in this event."

"I'm sorry, sir. As I said before, you can file an appeal, but the judging is done in secret, and a withdrawal is typically considered final."

"Oh fuck," I whispered as it all became clear to me.

Piper had been raving last night about how terrible Daddy Sinclair had been to her. How he'd called it "our" award and not hers. She'd done all the work, and he was going to take the credit for it. She'd been mad enough and stubborn enough. Even if it meant hurting her place at the winery, even if it meant losing the thing she had been working for all year, she'd do it.

"How could this have happened?" Daddy Sinclair demanded.

The woman looked down at her paperwork. "Officially, Sinclair Cellars withdrew from the competition by the organizer of the vineyard entry, Piper Medina, last night, sometime after eight p.m."

"Shit, Piper," I hissed.

Daddy Sinclair appeared to turn almost purple with rage. "That *bitch*," he snarled.

"Watch your fucking mouth."

But he was long past gone. "After all that I did for her family. After I spoke with her last night, assuring her that nothing was going to change. She goes behind my back and pulls this shit. There will be consequences for this deceitful, underhanded behavior. Forget tolerance. The old ways are out, and the new ways are in." He punched his fist into his other hand. "There will be restructuring after this stunt, and Piper will find herself out of a job."

I took a menacing step forward. "You will do *no* such thing."

"Excuse me," he snapped. "You have no say in the matter."

"No, but you haven't even talked to her. Maybe she was saving you from embarrassment because the winery was going to crash and burn."

"No," he said. "I know a judge, and they informed me that we were placing."

"Isn't that outside of the bounds of the award?" I pushed right back. "Couldn't you be disqualified for tampering?"

"Certainly not," he said, bristling at the implication.

"Piper must have had a reason for withdrawing."

"Insanity. She was mad that I'd purchased the winery and wanted to get back at me. I can't imagine any other explanation. So, you'll forgive me if I don't want to hear about your infatuation with the girl. She might need your defense, but she'll find only justice from me."

"Oh, I don't think so."

He looked half-ready to hit me. "You have no power here."

I smirked at him. "I think I do." I pitched my voice low, so only he could hear me. "Sugar daddy."

He narrowed his eyes at me. "You don't have anything on me." He looked me up and down with disgust. "You're just a boy. Congratulations on your win. Now, get the fuck out of my way."

He dropped his shoulder into me as he passed. Of course, I was a head taller than him, so it did nothing but push him backward. I watched him with a fire-breathing dragon rippling through my chest.

He wouldn't get away with this. Not after the shit he'd pulled on Piper. A man like him always won. He was sure of it. But he'd never dealt with me before.

And I knew just how to break him.

40

PIPER

"You ready, Piper?" Blaire called from the living room.

I was seated at my desk bright and early Monday morning, reading through the winner list for the award ceremony. I'd forced myself not to look all day Sunday as I drove back home. I didn't want to feel anything but sad that I'd been forced to withdraw from the competition.

It had been the only reasonable thing I could do. It wasn't giving up. It was taking back control. It was saying that all of my hard work wasn't in vain. I couldn't stand it if the thing was attributed to some asshole who hadn't done the work. So, I did the only power move I had left.

And Hollin had won.

If I couldn't, at least it had come back to Lubbock somehow. It hurt, not being there, not knowing how I would have done. But less than if I'd had to share the award with that bastard. I wouldn't give him the satisfaction.

"Piper," Blaire said, sticking her head in my door. "You coming?"

"Yeah. Just...finally checking the results."

"Hollin won!"

"You already knew?"

She laughed. "Uh, duh! It was hard as fuck not to tell you."

"I'm happy for them."

Blaire plopped down next to me. "You sound really sad when you say that."

"I know. But I am happy. I'm also...sad about everything." I huffed and finally revealed my plan. "I'm quitting."

Blaire gasped. "What?"

"The winery. I'm quitting. I decided on the drive home that I'm not going to work there anymore. I just...I can't do it. I can't work for that man. I'd rather find something else to be passionate about."

"Wow." Blaire's eyes were wide in horror. "But, Piper...it's your dream."

"Trust me, I know. I've thought about it. Dad's going to be pissed, too. I can't stay either."

"I'm sorry." Blaire stood and hugged me. "You still want to go to the Memorial Day party?"

I nodded, swiping at my eyes. "Yeah. It'll be good to be out. Plus, Hollin won't be there."

"Okay. Well, you look hot," she said.

I looked down at the pink bikini she'd thrown at me this morning. "I'm wearing your clothes."

"Exactly." She winked at me. "Let's go."

I followed her out of my room, grabbing my beach bag and heading out to my Jeep. I spent a few minutes removing the top, and then we drove out of town and toward Ransom Canyon. Jensen Wright had a lake house right on the water at the bottom of the canyon. It was tradition for him to have a giant party to celebrate the start of summer.

We parked behind Sutton's Range Rover and migrated inside. The Wrights were in full swing. Austin and Patrick stood with Julia. She was arguing with them about some old fight they'd had. Apparently, she'd left him at the top of the canyon after he made a move. I cracked up as I passed and found Jensen with baby Logan swaddled across his six-pack. My heart melted. Jensen Wright, baby, six-pack. Dear God.

"Thank you so much for having us," I told him with a smile.

"Of course. I like that the parties are growing," he said.

Blaire handed him a bottle of gin. "I brought the goods."

"Oh, gin," Morgan said with a smile. "The good stuff."

Jensen laughed at his sister. "Well, Morgan is thrilled. But you didn't have to bring anything. The wet bar is fully stocked."

"It's nice of them," Morgan said. "You get Tanqueray. Not Bombay."

"Forgive me," he said with an eye roll as he bounced the baby. "Maybe go offer that to Emery and Heidi. They look like they could use a break from the constant, 'Mom. Mom. Mom. Mommy. Mommmm.' "

I chuckled at the impression of all the kids out on the lawn that led to the dock and lake.

"On it," Blaire said, snagging a few limes.

I grabbed Solo cups, and Morgan headed outside with us. We found Emery, Heidi, and Sutton sitting on lawn chairs, supervising the brood of Wright children. Emery's one-year-old, Robin, was toddling along after Heidi's oldest, Holden, and Sutton's youngest, Madison. David was on his feet, running interference on the youngest ones to make sure no one fell into the lake. Colton, Jensen's oldest, who was now a teenager, held court with Emery's nieces, Lilyanne, who was closest to his age, and Bethany; Sutton's oldest, Jason; and Isaac's daughter, Aly. Aly and Bethany were best friends, and Isaac and Peyton had agreed to let her spend the day at the lake with Bethany while they were still on their honeymoon.

"We brought drinks!" Morgan cried, flopping down next to them.

"Please, dear God," Emery said. "Anything."

Heidi held out her hand. "Gimme."

Sutton held hers up with a sleepy smile. "I'm good. I'm nursing this one."

"Lame," Heidi said.

"Madison kept me up all night for no reason at all. The twos are absolutely terrible."

"I'll drink to that," Heidi said.

Emery sighed. "Robin is only one and so good."

"That's how they get you," Sutton said. "Have one, and they're a perfect angel. The second is a hellion, I swear. It's like they trick you on purpose."

Emery made a face that said, *Save me.*

"Speaking of, where are the twins?" I asked Heidi.

She pointed up the hill and back toward the house. Landon stood with both of the boys in a stroller, rocking them back and forth and doing some kind of silly bedtime dance. All the girls laughed but also simultaneously turned into a puddle of goo.

"That's adorable," Blaire gushed.

Jennifer skipped down the hill and grabbed another one of the chairs. "Hey, y'all. What a perfect day." She brought her camera up to her eye and took pictures of us as we poured out heaping amounts of gin to survive the mass of children sprawled across the lawn.

"Did you come with Julian and Jordan?" Morgan asked.

"Yeah. They're still talking to Jensen inside. Annie is

attached to Jordan's hip but should be down here soon, too," Jennifer said.

"That's that engagement excitement," Heidi said.

Morgan coughed. "Well, I'm not attached to Patrick."

Emery cracked up. "That's because you're not like other girls. You're a cool girl."

Morgan threw a pretzel at her face. "Shut up."

Blaire passed me a drink, and I leaned back against my chair. I wasn't feeling chatty, but it was nice to be among the Wrights. They took up so much space that I didn't have to take up any. A nice contrast to being around my family.

The day passed by in a haze of booze, snacking, and laughter. I was half-involved with everything going on. The kids bustling around. The parents rushing to help boo-boos and watching as they made silly jumps into the lake. At some point, half the girls got up to go out on the water with the older set of kids. I reapplied lotion and rolled over. Blaire made more drinks.

The day was exactly what I needed.

Tomorrow, I had a decision to make. The one I'd never, ever planned to make. I'd gone into business at Tech because all I'd ever wanted to do was run my winery. Now, I was leaving it all behind. I was cast adrift, and I'd have to find somewhere else to work. Maybe for another vineyard. I didn't have to figure it out today. In fact, I'd promised myself I wouldn't think about it at all. Yet here I was, thinking about it.

I downed the contents of another drink, rolled back over, and closed my eyes. I needed to stop obsessing. Things would work out eventually. All I wanted to do today was sit here under the bright rays and do nothing but get a tan.

I was nearly asleep when everyone around me fell silent.

The kids still yelled and cheered and ran around, but the girls stopped all their talking entirely.

My eyes popped open.

Then, I saw exactly what had forced them to quiet.

Hollin Abbey.

41

PIPER

I jerked upright. "What are you doing here?"

"Hey, Piper. Can I borrow you a minute?"

Hollin wasn't supposed to be here. He'd gotten the hotel for the entire weekend. There were still private events and such in Austin in the morning. This made no sense.

"Aren't you supposed to be in Austin?"

He grinned down at me, and something stirred deep in my belly. He looked...fucking gorgeous. He was in jeans despite the heat and a white T-shirt that clung to all of his muscles and revealed all the glorious lines of his tattoos. He'd always been tall, but him hovering over me made it feel like he was massive. And I was in nothing but a teeny bikini.

His eyes crawled my body, appreciating the naked lines of me. Before he met my gaze again. "I was. I came back early."

"Why?" I stammered out. "You won."

"I did."

"Congratulations," Blaire blurted out.

"Yeah! We're so proud of you," Jennifer threw out.

"Thanks." He shot them both a meaningful smile and returned to me. "So, can I steal you?"

"Uh...sure."

I was too curious to say no. And this was coming one way or another anyway. I just hadn't expected to see him today. In fact, I'd planned the day around not seeing him and dealing with it all after I quit tomorrow.

I snatched up my jean shorts and a crop top, drawing them on over the bikini. I stuffed my phone into the back pocket of my jeans as we walked to the lake house. Instead of heading inside, Hollin took the long way around the house. I followed him until we reached the front of the property and found his motorcycle sitting in the driveway.

"You drove your motorcycle in the canyon instead of the truck?"

He grinned. "It's a perfect day."

It was. I could only imagine how great it would be to disappear on that bike in this weather. Just ride around and have no cares in the world.

"So," I prompted, "what are you doing here?"

"You withdrew from the competition."

"Yeah, I did."

"After all your hard work, you withdrew. Why would you do that?"

"I needed to take control back," I told him. "I couldn't see another way."

"Daddy Sinclair was pissed. He was raging. You should have seen him. He planned to fire you."

I rolled my eyes. "I don't give a fuck about him. He can do whatever he wants. I'm done with it all." I crossed my arms over my chest. "Is this the reason that you came to talk to me? Because Daddy Sinclair was mad?"

"No," he said with a smile that I hadn't seen in a while.

One that was so cocky and full of shit that I nearly leaned right into him. I'd hated that smile in the past, but now, it was all I could see. It meant that I was going to be thoroughly fucked until I passed out. It meant that he knew exactly how to take care of me. And God, despite how angry I was with him, I wanted that. I wanted him.

He stepped up to his motorcycle and opened a bag he'd left here. "I came for this."

He extracted a few papers and passed them to me.

"What's this?"

"Just look."

I glanced down at the paperwork and froze. The first page was a letter of intent to *sell* Sinclair Cellars.

"What the hell?" I gasped.

"Keep going."

I flipped to the next page and nearly dropped everything. This page was the deed to the winery. A deed that I'd only seen once before with my father when he showed me where he kept everything, just in case. That had been years ago. And now, it was in my hands...with *my* name on it.

I looked up at him with tears in my eyes. "How? How is this possible?"

"I might have applied a little bit of pressure."

"What do you mean?"

"Might have made Daddy Sinclair realize that running Sinclair Cellars was too much of a hassle. That it might be easier and cheaper to give it back to the person it belonged to rather than, say, lose half of his fortune to his wife when she divorced him."

I gaped at him. "He would *never* buy that."

"He would if Eve agreed."

"She didn't," I gasped.

He smirked at me. "A little pressure with the right tool gets the desired result."

"Hollin, I can't believe you did this." I pressed the papers to my chest. "And you had it signed to *me*? Not to my father?"

"Like I said...the person the winery belongs to."

Tears flowed freely down my cheeks, and I didn't think; I threw my arms around him. He laughed softly and held me against his huge chest until the tears stilled. Finally, I wiped the tears free.

"Thank you. I don't know how I'll ever be able to thank you for this. It's too much."

He swiped one of the tears from my cheek. "Nothing is too much for you."

"Hollin," I said, pressing my cheek into his hand. "I can't believe you did this."

"It doesn't make up for hurting you, but I couldn't let him ruin everything you'd worked for. I had to do something."

I met his firm gaze, swirling with emotions. I slowly lifted onto my tiptoes and kissed his lips softly. He stilled completely at the touch, as if shocked that I would even do this. Then, he relaxed into it, tugging me tight against him and crushing our lips together.

The kiss lasted for an eternity, and I had no intention of ever stopping.

But finally, he pulled back with a soft laugh. "Well, I didn't expect that."

"I was so mad at the wedding," I said softly. "What you did was wrong, but I had already been so upset about my dad and the winery and the Sinclairs. It exploded out of me." I drew a hand down the stubble of his jaw. "You're getting help for what happened with Tori. You did *this*." I gestured to the winery paperwork. "I'm still mad, but...I don't want to live in a world without you."

He kissed me again. "I don't want to either. I promise that I am going to keep working to be the man that you deserve."

"You already are."

He grinned down at me. "Well, I wasn't sure how this was going to go down, but I have another surprise...if you'll come with me."

I arched an eyebrow. "What other surprise? Bigger than this?"

"Maybe not bigger, but you'll like it."

"All right," I agreed. "Just let me tell Blaire."

I rushed back down the lawn, handing off my keys to my best friend, who squealed with delight when I told her the news. Then, I rushed back into his arms. He passed me a second helmet, and we were off into the wind. The motorcycle handled the canyon better than I'd expected, and I let all the stress melt off of my shoulders.

We drove back into town and south toward the wineries. I straightened in my seat, wondering what he had in store. I couldn't imagine anything I wanted more than what he'd already given me.

Finally, he approached the Sinclair Cellars property. This morning, I'd woken up, thinking that it would be my last as a Sinclair Cellars employee. And now, I was driving here as the *owner*. It felt unfathomable.

But before we reached the entrance, Hollin slowed. My dad's truck was parked near the entrance. What was my dad doing here on a holiday? Had Hollin told him about what he'd done?

Hollin parked in the field next to my dad and killed the

engine. He helped me off the motorcycle. My dad stood there, as if waiting for us.

"Hey Dad."

"*Mija.*"

"What's going on?"

He smiled. "You have a good guy here." He clapped Hollin on the back. "I'm glad you came to me." His eyes met mine. "He did what I didn't know how to. But it's settled now. The winery is yours. And...he had another idea."

I looked between them. Hollin looked ecstatic. My dad as proud as I'd ever seen him.

Hollin gestured for me to look up. I blinked in confusion as the sun brightened behind the Sinclair Cellars sign I'd seen almost every day as I drove into the winery.

I shaded my eyes and then gasped. Because the sign no longer read *Sinclair Cellars*. It had been changed, and now, it read *Medina Cellars*.

My hands flew to my mouth. "*Ay Dios mio!*"

Hollin put a hand around my waist. "As it always should have been."

My dad smiled at us both. "I never had the heart to change it. But this feels right for you. No more hiding behind someone else's name."

My heart swelled with joy at the words on the sign. It was such a simple thing. A small thing that I'd never believed would happen. We'd kept the Sinclair name because it came with prestige. It would be hard, starting all over again with a name change, but I was up for the challenge. Anything to scrub the Sinclairs from every inch of this place.

It was ours.

Medina.

Now, it was reflected in the name.

I dropped my head onto Hollin's shoulder. "Thank you."

"Anything for you, Medina."

"And you, Abbey? You're mine?"

"For as long as you'll have me."

"Forever then."

He kissed the top of my head. "Forever it is."

EPILOGUE

ONE YEAR LATER

"*C*an't keep your hands to yourself for five minutes," I joked.

I didn't push Hollin back. He still had his hands under my skirt, and maybe we could skip the award ceremony.

"Are you complaining?" he asked.

Those blue eyes smoldered as he dropped to the ground in front of me. He pressed his mouth hot to my core, and I shuddered.

"No. No complaints."

"That's what I thought."

He pushed the skirt of my maroon dress around my hips. The same maroon dress that I hadn't gotten to wear last year, but I was putting it to good use this year.

Hollin pulled aside the lace of my thong.

"We're going to be late," I gasped.

"We'll make it."

"Oh God," I moaned at the first thrust of his finger inside of me. The second followed almost without hesitation. I gripped one of the bedposts and tried not to ruin my hair as he began to finger-fuck me.

"Now, isn't that better?" he asked with a chuckle that brooked no response.

His mouth returned to my clit and flicked against it until I was screaming into the hotel room. I hoped we didn't have any neighbors right now. It was hard to sate my desire for Hollin Abbey.

A year earlier, we'd almost ruined everything. Now, things were better than ever. The sex was somehow better than ever, too.

Hollin released the buckle on his belt. His fancy suit pants followed, and I was scrambling for his heavy cock, falling to the floor before him. His eyes widened in wonder as I slicked the head of him with my tongue.

"Fuck, Piper," he growled. "I want to fuck you."

"Let me taste at least," I teased.

And how could he argue?

I jerked him off with one hand as I brought him deep into my mouth. His hands fisted in my hair, holding me in place as I worked to get him deeper. He was so massive that it had taken months for me to get anywhere close to deep-throating him. I still sometimes gagged and had to give up. He never minded because that meant he got to punish me by bending me over his knee. Both of us liked it enough that I always fought to try again the next time. Either I succeeded or I got the spanking I deserved. Win-win.

I tried to get him all the way this time, but he was impatient. He jerked into my mouth.

"Babe," he groaned. "No time."

"Now, who's complaining?"

He growled something about me being a bad girl, and it went straight to my greedy pussy. Did I want to give this blow job, or did I want him to take it out on my body? Toss-up.

Finally, he got fed up and withdrew from my lips. "Over the bed."

I grinned devilishly. He rammed me forward until my ass was in the air and my pussy was on full display. He tugged my panties all the way down my legs, dropping them to the floor. Then drove deep inside of me.

I moaned around the sharp pain of him filling me. He was huge, and sometimes, he forgot that I was relatively small. Or maybe he liked the way I squirmed around the pain. I knew that I did.

"Going to come for me again?" Hollin asked.

My answering response was to tighten all around his cock as he hammered harder and faster inside of me. I'd been hanging on a thread before, and it all came undone.

"Fuck," he spat. Then, he came alongside me, spending himself thoroughly. "That's my good girl. So fucking good."

We both grew still, panting in the hotel room. He withdrew from my body and went to clean up. I followed him, and when I came back, I looked around for my underwear.

Hollin gave me a shit-eating look. He patted his pocket. "I'm keeping these."

"Hollin," I chided.

"I want you to be commando under that dress. Makes me think about fingering you under the table."

I flushed. "At the award ceremony? In front of all those people?"

"Who's going to know?"

"Oh, I don't know. Everyone?"

He smirked. "How good is your poker face?"

I rolled my eyes at him but was thrilled at the thought. It wasn't the first time I'd gone out without underwear. Just knowing I had on nothing underneath this would make the sex amazing when we got back. It would heat us both up all night long.

"Fine."

We headed down to the award ceremony. I'd missed it last year after pulling Sinclair Cellars out of the running. This year, Hollin and I were in it together. We each had individual wines in the running. Luckily, he was putting forward a chardonnay for Wright Vineyard while Medina Cellars had a new merlot that I hoped would top the category. But *together*, we'd decided on a whole new blend vintage. A pinot noir mix with grapes from both vineyards that we were calling the *Medina-Abbey*.

We'd commandeered an entire table this year. Jordan and Julian were seated with Annie and Jennifer beside them. My dad, mom, Peyton, and Peter took up the rest of the seats. Hollin's family along with Blaire and a good number of the Wrights had a table farther from the action but hollered as we passed by. We had an entire entourage this year, and I loved it. All of us together.

"Took you long enough," Julian said, coming to his feet and shaking Hollin's hand.

"Yeah. We had other plans," Hollin said with that same smile.

Julian rolled his eyes. "I bet."

Jordan shook his hand next. "What do you think is going to happen this year?"

"I'm going to win," I told him with a wink.

Jordan laughed. "We'll see about that."

Hollin tugged me closer and kissed me hard one more time. "I don't know what's going to happen," he admitted. "But it doesn't matter."

"No?"

"I've already won." He pressed our lips together one

more time in front of our entire family and all our friends and the entire Texas wine world. "I've got you. What more could I want?"

My cheeks heated again at those words. "Oh, Hollin, I love you."

"I love you, too."

And though we *did* win Best in Class for our blended wine, the *Medina-Abbey* vintage, all that mattered was that we had each other.

The good girl and the reformed bad boy.

The End

ACKNOWLEDGMENTS

The idea for this story came as one of the very first books when I came up with the idea to write a vineyard for the Wrights. There are dozens of vineyards here in Lubbock, and I'd like to thank all of them for giving me inspiration for this story.

Also everyone who helped me with this one: Danielle Sanchez for a sensitivity read; Rebecca Kimmerling, Rebecca Gibson, Anjee Sapp for early reads; Jovana Shirley for editing; Devin McCain for graphics and all the things you do to keep me sane; Sarah Hansen for the incredible cover design; Michelle Lancaster for taking the cover image.

Especially Staci Hart for the hours and hours of plot talking and joking and sprinting. All the laughs and tears and everything in between. Thank you friend!

Also Nana Malone and Bethany Hagen for all their help while writing this one and being there when Hippo was diagnosed with cancer.

My sister, Brittany, for her help with alcohol distribution in the state of Texas. Thank you for all the proprietary information!

Finally, Joel who is always there for me through everything. I love you so much!

ABOUT THE AUTHOR

K.A. Linde is the *USA Today* bestselling author of more than thirty novels. She has a Masters degree in political science from the University of Georgia, was the head campaign worker for the 2012 presidential campaign at the University of North Carolina at Chapel Hill, and served as the head coach of the Duke University dance team.

She loves reading fantasy novels, binge-watching Supernatural, traveling to far off destinations, baking insane desserts, and dancing in her spare time.

She currently lives in Lubbock, Texas, with her husband and two super-adorable puppies.

Visit her online:
www.kalinde.com

Or Facebook, Instagram & Tiktok:
@authorkalinde

For exclusive content, free books,
and giveaways every month.
www.kalinde.com/subscribe

CPSIA information can be obtained
at www.ICGtesting.com
Printed in the USA
LVHW090741120122
708211LV00002B/97